ROSE EDMUNDS

Exposure

CRAZY AMY THRILLER 2

Published in Great Britain by Mainsail Books in 2017

First Edition

Paperback formatting by Clare Davidson www.claredavidson.com
Proofreading by Julia Gibbs www.juliaproofreader.wordpress.com
e-book formatting by Ben Bryant www.makemyebook.com
cover design by Ana Grigoriu www.books-design.com

To my loyal test readers
Thank you for your thoughtful (if sometimes contradictory!) feedback,
which has helped me to make this book my very best work.

1

Amy paused to admire the glorious London panorama stretched out in front of her.

Tower Bridge, The Shard, The Gherkin, The London Eye, Big Ben—even the glassy splendour of her old offices at Pearson Malone.

'The City belongs to you,' said the voice in her head.

Hey—welcome back, Little Amy—where've you been hiding?

'Should have gone higher,' urged her teenage alter ego. *'Right to the top.'*

There were barely two hundred more steps to the Golden Gallery, the pinnacle of St Paul's Cathedral. But it might be too windy higher up, with a greater margin of error. She would stick at the lower Stone Gallery.

'Hope you know what you're doing.'

Far above the traffic fumes, the air had an Alpine freshness. And it was early yet, with the tourists still circling like vultures round their prepaid hotel breakfast buffets. Greed for food, greed for money, and greed for material possessions—the same phenomenon in different guises—people didn't realise when they had enough.

Far below, the anti-capitalist protesters camped outside the cathedral went about their business. They railed against corporate immorality and City fat cats, but Amy bet that if they could join the 1% elite, they'd have no beef with capitalism.

A light breeze wafted a stray wisp of hair across Amy's face.

'See—not too much wind. Even God is on your side now.'

Amy fished into her rucksack for a wad of notes. The bank's money-laundering neurosis had failed to thwart the twenty thousand cash withdrawal, despite their best endeavours.

'Give it to those dumb peasants,' said Little Amy. *'See if it makes them any happier—because it didn't do much for you, did it?'*

True enough. Amy had never been gloomier than when she'd been earning half a million plus a year in the City.

The first notes fluttered to the ground—landing squarely in the target area. Encouraged, Amy reached over the parapet and tipped the remainder out of the bag. They came to rest on a small ledge a short distance below the stone balustrade, before the wind picked them up and propelled them towards the crowd.

'Whee! Such fun!'

From her lofty viewpoint, Amy watched the people scurry to retrieve the cash. Some looked doubtfully towards the heavens, as if suspecting divine intervention. But disbelief morphed into unbridled avarice as more joined the party, pushing each other out of the way to grab their share of the spoils.

'See, everyone worships money, whatever they say. They believe more will make them happy, just as you did.'

Yes—the theory that money buys happiness was the big lie oiling the wheels of capitalism—a lie so seductive not even the protesters could rise above it. Point proved.

'But I'm different now,' Amy replied under her breath. 'I had the guts to walk away.'

A sense of power surged through her like a powerful narcotic as the sun emerged from behind the clouds in a signal of validation.

'And now we're free. We can do anything. Why, if we only have faith in ourselves, we can fly.'

Little Amy materialised from the shadows to stand triumphant atop the high stone balustrade, her arms spread like the statue of Christ the Redeemer. She wore her school uniform, with the hat dented defiantly, trilby-style.

'Come on!' she shrieked. *'Come up and fly with me!'*

Her bravado was compelling. Oh to have Little Amy's confidence, the absolute certainty of boundless possibilities, even when life had dealt you a duff hand. Amy hadn't felt so self-assured in ages, but it was never too late to regain your mojo.

And invigorated by this notion, Amy hauled herself up the balustrade.

2

'When did you last have an alcohol-free day?' asked the duty doctor, peering at Amy over the rim of his tortoise-shell glasses. He reminded her of a geeky tax specialist from her Pearson Malone 'glory' days, steeped in professional certainty, but lacking any real understanding of the world. Even leaving aside the patronising body language, his voice had an accusatory tone.

Amy resisted the temptation to reply "Sometime in 1995." Flippancy was unlikely to help her cause.

'A couple of weeks ago, I think,' she mumbled instead.

The humiliation of being carted off to the world-famous Priory, where celebrities came to dry out and City weaklings to regroup, stung Amy hard. Still—better here than sectioned under the Mental Health Act in some NHS shit-hole. And at least she was calmer now Little Amy had vanished.

The doctor peered again.

'While hospitalised after the last bender, no doubt.'

Bender? How grossly unfair—had he not read her notes? But arguing was futile, because trying to explain would make her look crazy and paranoid. And the arguments in defence of her sanity were weak to begin with.

'It may have been,' she conceded with reluctance.

'Even though...' said the doctor, moving in for the kill, '...you were specifically told to avoid alcohol with the anti-psychotic tablets you were prescribed.'

Amy let the accusation hang there before delivering her riposte.

'Actually, I came off the tablets a few days ago.'

Although needless to say, she hadn't avoided drinking while she had been taking them.

'Aha,' he said, peering over the glasses again.

He scribbled something onto his notepad. And though upside down reading had been a valuable skill in corporate life, Amy was unable to decipher what he'd written. She suspected it would be equally illegible the right way up.

'And what were your reasons for stopping?'

Another tricky, no-win question. Though the "delusions" from which she'd allegedly been suffering had turned out to be true, suggesting this would only make her sound even more deluded.

'I decided I didn't need them.'

'I'm inclined to agree,' he admitted, to Amy's astonishment. 'In fact, I doubt if I would have prescribed anti-psychotics in your case.'

He sounded like the Pearson Malone geek again, critiquing another firm's shoddy tax advice.

'Did no one tell you it's dangerous to stop the medication suddenly?'

'Dangerous—how?' she asked, realising as soon as she'd opened her mouth how mindless she sounded. What was more dangerous than a narrowly averted leap to oblivion?

'Sudden withdrawal can lead to a manic episode. Now tell me honestly—what were you thinking up there?'

'Ridiculous as it seems now—I believed I could fly.'

As before, she didn't mention Little Amy—it seemed somehow disloyal.

'That's entirely consistent with my diagnosis,' said the doctor. 'The attendant who saved you thought it was a suicide attempt. But even he said you'd gone a crazy way about it, climbing up the stone balustrade. When he told me about the money, I was 99% certain you were gripped by mania. Now I know for sure.'

This came as something of a relief. She'd been suffering from a temporary chemical unbalance, and already she'd recovered her equilibrium. Sorted.

'Well everything's fine then, isn't it?' Amy ventured with optimism. 'If it was only a reaction to stopping the medication, then there's absolutely nothing wrong with me and I can go home now…'

'I can't stop you, but I wouldn't recommend it,' the doctor replied, shaking his head. 'Your blood alcohol level on admission was alarmingly high.'

Idiot man. Over the years, Amy had learned to assess with pinpoint precision how much alcohol she could handle. And yes, she had been drinking more than usual, but only to slow her galloping mind at night.

'Yes, but that'll be normal again soon,' she countered.

'Until the next time.'

'But…'

'I'm afraid the questionnaire you filled out on admission shows conclusively that you're an alcoholic.'

'But…'

Impossible—she'd calibrated her answers with the utmost precision to avoid such an outcome. Clever people like her did not get labelled as alcoholics unless they wanted to be.

'And so we're advising you to check in for our twenty-eight-day rehab program,' the doctor continued, ignoring Amy. 'During your stay we can monitor your mental health generally. Now what do you say?'

Although Amy was reluctant, in hindsight this so-called manic episode had unnerved her. An electric, euphoric energy powerful enough to propel her to a certain death was a frightening force, and next time she might not be so lucky. Twenty-eight days without a drink seemed a small price to pay to avoid a recurrence.

'You do have private medical insurance?' asked the doctor, misinterpreting her hesitation.

'Yes, of course.'

Her Pearson Malone health insurance policy had another six months to run, even though she'd left. And the opportunity to screw those bastards for all they were worth clinched it.

'So what do you think?'

And Amy heard herself say, 'What a great idea.'

3

Toby Marchpole thrived on confrontation, and today he was in his element. He'd come to the IPT Plc Annual General Meeting to ask questions of the board, and he didn't plan on leaving without satisfactory answers.

IPT was a distributer and retailer of plumbing components. With skyrocketing profits and share price, it was a star of the Alternative Investment Market, and would soon be listed on the FTSE 350. But Toby didn't buy the hype because, in his opinion, the IPT business empire was riddled with fraud, and he intended to prove it.

Toby had tried all the conventional ways to get the information he wanted, but IPT's staff had been unwilling to answer his ostensibly simple questions, in itself a warning sign. They passed him around, until finally he'd come up against the formidable Roxanne, from IPT's PR agency. She'd informed him in her smooth transatlantic tones that he would find the details he required in the company's annual review.

In Toby's view, the review was a glossy piece of obfuscation designed to convey an illusion of prosperity, just like the plush AGM venue. Indeed, the contents of the document raised further questions. Which left him no alternative but to challenge IPT in this public forum.

Only shareholders can attend an AGM, so Toby bought a small holding and came armed with the contract note showing his purchase, a technique he'd frequently used in the past.

'Sorry—we can't let you in,' said the dragon woman at the door as he showed the document. 'Your shares are in a nominee account.'

'But here's my name.'

'According to our rules, it's not good enough.'

'But I do this all the time.'

'Not with us. If you're unhappy, I'm afraid you must take it up with the Registrars.'

Fat lot of good that would be. He needed to be in there now, putting those shysters on the spot, not sometime next week.

'Don't worry, it's not just you,' said a guy Toby recognised as an FT journalist. 'They said the same to me.'

This was little short of outrageous. Many regarded Toby's Shareguru blog as a crappy troublemaking site, but to exclude a journalist from a premier publication was in a different league of shoddy behaviour.

The FT guy would slink away and write platitudes, but Toby had no intention of leaving quietly. He spotted Roxanne, or Foxy Roxy as he'd nicknamed her, sashaying across the foyer in a snugly fitting purple dress and black patent stilettos.

Half-Chinese, Roxanne's regal bearing and well-proportioned body deceived many into believing she was a great beauty. But while Marchpole hadn't fallen for this confidence trick, others had. Not only did she handle IPT's PR, but he'd heard she was the CEO's live-in girlfriend.

'Excuse me,' he said. 'I'm Toby Marchpole.'

To Toby's satisfaction she flinched slightly—she knew him alright.

'How may I help you, sir?' she asked in tones suggesting a reluctance to do so.

'I'm having a problem getting into the meeting.'

'Oh dear—why?'

She gazed at him, her brown eyes unblinking and apparently unknowing.

'They won't accept I'm a shareholder.'

'I'm afraid they're correct. Our Registrars have issued us with specific instructions. Contract notes from brokers are not sufficient proof.'

The speed of her response and hint of triumph in her voice confirmed Toby's suspicions. He hadn't even mentioned the note.

'This document has my name on it.'

'You'll have to take that up with the Registrars—it's an issue for them,' she said, repeating the gatekeeper's mantra.

'No—it's an issue for the company. You're manipulating the rules to keep journalists out—how is this shareholder democracy? I've asked some simple questions and all you've said is "no comment" or to consult the annual review. I'm forced to come here for the answers. Why do you refuse to respond? What are you scared of?'

'It's a matter for the Registrars,' she chirruped like a well-rehearsed parakeet. 'They have their parameters…'

'The main parameters being not to let in awkward buggers like me,' Toby interrupted her. 'I have documentary proof of my shareholding.'

'Our Registrars have advised us to the contrary.'

'What crap—are you proud of defending the indefensible?'

He waved the piece of paper theatrically in the air. Although he'd get nowhere with Roxanne, he'd attracted a pleasing level of attention from the other shareholders drifting in.

Roxanne's eyes lighted on Gus, Toby's chum, and in particular the camera focussed on them.

'Are you filming this?' Without waiting for an answer, she beckoned to a security guard across the room.

It looked as though the game was up, when Toby saw an opportunity to make a real impact. Richard Pedley, the founder, CEO and majority shareholder of IPT, walked through the door with John Venner, the most recent addition to the crooks on IPT's main board.

Toby had done his due diligence, and concluded that both men sat on the wrong side of the fine line between debonair and slime ball.

Pedley had established IPT five years earlier, having fleeced the shareholders of his previous company before bailing out. Toby had never fully unmasked the fraud triggering this fiasco, and he doubted anyone else would either. Frankly, no one cared, least of all the regulators. The only people who'd lost out were small investors left holding the worthless shares—the big City boys had cashed out long before.

Venner, the finance director, had come from the global accountancy firm of Pearson Malone, and it was plain to Toby why he'd been hired. His impeccable City bean-counting credentials lent an unwarranted veneer of respectability to a shady organisation.

Toby dodged the security guards, and stood with Gus, barring the two men's way.

'Toby Marchpole,' he announced. 'I'm a journalist who's been excluded from this meeting because you don't want to answer my questions.'

'That's not true,' said Venner smoothly. 'My understanding is there's a technical issue regarding the validity of your…'

'Rubbish!' shouted Toby, wondering how everyone had been aware of the contract note in advance. 'You're keeping me out because you and your crooked friend…' he pointed at Pedley, '… have got something to hide.'

'Let us pass please,' said Venner, trying to manoeuvre himself through the crowd. A film of sweat had formed on his forehead.

The security goons were rapidly approaching, but while Pedley had slunk off, Venner remained, apparently rooted to the spot.

'OK, well here's what I planned to ask if you'd let me in,' Toby began, taking advantage of the few seconds remaining before being escorted from the premises. 'And let's kick off with two easy ones. Why are you making double the gross margins of your competitors? And why do you carry enough inventory for a year's sales?'

'This public haranguing is completely inappropriate.'

For a City smoothie, Venner sounded uncharacteristically alarmed.

'Security please!' he shouted, looking around him in sheer panic, his voice hoarse and his face a curious chalky grey.

He clutched at his throat and gulped for breath. Wow— Toby thought. He'd induced a panic attack—totally freaked the guy out! This was beyond his wildest expectations. And capturing it on video, the icing on the cake.

'Keep filming, Gus,' he shouted. 'This is dynamite!'

Venner rocked unsteadily, before collapsing to the floor, gasping.

'Tell Amy…' he spluttered, his eyes wide open in terror. And then he lay still.

4

Amy was an expert at pretending.

She'd pretended to come from a normal family, pretended to be the perfect wife, and pretended to be a high-flying tax partner. In Amy's view, you could pretend anything as long as you made it convincing.

After so much practice, pretending to be an alcoholic ought to have been a doddle—a role merely requiring a plausible mix of denial, contrition, embarrassment, sadness and acceptance. But the game turned out to be harder to play than she'd predicted.

In the group therapy, Amy maundered on about stuff that *might* have bugged her if she'd let it, such as her father dying when she was eight and growing up with her mother's compulsive hoarding. When she'd done with those aspects of her life, she moved on to the ten-year estrangement from her mother, the breakdown of her marriage, her stressful high-flying job and bullying boss. Then to cap it all came the murder of a colleague and subsequent traumatic events. There was certainly no shortage of material to discuss.

But underneath, none of it touched her, because she wouldn't let it. If she yielded to long-supressed emotions, she wouldn't be pretending anymore—she'd have lost the game. And Amy liked winning.

As a concession to the ethos of the group, Amy was relatively open about the hoarding—they wouldn't get it anyway, because people seldom did. Could growing up in a messy house really be *that* terrible? Her instincts proved correct. Not even the trained therapist empathised with the shame, the broken plumbing and the secrecy. Hoarding had been the most important influence on her life, from relationships to career, even the clothes she wore. And they dismissed it.

But they questioned her on the rest. A bunch of addicts who'd put on their own Oscar-winning performances for decades had a nose for those who weren't fully engaged. And as they challenged her, she ramped up her acting routine to keep them at bay, while avoiding any genuine emotion. The struggle exhausted her, but she resisted the temptation to capitulate.

The group was an eclectic mix. Roger the advertising guy was pushing sixty and on his fourth wife. She'd threatened to leave him if he didn't get a handle on his serious cocaine problem. Amy reckoned he'd been lucky to live so long.

And Cathy, a drug-raddled D list celebrity who was "resting", but still made ever more frenzied calls to her agent. She appeared not to grasp that her career had imploded.

Next was Eleanor, who'd been drinking a bottle of Jack Daniels a day to assuage the pain after her husband had left her for a twenty-year-old nymphet. Although Amy had also lost her man to a nymphet, she found Eleanor's "poor little me" victim mentality annoying.

Weirdest of the lot by a considerable margin was Colin, in his forties, still living with his mother and never gainfully employed in any capacity. Crippled by severe anxiety, he'd developed an addiction to painkillers, which the mother was now paying to unravel.

Amy at first dismissed them all as worthless losers, but soon felt her assessment had been harsh. Sure, they'd all hit rock bottom, but so had she, and Amy's bottom was just as rocky as anyone's. Moreover, even when she admitted this, no one condemned her. For years, she'd been afraid to show any weakness, because of the toxic people around her who seized on any perceived frailty to bolster their own position. Here her foibles were not only tolerated, but embraced. But even so, she still couldn't quite bring herself to lay her emotions bare.

In one session, amusingly, the group therapist instructed them to have a dialogue with their inner child.

'How old is she meant to be?' Amy asked the therapist.

'Whatever age feels right.'

'She's fourteen, for sure, although she's dead now.' This was as close as she would ever come to disclosing Little Amy's existence.

'How did she die?' asked Colin in his trademark doom-laden tones.

'She jumped off the roof at St Paul's.'

This seemed probable, for there'd been no sign of her since. But Grown Up Amy didn't need her presence to write the script—she'd heard the entire repertoire of Little Amy bullshit in the past few months.

After she'd finished, everyone sat quietly.

'Very authentic, Amy, very heartfelt,' said the therapist, breaking the silence. 'It must have been painful to explore that dynamic.'

Amy silently congratulated herself on having upped her game to a new level.

'Does anyone else have any observations?'

'She's disappointed in you, and so judgemental,' said Roger, with a sniff suggesting he'd managed to smuggle in a supply of cocaine. 'I mean—who's in control here, you or her?'

An insightful question, and difficult to answer.

'She's hoping to grow up a better person than me,' Amy replied. 'But she doesn't understand the realities of life. So she'd like to be in control, but it would be dangerous to give her free rein.'

'You were very harsh with her,' Eleanor observed. 'Given all she's been through, doesn't the poor kid need someone to love her?'

'Yes, well, she's not exactly loveable herself.' Only after the words were out did Amy remember—wasn't this what her mother had always claimed, when blaming Little Amy for the deplorable state of the house?

Amy half-expected the therapist to delve deeper into the question of whether Grown Up Amy considered herself loveable, a topic she would rather avoid. But fortunately, Colin diverted the conversation.

'You say she's dead,' he chimed in. 'But you don't grieve her loss. It's like when your father died—you're not being open about your sadness.'

'I agree,' said Cathy. 'Maybe it's time to confront the scale of your loss.'

Sod them—Amy didn't do grief, let alone confronting the scale of it. Someone's there one minute and gone the next—tough shit. Human existence is transitory—get over it and move on. Had her father's death not sparked off her mother's hoarding, her life would have continued as normal. She knew this analysis would not be well received, but she'd faked enough emotion for one day.

'I'm not ready to discuss this,' she said, feigning a little sob. 'Surely it's someone else's turn.'

And to her profound relief, the therapist agreed, pointing out only that our inner child is always with us, and we neglect her at our peril.

***

Aside from the therapy sessions, the days slipped by pleasantly as Amy read, slept, ate and smoked, paying little attention to the outside world. She didn't miss drinking much, which proved she wasn't addicted, although she didn't dare express this view to anyone, as they'd jump on her for being in denial.

Halfway through her stay, when she'd begun to focus on what she might do with her life after the Priory, events conspired to force her hand. One afternoon, as Amy sat in the lounge reading, the TV news played in the background.

'John Venner…'

On catching her one-time boss's name, Amy leapt up, seized the remote control and backed up to the start of the bulletin.

'This afternoon, questions are being asked regarding the death of a senior executive at his company's Annual General Meeting. John Venner, the fifty-eight-year-old Finance Director of IPT Plc, collapsed at Lancaster Gate Hotel in London at around eleven yesterday morning. Paramedics pronounced him dead at the scene.

'As Venner fell dramatically to the floor, he was being interviewed on film by a controversial financial blogger. The video went viral amid howls of protest that it was in poor taste and disrespectful to the family. It has since been taken down.'

They showed a clip from the video, cutting out tastefully at an appropriate point. The taboo against broadcasting someone's death perplexed Amy. No one bats an eyelid when babies are filmed being born, and conceptually, how was the end of life any different from its beginning?

Admittedly, Venner appeared unwell, but Amy had seen him look considerably worse. Certainly, she wouldn't have bet money on his imminent demise.

'Venner's death appeared to be due to a massive heart attack. However, speculation is mounting that he was poisoned. Prime mover in these accusations is Dr Gordon Pexton, a retired anaesthetist, who took to Twitter to vent his suspicions. We have him in the studio now.'

Cut to Pexton, who seemed far too erudite to be sparking off Twitter conspiracy theories.

'Dr Pexton, thank you for joining us this afternoon. What makes you say Mr Venner might not have died a natural death?'

'I've been following the Shareguru blog for a while, as they've been making various accusations against IPT Plc, a company I'm invested in. Once I saw the video, I became suspicious.'

'Why so?'

'It looked as though he died due to paralysis of his muscles.'

'And the cause?'

'A drug overdose.'

'Can you tell us which drug?'

'In my opinion, the most likely candidate is succinylcholine. It's a drug commonly used as an anaesthetic, but can cause a horrible death if misused. The muscles are paralysed one by one, and finally the respiratory system shuts down. On the full version of the video, you can see Venner gasping for breath.'

'But mightn't this happen during a heart attack?'

'Possibly, but not with the other signs he displayed.'

'So, in your opinion, should the autopsy include toxicology tests?'

'Certainly, but if they haven't tested yet, it's already too late. The drug has an extremely short half-life.'

'So is this drug the ideal murder weapon?'

'In some respects, yes.'

'And how easily can it be obtained?'

'Very easily, by someone who works in a hospital.'

'Thank you again for joining us, Dr Pexton.'

'So, was John Venner murdered?' asked the presenter. 'Many are inclined to think so, especially in the light of recent posts on Shareguru suggesting fraud at IPT. Supporters of the murder theory believe Venner planned to blow the whistle, despite a lack of evidence to support this. One final little twist to the mystery comes with Venner's last words. As he lay struggling for breath on the floor, he was heard to croak, "Tell Amy".'

Amy sat bolt upright.

Shit—had he meant her?

'Amy's identity is unclear, but sources close to Venner have suggested the woman in question may be Amy Robinson, a former colleague of Venner's.'

An image of a professional and serious-faced Amy, copied from her LinkedIn profile, flashed up on screen.

'To add to the mystery, Amy Robinson has disappeared.'

'I'm in the Priory!' Amy shouted, as though they were listening.

'This has further fuelled speculation, as two weeks ago Ms Robinson was rescued from St Paul's Cathedral after a bizarre suicide attempt.'

Cut to irrelevant footage of the cathedral.

'So, given the level of public interest, what have the police been doing to investigate this matter? I spoke earlier to a spokesman for the Metropolitan Police, who said there was no indication of suspicious circumstances. Nevertheless, the story has captured people's imagination, and the controversy seems unlikely to die down any time soon.'

Amy sat back in her armchair, flabbergasted. The murder accusations seemed ludicrous. Venner was in his late fifties, smoked forty cigarettes and drank several bottles of wine a day. It was much more likely a dodgy heart had finished him off than poison, though murder made for a juicier news story.

Later, in the group session, she confided her fears of press harassment, but the therapist hijacked the discussion.

'So how do you feel now this guy is dead?'

Oh no—not again. Whatever she ought to feel, she sure as hell didn't. Venner had been Amy's boss for six years, until evil Ed Smithies, her nemesis, had supplanted him. Venner was not quite a friend, but more than an acquaintance. They weren't talking about her dad here.

If she'd expressed these views, they'd have accused her of being in the denial phase of the five steps of grieving, and would be waiting for the uncontrollable sobbing to kick in at any moment. They would be disappointed. And in all honesty, how did her emotions benefit Venner or indeed anyone else?

'I'm sad, of course,' said Amy, trying to strike an emotional balance. 'And sorry for his widow and his kids. I wish I had the chance to see him again and tell him how much I respected him.'

Amy never discovered whether this passed muster as a fitting level of distress, because the others had latched on to the potentially salacious elements of the story.

'The *Daily Globe* website says you were having an affair,' Eleanor said, no doubt hypersensitive to any sniff of hypocrisy in Amy's pity for the widow.

'We were not.'

'So why mention you in his last breath?'

'I don't know.'

'And what did he want to tell you?' Roger chipped in.

'I've no idea.'

'You were sweet on him,' Eleanor said, with a simper. 'Even if subconsciously.'

'Or maybe he was a father figure to you,' added Roger.

Ah well—he'd be the expert, with his fourth wife practically a child bride.

'I'm worried about this drug they used on him,' said Colin. 'Suppose I have to go into hospital for an operation…'

Enough was enough. Amy loathed the undercurrent of voyeuristic pleasure she'd detected at various points of the programme, and today she'd reached her limit. These bottom feeders were actually disappointed there had been no love affair, latent sexual attraction, or other emotional drama.

'Will you shut up, all of you,' Amy shouted, and stormed out of the room, slamming the door behind her.

***

Whatever enjoyment Amy derived from her dramatic departure evaporated instantly when reception informed her that a journalist was waiting for her.

Damn. It was inevitable they'd track her down sooner or later—her whereabouts weren't secret. But still, she had no desire to feed the media frenzy.

'No way am I talking to anyone.'

'But he felt sure you'd speak to him once you knew his name.'

'It won't make any difference, but go on—tell me.'

'Toby Marchpole,' the receptionist replied.

'Toby Marchpole?'

Incredulous, Amy repeated a name she hadn't heard in over twenty years. She wavered, curious about how he looked now, before outrage kicked in. How *dare* he assume his name had any power over her? And after the shabby way he'd treated her, she had no wish to flatter his ego.

'The name doesn't ring a bell, I'm afraid,' she told the receptionist. 'So the answer's no.'

She replaced the telephone in its cradle, for once craving a gin and tonic.

5

Oak casket and *Abide with Me*.

Venner was nothing if not a traditionalist.

The Priory rehab program rarely allowed anyone out without a minder. But the group had misconstrued Amy's door-slamming pique as a sign of her true grief—perhaps the anger coming first—and their collective sympathy had moved those in charge. They bent the rules and permitted Amy to attend the funeral.

In truth, this was a Pyrrhic victory, as she'd have loved to have an excuse to miss it. She'd even considered whether to venture out but skip the ceremony, returning suitably subdued and ashen at the requisite time. She could even—shock, horror—go to the pub. No—they'd likely breathalyse her when she got back. And it would be a pity to flunk a rehab program she didn't need. So with nothing better to do, she found herself surrounded by a depressing crowd of former colleagues, all deeply unpleasant people she'd hoped never to encounter again.

Amy walked past them, ignoring the whisperings as their eyes bored into her, judging and condemning.

'Shocking instability…'

'Tried to jump off St Paul's, of all things.'

'I always suspected she had a serious drink problem…'

'She's finished. Never work in the City again. Who'd trust her now?'

It was far easier for them to disparage her than face their own deficiencies, but this knowledge didn't make the experience any more comfortable. After two weeks cocooned in a supportive environment, Amy wobbled back amidst the bitching and sniping, before remembering she'd been just as spiteful herself in the toxic cesspit of Pearson Malone.

At the reception, Amy was nobbled by Venner's son David—a young man whose privileged life had given him delusions of grandeur.

'Oh—so you're Amy. I didn't appreciate you and my dad were so close,' he said with more than a hint of sarcasm.

Amy was "rescued" from this conversation by evil Ed Smithies. Even though he'd shafted Venner and usurped his job, Smithies had the brass neck to show up, full of faux sympathy and mawkish remarks. The therapy group had denounced him as a bully, with self-esteem issues of his own. But for every bully, there is a willing victim, and Amy had been it.

For old times' sake, Smithies sidled over to bait his former victim once again. Amy's stomach heaved in a Pavlovian reaction at the sight of him.

'*Do* have a glass of wine,' he urged, taking one from a passing tray and handing it to her.

On autopilot, Amy reached for it, before checking herself. What a tactical error that would have been—she'd be forced to sit dissecting her 'failure' with the therapist on her return.

'No thanks, just orange juice.'

'Oops—sorry.' He gave a sly little grin as he replaced the glass on the tray. 'I forgot you're in rehab.'

Smithies was playing the same game of cat and mouse he'd always enjoyed. He didn't appear to have focused on her transformation from a mouse. She had in her possession an incriminating recording, implicating him and his brother-in-law in a massive fraud. It had been the trump card in her exit negotiations at Pearson Malone. Maybe it was time to remind him.

'Hey—don't wind me up too much, Ed. Remember I've got the dirt on you.'

It had been Venner who'd bugged Smithies' office, for reasons of his own, then generously given the recording to Amy when she was in the shit. She should raise a glass to the dead man for that alone, even if he'd have heartily disapproved of the orange juice.

'My goodness, what an over-aggressive response,' Smithies replied, sounding pained. 'I made an honest mistake—and I apologise. Anyway, I fear you misunderstood those recordings, possibly because you weren't in the best frame of mind. They were highly ambiguous.'

There was a grain of truth in this. The recordings were damning only if the listener understood the context, but there were enough people in the know to finish Smithies if they ever saw the light of day.

'Besides,' he continued. 'If you were planning to release them, you'd have done it by now. Afraid they might show you up in a dismal light as well?'

'Not in the slightest,' Amy replied. 'Now if you'll excuse me, I must speak to Susan.'

John's widow wore a black silk dress a fraction too foxy for the sombre occasion. Her nails were blood red, with matching lipstick, and no trace of emotion disturbed her immaculate façade. Amy caught herself thinking maybe Venner's sudden death hadn't come as such a surprise to her as to everyone else.

Susan's elegance only highlighted Amy's own frumpiness. Once Amy's impeccable designer wardrobe had been part of her corporate armour, props in a gigantic con act. Now she had no need of these accoutrements of corporate life, and she'd lost the habit of snappy dressing. Her black trouser suit was more suitable attire for a job interview where she didn't much care about the outcome.

'Please,' Susan said after the obligatory exchange of condolences and pleasantries. 'It's been bugging me—what did John want to say to you?'

Even by Amy's glacial standards, there was a clinical coldness, unfitting for a new widow, in Susan's manner.

'Not a clue—can't you shed any light on it?'

'Me?' She gave a self-deprecating shrug. 'What do I know of his business dealings?'

'Who says it *was* business-related?' Amy asked. 'Your son appears to think…'

'What rot!' Susan rolled her eyes. 'I'm well aware of who John was screwing over the years and you're not on the list.'

Amy resisted the considerable temptation to ask who was. If Venner had been unfaithful, he'd been very discreet—there'd never been a breath of scandal until brazen lies about his use of pornography had hastened his departure from the firm.

'He trusted you as a colleague,' Susan added. 'He always said you had commercial savvy.'

'Well that's uplifting to hear.'

'Have the press been onto you?'

'Incessantly. And it's not as though I can add to the story, but they don't care. In my opinion, they've gone overboard, and those absurd theories about John being murdered must be so distressing for you.'

'For sure,' she replied, although she didn't seem distressed. Amy sensed that Venner's death had been inconvenient, rather than traumatic, for Susan. In a strange way, she found this encouraging—perhaps her own absent grief was less abnormal than those at the Priory believed.

'Although,' she went on, 'in a manner of speaking, John *was* murdered.'

'*Really?*'

'Hounded to an early grave by Toby Marchpole.'

'What's he got to do with it?' asked Amy, startled to hear Toby's name again.

'He's the vile little jerk who writes the blog.'

'Ah—I didn't realise.'

After watching the initial TV report, Amy had made strenuous efforts to avoid the media, for fear of reading harsh commentary about herself. So she hadn't twigged that Marchpole was behind the blog, and nor had she checked out the website.

'The allegations were dreadful,' Susan continued. 'John was trying to coordinate a lawsuit, which stressed him out hugely. And don't forget Marchpole was there when John died, heckling him on film.'

'How awful,' said Amy.

'Apparently Marchpole's talking the company down because he stands to make a shed load of money if the share price plummets.'

People sometimes changed, but Amy couldn't envisage the Marchpole she had briefly dated two decades earlier maturing into a brutal profiteer. Whatever his faults, and they were legion, he was indissolubly wedded to the concepts of truth and honesty.

'Shocking,' Amy said, revealing neither her connection with Marchpole nor her views. 'They should arrest him for market manipulation.'

As she muttered these platitudes, Amy's mind raced. Was there more to Venner's involvement than met the eye?

6

'You've got another visitor,' said the woman on reception as Amy made her triumphal and sober return to the Priory.

'Not another journalist?'

'No—not a journalist.'

This evasive answer rattled Amy, who hoped fervently her mother hadn't come to call. After the rigours of the funeral, she'd be the last person Amy needed. And given her mother's own lunacy, surely she'd be loath to risk visiting a place awash with shrinks. Catching the anxious expression on Amy's face, the woman added, 'It's a policeman. He's waiting in the lounge.'

Amy found this reassuring, until she saw which policeman. For sitting in an armchair working on the *Telegraph* crossword was Amy's next least favourite person after Ed Smithies—Detective Chief Inspector Dave Carmody of the Metropolitan Police.

She fought the impulse to turn and flee from the man who'd betrayed her to satisfy his lust for professional advancement, as she suspected this was no social visit. If she'd be obliged to speak to him sooner or later, better to face the ordeal now.

'Dave—what the hell are you doing here?'

He looked up. With his aquiline nose and bright eyes, he'd always reminded her of an intelligent budgerigar. And in spite of the man's total unsuitability by any rational measure, her hormone-driven, physical attraction to him still endured.

'The crossword—tough one today.'

She peered at the quarter-completed grid—maybe he was more of a birdbrain than she'd supposed.

'I assume there's some professional reason for your visit.'

'There is,' he replied. 'Although it's nice to see you.'

Amy was damned if she'd reciprocate.

'How are you?' she asked instead.

'Oh, can't complain. And you?'

'As you can see, I'm in rehab.'

The St Paul's incident hung as an unspoken subtext to the conversation. Did this account for his presence—had he come to charge her with an offence?

'You're far too smart to be an alcoholic.'

'Shush—you can't say that here—they accuse you of being in denial. Will this take long?'

'Why?'

'I need a cigarette. Shall we go in the garden?'

'So we're back on the fags again, are we?' he said, in his most chilly, judgmental tone.

And nobody did chilly and judgmental like DCI Carmody.

'It's the only legal way to get a buzz in here.'

Almost everyone smoked, except for Colin, who feared contracting some dread but unspecified disease even from the toxic chemicals clinging to the clothes of the smokers.

The chill air, long autumnal shadows and first leaf fall on the grass signalled that soon winter's icy grip would tighten around them. They sat on a bench inscribed with the name of a former patient.

'So why are you here?'

'To discuss John Venner.'

She lit up her cigarette and gave a throaty chuckle as she exhaled the first lungful.

'If you're investigating his murder, you're too late. They cremated him today.'

'No problem, the autopsy's all done.'

'And what did it show?'

'Significant signs of cardiovascular disease and a clean toxicology report.'

'As expected—so why isn't the case closed?'

'Venner's family released the report to the media hoping to kill the story, but it didn't work. Dr Pexton's theory about an undetectable poison has struck a chord, and it's escalated into a story on police incompetence. So to scotch that, we're now making full enquiries.'

Amy couldn't help but notice his low enthusiasm for the task.

'I do have an alibi if I'm a suspect. And if I'm not, I don't see how I can assist.'

Amy's voice had a bitter edge.

'Do you have any idea what Venner was so keen to tell you?' Carmody made an elaborate show of wafting away a plume of smoke.

'Why no. How could I?'

How unreasonable of everyone to persist in asking. Self-evidently, if she'd known, there would have been no need for him to tell her.

'Did you seen him after he joined IPT?'

'We met up just after he started.'

'What did you discuss?'

It was awkward to answer fully, for it was the evening Venner had handed over the incriminating recording of Smithies—a topic best avoided for now.

'Oh just chitchat—he was sorry I'd left Pearson Malone—his cruise holiday. Nothing much.'

And besides, as they'd sunk four bottles of wine between them, the memories of the evening were fuzzy round the edges.

'Did he suggest anything was amiss at IPT?'

'No—he seemed pretty chipper.'

'And do you think he died of natural causes?'

'Without a doubt. The booze and fags got him, although perhaps hastened by the stress of being hounded by the blogger guy.'

Amy watched as Carmody transcribed her words with painstaking care. He could have sent a junior officer to obtain a routine statement, but had chosen not to. And much as she loathed him, she felt a frisson of pleasure at the possibility he still held a torch for her.

He closed his notebook.

'Thanks—that's helpful.'

Amy doubted if it had been.

'Oh and incidentally, we recovered part of the cash from St Paul's.'

'Who cares? It was only a miserable twenty grand all told. Give it to the police benevolent society or something.'

'That's a very lofty attitude,' said Carmody.

'I'm a very lofty person. Just because *you* earn a poxy police salary, you place an over-exaggerated importance on money. I *know* what it is to earn big bucks, and it doesn't buy you happiness.'

'Yes, but even so…'

'I'm done with capitalism in any case.'

'So remind me—who's paying for your treatment here?' Carmody asked, his gaze sweeping round the elegant grounds.

'BUPA—I'm still on the Pearson Malone group policy.'

'But *you* have left the firm?'

'Yes, of course.'

'Ed Smithies tells me they offered you the chance to change your mind, because of your mental state when you resigned.'

A responsible employer might have done this, though Pearson Malone had chosen not to. And Smithies had once again lied to present himself as a decent human being.

'They didn't, but I'd made up my mind, crazy or sane.'

Carmody said nothing, as Amy justified her decision.

'OK—I get it—in your eyes Crazy Amy failed the ultimate sanity test by walking away from a huge salary. But I was so unhappy, and it's the right answer for my mental health.'

As Carmody patted her arm, perhaps by way of reassurance, Amy shrank away, hyper-aware that any physical contact would weaken her resolve. Intellectually, she understood the man was disastrous for her, but her emotions and hormones were still catching up.

'I'm sure it is,' he said, unable to avoid coming across as patronising.

The strength of Amy's feelings unsettled her. They had never even kissed, their one date had ended in disaster and the narcissistic streak driving his actions would alarm any sane woman. Yet still...

'There was something else,' Carmody began.

'What?'

'You can probably guess.'

Amy softened for a moment, before recovering.

'The answer's still the same. Please don't ask me again.'

Amy was sure the pain in his eyes signified nothing more than a bruised ego, but still she felt guilty.

'I respect your decision but your reasoning is faulty.' He sounded strangely formal, as though dealing with a superior officer with whom he disagreed.

'I don't trust you, and there's an end to it.'

'Your problem,' Carmody pronounced, 'is that you don't trust yourself.'

Right.

After a few moments' silence he picked up his raincoat and stood up.

'Ah well. At least I tried.'

As he made to leave, Amy considered calling him back, but thought better of it.

7

They'd told Carmody his promotion to superintendent had been deferred indefinitely owing to "the economic climate". But these weasel words were merely a cover for internecine departmental politics.

In essence, he'd traded off an embryonic relationship with Amy for a promotion, which his superior officers had in turn traded off for something else. There was a poetic justice in that, he supposed, but Amy's reaction had always struck him as being disproportionate. If *her* promotion had been at stake, wouldn't she have taken a pragmatic view, just as he had? Meanwhile, she required him to accept her many flaws without question—emotional instability, promiscuity, weird hang-ups, substance abuse, to name but a few. Hell, he had bent over backwards to help her, and she'd repaid him by rejecting him.

Carmody hated to lose, especially the one woman he'd ever truly loved, but now he tried to persuade himself it was for the best. How draining to have a partner who took umbrage at every perceived slight, and how damaging for his career to be hitched to a crazy woman. Though on reflection, perhaps the damage had already been done. On top of his "deferred promotion", this Venner enquiry was far from a prestige assignment. They'd left him in no doubt about the "correct" answer—natural death and an early closure of the file. Which, he presumed in his more cynical moments, left the field clear for them to pin the blame on him if a different story surfaced later.

Half-heartedly, he set to the task of complying with their requirements.

***

Marchpole responded to Carmody's email with alacrity, calling back within five minutes on the number he'd provided.

'So, am I number one prime suspect?' he asked, with an edgy little laugh.

'Of course not,' Carmody reassured him. 'I just need to ask you a few questions.'

'I must say you're late to the party. Venner's been dead more than a week and the funeral was yesterday.'

Carmody had only been asked to begin enquiries the day before. But to admit this made the Met sound even more like bumbling fools than Marchpole no doubt imagined.

'We're following due process,' he said.

'So—how can I help?'

'Did you see anyone close by Venner, who might have injected him with poison? Or did he flinch?'

'No—nothing untoward. Obviously he was unwell, but if anyone got to him, I'm positive it happened before Gus and I came on the scene.'

'And Gus is?'

'The guy with the video cam.'

'May I have a copy of the video?'

'Sure,' Marchpole replied. 'I presume you're planning to study it frame by frame—see if you can identify any of those shadowy characters in the background as known assassins.'

Carmody couldn't decide if Marchpole's nervous, jokey banter concealed an underlying anxiety. Did he somehow feel responsible for Venner's death?

'It's an exercise we must undertake.'

'Well, if you must, although the conspiracy theorists have already picked over it exhaustively.'

'You never know—they may have missed something.'

'Unlikely, because if you ask me, DCI Carmody, your whole enquiry is pointless.'

Though he didn't disagree, Marchpole's manner annoyed Carmody.

'I didn't ask you, but no doubt you'll tell me why.'

'Venner wasn't murdered.'

'How can you be so sure?'

'He was a ticking time bomb. He croaked because he smoked, drank, ate too much, and exercised too little—a lesson to us all—although Lord knows, who am I to talk?'

'Unhealthy people can be murder victims too,' said Carmody, trying to re-exert his authority over the discussion.

'But even if he was killed, Richard Pedley is not your man.'

'Why not?'

'He's old pals with Venner from way back. Pedley picked Venner as finance director to lend credibility to the whole shabby set up. So you tell me—why would Pedley kill his most useful asset?'

'Because Venner joined them in innocence, and when he learned the truth he felt obliged to disclose it.'

'I severely doubt that—I'd say Venner was in it right up to his neck. But even if you're right, announcing it at the AGM is *not* Venner's style. Remember, he's a bean counter not a showman. He'd make proper reports through the proper channels, not blurt it out, as Pedley would be aware. So there'd be no need for Pedley to kill him so publicly— he could have bumped him quietly off in the privacy of his own home.'

Irritating as Marchpole was, Carmody had to concede that his arguments seemed cogent.

'You know,' Marchpole added. 'If you're after something meaty to investigate, you should scrutinise these fraudulent AIM listed companies, rather than a non-existent murder. The system is rotten right through—brokers, advisors, lawyers, fund managers, accountants—all skimming off money and playing pass the parcel with the shares. Then suddenly the companies are delisted and everyone's holdings are worthless. And who's the loser when the music stops? The small investor who doesn't understand the rules of the game. IPT is one of many dodgy firms, but none of the establishment elites will call them out, because they're too busy lining their own pockets.'

'I'll bear it in mind,' said Carmody sourly. 'Although it would be helpful to know what proof you have about IPT.'

'Ah well, I'm a few steps ahead of you there, DCI Carmody, and you'll have to wait till I publish my next article to catch up. And there'll be no holds barred where Venner is concerned, because you can't libel the dead.'

'It would be more to the point if you shared your evidence with the appropriate authorities.'

'And I fully intend to. Once I'm done with my investigation I plan to hand over the dossier to the Financial Conduct Authority and possibly the Serious Fraud Office to boot.'

'Well, I'm glad to hear it,' said Carmody.

'But whether they'll act on it is another matter—their reluctance has been a big problem historically.'

'Part of the rotten establishment, eh?'

'You said it—not me,' Marchpole replied. 'Incidentally, have you interviewed Amy Robinson yet?'

'Yes.'

'She still mad as a box of frogs?'

'How do you mean *still*?'

'Oh, I dated her for a while twenty odd years ago—she was nuts then, and no better now from the sound of it.'

'I couldn't possibly comment.'

Carmody desperately wanted more details. How long was a while? Had they slept together? But there was no justification for asking either of these questions.

'Did you find out what Venner meant by "Tell Amy"?'

'It wouldn't be proper for me to discuss it with a journalist.'

'Ah—I'll take that as a no then,' he replied, with remarkable insight.

Infuriating as the discussion had been, it had prompted a useful idea. It might be worth checking whether Venner had contacted the FCA. After a quick phone call, he'd eliminated this option.

***

After Marchpole's anti-establishment bravado, the urbanity of Richard Pedley, IPT's CEO, came as a welcome respite.

Carmody struggled to visualise Pedley as a fraudster, let alone a murderer. And although he was not easily swayed by superficial charm, Carmody sympathised with Pedley's portrayal of himself as the victim of baseless online allegations.

'That chap Marchpole is an absolute menace,' Pedley told him, 'spreading his lies to line his own pockets. Why we've been nominated for awards, and there's every chance we'll be a FTSE company in the next few months. The facts speak for themselves.'

'And what about the suggestion you had Venner killed?'

'I'm appalled. I find it deeply offensive that anyone should think I caused John's death. Why, he was a dear friend.'

'Yes, I understand how absurd these suggestions are, but people will speculate.'

'Oh yes,' said Pedley. 'And nowadays gossip can spread like wildfire on social media.'

'It certainly can. Though Marchpole isn't responsible for the murder rumours, is he?'

'I beg to differ. If that stupid blog hadn't accused us of fraud, the question of murder would never have arisen. And then you see, it's a vicious circle, because the murder proves the fraud exists.'

'Yes, it must be awkward for you.'

'Well, Marchpole will rue the day he ever crossed me. I'll sue the pants off him for what he's done, and Venner's widow plans to do likewise.'

'I assume from what you're saying,' said Carmody, getting to the nub of the matter, 'you don't believe Venner was murdered?'

'Absolutely not,' Pedley replied. 'I was standing right next to him when it happened. The stress of the heckling got to him. John was never one for flapping—could see the poor chap wasn't well. And I'm no medical expert, but it looked awfully like his heart to me.'

***

A brief discussion with Susan Venner established that she too accepted this explanation. And yes, she admitted, the link between Venner's death and Marchpole's activities was tenuous, but she had to play it up to reinforce the pending lawsuit.

It seemed like the whole world was out to get poor old Marchpole, not that Carmody had much pity for him.

Now there was only Ed Smithies left on Carmody's list. 'Ed—Dave Carmody here.'

'Hey, Dave, good to hear from you, buddy. How's it going?'

Carmody had always been at a loss to understand Amy's visceral loathing of Smithies, who'd been unfailingly helpful to Carmody in his last enquiry. But today he tuned in immediately to the nasal droning voice that grated on Amy so much—he'd never noticed it until now. And what was all this pretentious "buddy" stuff—the latest in corporate speak?

'Oh, can't complain—could be worse,' he lied. 'Listen, I won't take up much of your valuable time, but I'm investigating this John Venner affair and I gather you knew him well.'

'Odd you're asking now. I attended his funeral yesterday.'

'So, I expect everyone was talking about speculation surrounding his death?'

'No, not so much. They were all pretty clear on what killed him—a total lack of self-discipline.'

No trace of compassion from Smithies as he delivered this damning verdict.

'Although I'm told his widow is lodging some spurious lawsuit against the blogger guy,' he added.

'How long had you known him?'

'Since I joined the firm, twenty years ago, but I worked with him more closely the last few years. I took over his job after he left—a mammoth task because everything was in a terrible muddle. I've been working round the clock to correct his cock-ups. If all the rumours about him were true, he'd been very distracted.'

'What rumours?'

'I shouldn't speak ill of the dead. And nothing was ever proven.'

For all his reticence, Smithies had nevertheless cast a shadow of suspicion over Venner.

'What's your view on the reports of possible misconduct at IPT?'

'Ah well, let me put your mind at rest. As it happens, I'm acting for IPT now, and I would never accept a questionable client. Besides, these reports as you call them were only the ramblings of that lunatic blogger. No one else has any doubts whatsoever.'

'And in your opinion, was Venner ethically sound?'

'Well, I guess you can never be sure of anyone.'

For the first time, Carmody glimpsed the obnoxious facet of Smithies. He protected his own backside by rebutting the allegations against IPT, but couldn't bring himself to issue an unequivocal endorsement of his dead former colleague. Carmody could almost see Amy's point of view, although, as with everything else, she'd grossly overreacted. Wasn't it part and parcel of professional life to stand up to disagreeable people?

'And you may not be aware,' Smithies continued, 'but that blogger's taken a short position in the shares, so he'll make a packet if the price falls.'

'Yep, so I'd heard.'

Carmody made a mental note to document these aspects of the enquiry with care. If IPT was a paragon of corporate virtue, then the murder theories crumbled to dust—the polar opposite of the vicious circle Pedley had bemoaned.

'Though if there had been anything amiss, Venner could have got caught up unwittingly—he wasn't the sharpest tool in the box. Between you and me, we weren't sorry to let him go.'

With that, Smithies completed his hatchet job on Venner.

'I do hope I've helped. Oh, and if you fancy catching up sometime…'

'Great,' Carmody said, feigning enthusiasm. 'My diary's rather clogged at present, but I'll give you a shout.'

'I've just completed on a super penthouse flat in a new waterfront development in Chelsea—my little city pied-à-terre. It's Churchill Tower—perhaps you know it.'

Carmody did not. Even for Smithies, he reflected, a Chelsea penthouse would be a stretch financially.

'Do drop round one evening and I'll show you round—it has a super roof terrace, with some of the finest views in London.'

'Thanks—I may take you up on that,' said Carmody, although he had no plans to do so.

Now he wished he'd identified Smithies' poisonous side at an earlier stage, when he still had a chance of winning Amy over. *Note to self for future reference.* If the woman you're after detests a casual acquaintance, it's sensible to ditch the acquaintance, at least until after you've closed the deal. This rule applies no matter how illogical the woman's stance may be.

Out of sheer detective's nosiness, he checked the value of the apartment—four million pounds. In isolation, it was affordable on Smithies' million plus profit share—but with his naff pile in the stockbroker belt, kids' school fees, wife's designer wardrobe, and flashy holidays? Doubtful.

Two days later, after a detailed analysis of the video had shown nothing conclusive, Carmody wrote a compelling case to close the file. He prayed his decision wouldn't come back to haunt him.

8

The funeral, combined with Carmody's visit, had left Amy jittery and scouring the internet for information.

The picture on the Shareguru blog showed a vastly different Toby from the gawky ginger-haired lad Amy remembered. His asymmetric features remained, but straightened teeth, hair rendered less vivid by age, and a smart suit, all combined to give the mature Toby an aura of authority. Here was a man no longer troubled by his physical shortcomings.

The blog's attitude to IPT was hostile. It claimed the stated financial results were too good to be true and suggestive of fraud. It cast aspersions on both the CEO Richard Pedley and Venner—Pedley because of his shady past, Venner because his City pedigree was a smokescreen.

In the comments section, much vitriol was poured on this analysis. Those who'd invested in IPT pointed out how much profit they'd made and cited the company's forthcoming promotion to the FTSE 350 as further proof of Marchpole's idiocy. Inevitably, there were those who suspected Marchpole of deliberately driving down the value of the shares for his own nefarious purposes, as Susan Venner had suggested. There was strong sentiment in favour of Venner too. Marchpole had killed him as surely as if he'd murdered him, and what a pity someone hadn't rid the world of this evil peddler of malicious lies.

The Twitterverse took a different attitude, and was all over the murder theory like a rash. The fraud was a given, and Venner an unlikely hero in the fight against the corrupt elite.

Faced with such conflicting pictures, it was impossible to say where the truth lay. It troubled Amy to contemplate Venner as dishonest, and she preferred to buy into the whistleblower scenario, or to argue there was no fraud.

Amid the chaos in her head, one question stood out.

How reliable was Marchpole?

Twenty-two years ago, many expressed their incredulity at Amy and Toby's fleeting relationship. Most of the girls in her class at school swooned over alpha football types, the antithesis of Toby. She told everyone he made her laugh, and she loved his passion for the causes he championed. While this was true, she'd also calculated he'd be so grateful to have her that he wouldn't rock the boat by asking too many questions. Only now did Amy see how the urge to keep her mother's hoarding a secret had driven all her decisions. Ironically, Toby had shown himself to be one of the most inquisitive people on the planet, and his zeal for the facts had killed their brief romance.

Had he carried this trait into adulthood? As he'd become a journalist, probably yes, but the suggestion of him being a short-selling opportunist could not be rejected out of hand.

Marchpole had his own Wikipedia page, which gave a basic account of his life. After gaining a lower second in English at Oxford, he had begun a promising career as a financial journalist on the *Daily Globe*, followed by a spell with the BBC. For reasons shrouded in mystery, he'd reinvented himself as an entrepreneur, setting up an online jewellery boutique. The company had collapsed in spectacular fashion, leaving shareholders nursing huge losses.

After this debacle, he'd ventured back into freelance journalism, but his main business was now Shareguru, known for its investment seminars and state-of-the-nation blog posts decrying corruption in the markets. Toby styled himself as a self-appointed watchdog of the AIM market, seeking out the fraud and malpractice he claimed were rampant. Indisputably, his many detractors had a point. Over the years, he'd frequently been too enthusiastic with his accusations—bordering on market manipulation, some said. But was he merely over-zealous in his pursuit of truth, or cynically putting out lies for his own gain?

From all this ambiguity two points of certainty stood out.

One—before he died, Venner had something to tell Amy. And two—Amy was determined to discover what.

9

Toby sat in his racing green MG sports car, waiting for Amy to emerge from the Priory.

He knew she hadn't forgotten him. And he hadn't been surprised when she'd relented and contacted him—in fact, he'd counted on her curiosity getting the upper hand. And he was intrigued too. Venner's death was only the latest in a string of recent media stories involving Amy.

Most recently, there had been St Paul's. But earlier media reports suggested she was fired from Pearson Malone after exposing a huge fraud committed by a client. Not to mention the ex-husband.

Toby wasn't so much shocked by recent developments, as amazed by the sustained period of normality beforehand. At sixteen, she'd been one crazy chick. How on earth had she acted sane for long enough to become a partner in a leading financial firm, earning a humongous salary and looking every inch the successful businesswoman? And what had happened to tip her over the edge? But while there were plenty of questions to ask Amy, he didn't expect many answers. Transparency had never been her strong suit.

Amy came out wheeling a large suitcase. She was slightly thinner than he remembered, but with a jaunty walk and cheeky smile still familiar to him after two decades. She wore tight white trousers, a fuchsia pink top, matching nails and a black leather biker jacket. Her hair was loose and immaculately blow-dried. A guy knows when a woman's made an effort for him, and Amy had—big style.

She was accompanied by an entourage of fellow patients, who hugged her and swore to stay in touch forever. But unless Amy was drastically changed, Toby predicted they'd never hear from her again.

'Now you take care of her,' a plump motherly woman in a kaftan chided him. It seemed odd advice to a journalist after a story, but who knew what tale Amy had spun? Though as Amy flung her arms around him in an overblown, possessive gesture, the probable storyline became clearer.

She wore the same perfume—Coco by Chanel, still instantly recognisable. It was a scent too sophisticated for a sixteen-year-old girl, but one she'd now grown into.

'Adore your perfume,' he said. 'Always did.'

'Haven't worn it for years. Too strong for the office, but I don't care now. Oh I do love an open top car!'

She adroitly put up her hair with a scrunchie as they pulled out of the drive. As he observed her more closely, the illusion of youth began to unravel. Fine lines on her forehead and round her eyes hinted at the physical toll of a high-flying work-hard, play-hard life.

'Never thought I'd see you again.'

'And likewise,' Amy replied, lighting a cigarette without asking. 'Funny how life works out. By the way, I hope you didn't mind me telling them you were my new boyfriend. I said we'd met at Venner's funeral—easier than going into everything.'

Back in the day, Amy had lied non-stop. She lied to make herself more interesting, she lied about her problems, and she lied when it would have been just as simple to be honest. And she was still lying now.

'Where to?' he asked.

Amy exhaled a long jet of smoke.

'Well. As I'm officially out of rehab, let's celebrate with a drink.'

10

'Cheers,' Amy said as they clinked glasses.

Her first sip of Chablis tasted like nectar, and she gave a murmur of pleasure as she contemplated the rest of the glass.

'Crazy,' said Toby shaking his head. 'Still barking mad. You go through a whole addiction programme and within the hour you fall off the wagon. No—it's even more insane— you throw yourself off, in an act of sheer defiance.'

'I can do what the hell I like,' Amy replied, taking a larger slurp. 'They only put me on the rehab programme because they couldn't agree on a diagnosis.'

'I should have thought they'd have plenty of options to choose from.'

'That's unkind,' Amy rebuked him, although she understood what lay behind his remark. To him and the world, she was Crazy Amy whose insanity had culminated in a dramatic suicide bid. Never mind all the years she'd pretended to hold herself together—they were irrelevant now.

'But they may be onto something. I mean, if you're not an alcoholic why else are you gagging for a drink?'

'I'm not gagging—just keen to prove their brainwashing didn't work.'

'That makes no sense whatsoever,' he told her. 'But, hey, it's your life.'

Amy appraised Toby with a critical eye. He wore a saggy cardigan, a shirt with a loud checked pattern reminiscent of a tablecloth in a downmarket diner, and ill-fitting chinos.

His well-worn deck shoes were dusty and scuffed, his hair thinning. His photographs had flattered him, projecting the image of a man who didn't exist.

'So,' she said. 'What's happened to Toby in the last twenty-two years?'

'Didn't you search online?'

'I did, but I'd prefer your version.'

He repeated the Wikipedia content, putting a positive spin on his business failure, and adding that he was married with three-year-old twins and living in Acton.

'In fact, my wife was in your class at school.'

'Who?'

'Celia Holland. Perhaps you remember her?'

Jealousy stabbed at Amy like an ice pick in her heart. How could anyone forget Celia? She'd been the head girl, beautiful, clever, a talented pianist, an exceptional athlete, who'd led a charmed existence in an immaculate house. In fact, Amy had once pretended to Toby that Celia's house was hers, as part of her ongoing quest to conceal the dump where she actually lived. She doubted if he'd remember this though.

Unwilling to admit she'd checked on Celia's progress in the intervening decades, Amy feigned a gradual process of recollection.

'Oh yes—wasn't she the head girl, or am I mixing her up with someone else?'

'No—that was Celia.'

'Ah yes, I saw something about her in the school Old Girls' magazine, she's a criminal barrister, isn't she?'

'A QC,' he said proudly. 'Appointed very young, too.'

Odd. Celia could have landed any man she wanted, so why did she end up with an offbeat misfit like Toby?

'I didn't even realise you were friendly with Celia back then,' Amy said, stifling her incredulity.

'I wasn't—we met by chance at Oxford before realising we'd lived a few blocks apart most of our lives. We must have rubbed shoulders dozens of times without realising.'

'And you lived happily ever after.' Amy was unable to keep the edge from her voice.

'Yes, very happily.' But his voice sounded flat and lacked conviction.

'I'm happy too,' she replied, twirling round the splash of Chablis remaining in her glass.

And indeed, in that moment, she was. With the first glass of wine, she'd felt the buzz of being reacquainted with a friend older and more familiar than Toby.

'So what's your back story then?' asked Toby, topping her up.

'No doubt you checked me out too, but here goes. Maths at Southampton, qualified as an accountant, ended up head of the Entrepreneurs Tax Advisory Group at Pearson Malone—got married, got divorced. No kids.'

'That précis of your life almost makes you sound normal.'

'Well, I did try.'

'Until it all went pear-shaped.'

'It didn't go pear-shaped.'

'No? Leaving aside the fraud case, and your ex-husband, what could be worse than attempted suicide?'

'Now, Toby—you know the mainstream press is full of shit. It says so on your blog.'

'Touché. We'll return to those aspects of your life later.'

'We will not,' said Amy firmly. 'We're here because of Venner. And don't ask me what he wanted to say, because obviously I don't know.'

'Not even an inkling?'

'No.'

'But you can still dish the dirt on him.'

Amy shook her head. The only potential dirt was the vile lies Smithies had concocted to drive Venner out of the firm.

'I'm afraid there is none—he was a decent guy.'

'Are you certain?'

'I worked with him for six years and saw nothing to suggest any unethical tendencies.'

'A politician's reply if ever I heard one.'

'But what else can I say? I can't prove he wasn't a rogue, but equally you can't prove he was.'

Toby paused.

'Well, let's put it this way, I have a hard time believing Venner wasn't aware of something wrong at IPT. Now, you've read the blog, I'm sure. As a qualified accountant, do you not find the high profit margin suspicious?'

'Yes, but there may be a rational explanation.'

'For fuck's sake,' said Toby, banging the table for emphasis. 'They sell plastic pipes and plumbing components. It's not a cutting-edge industry sector. They should make the same margins as their competitors.'

Never one to attend a meeting under-prepared, Amy launched into a spirited response based on her research.

'Well I hear they have a uniquely efficient supply chain, an incentivised sales force and...'

'Amy—that's crap,' said Toby, slapping the table again. 'The margins are not only too high, they're way too smooth—you'd expect a degree of volatility, like their competitors.'

'So—they run their company better—they genuinely are the best in class.'

'Oh please. They feed this garbage to the numpties who buy the shares. But you're a trained professional. And here's another oddity—why do they carry more than a year's inventory?'

'It's because their Chinese supplier shuts down shipping in January, plus the capacity of the new distribution centre near Beijing. I read the annual review and it sounds reasonable to me.'

'It's meant to sound reasonable to morons, but not to people with brains. I've got hold of shipping records, which prove the January shutdown is bollocks. And if you'd paid more attention, you'd know that the distribution hub merely centralises their holdings for the Asian and North American market.'

Amy topped up her own glass without saying a word, and let him continue.

'Now as I see it, Venner and Pedley are chums in this together. And Venner may have been superficially affable, but still crooked. Now was he stupid?'

'No—razor-sharp.'

'Well there you go—he had to have been aware of the fraud.'

'What fraud? Where's your proof?'

'The reality is,' he prattled on, ignoring Amy's objection, and with a splendid disregard for the facts, 'they hired him to lend an air of respectability to IPT at a time when a few awkward buggers like me started sniffing round. And, you've got to ask, why did the previous finance director leave so suddenly? Isn't that a red flag?'

'Ill health.'

'What a perfect excuse. And why have they chewed through three different auditors in recent years? Isn't that another warning sign?'

'Well, it passed Pearson Malone's take on procedures.'

'Good grief. Why are you defending those shysters after what they did to you?'

To be honest, Amy wasn't sure.

'And even PM have resigned now.'

'Only so they could advise IPT on tax planning without conflicts of interest.'

'Oh phooey. They got windy about it—they know as well as I do there's something afoot. I'm only scratching the surface, but I'll get to the bottom of it if it kills me, with or without your help to discredit Venner.'

Though Amy had never offered to help discredit Venner, clearly this had been Marchpole's intention all along.

'But it's still possible Venner planned to blow the whistle, like everyone's saying.'

'You don't get it, do you,' Toby said, continuing with his rant. 'There are plenty of companies like IPT. It's a big money-go-round. They float the company and raise a shed load of cash. The big boys invest and pass on the shares to someone who'll pay more. The directors milk the business, the brokers and advisors render their inflated bills, and creative accounting disguises the woeful financial performance. It's all smoke and mirrors and when the music stops, the shares are delisted and it's the little investors who get stiffed.'

'Well they know the risks. And aren't they just greedy little people who want something for nothing?'

'But aren't they *entitled* to a return on their investment? Or is that only for the elite City boys?'

Amy shrugged.

'Sophisticated investors will always outperform the amateurs. It's how the world works.'

'Yes, because the system's rigged against the ordinary folk. And these scandals don't shock you because you're part of the same rotten culture, like Venner. Which is how I know he was no whistleblower.'

'That's *so* unfair,' Amy protested. Most of the firms she'd worked with had been decent, professional—even Pearson Malone most of the time. At any rate, she'd seen no signs of systematic collusion to stitch up the little guys.

But it was pointless to argue with Toby. Like most conspiracy theorists, he regarded an absence of evidence for the conspiracy as further proof of how dastardly it was.

'Oh come on, Amy. Have your brains been addled while you've been navel-gazing in that plush private hospital? Have they lobotomised you or something? Because I had you pegged as a girl who asked questions, who exposed a dodgy client.'

'I'm not allowed to discuss it.'

'What the heck? Who's stopping you?'

'As part of my termination negotiations I've signed an agreement not to talk to the press.'

The agreement was not specific to the particular issue and its enforceability was, according to Amy's lawyer, debateable—but Toby didn't need to know that. He'd love to have the inside story, she was sure—exclusive access to the damning recordings, the whole shebang—and would be horrified to know what she was holding back. Which was all the more reason for saying precisely nothing.

'Oh, bloody marvellous. You go to considerable trouble in exposing a fraud and then the bastards buy you off! And don't tell me—you're so naïve you're hoping for a great reference and to walk into another plum job. Let me enlighten you, Amy—you're unemployable. You've broken ranks with all those other City crooks and you're finished.'

Amy's eyes smarted. His barb had cut to the heart of her worst fears—that everything she'd striven for in her life had been in vain. She topped up her glass again and took a big gulp, hoping to swallow her emotions along with the wine.

'Hey, yeah, like you were finished after your business venture collapsed.'

She'd jabbed at his sore point, hoping he might see how he'd hurt her, but he continued unabashed.

'Look, I admit I made mistakes. I didn't foresee that the model wasn't sustainable. Heck, I'm not perfect, and I apologised to anyone who lost money. But you—you spent years as a parasite, selling dodgy tax schemes and raking off huge fees with each revolution of the money roundabout. You suppressed your moral compass. And naturally you think Venner was OK—because you're just as corrupt.'

To be accused of being a moral vacuum after everything she'd sacrificed in the name of her principles was too much to bear. To Amy's chagrin, tears coursed down her cheeks. And finally, Toby recognised he'd overstepped the mark.

He put his hand on hers—familiar and comforting. This was the Toby she'd fallen for at sixteen, who was passionate about justice and equality. And who didn't shrink from expressing his displeasure at anyone who violated his moral code. She shouldn't take it personally.

'Hey, I'm sorry,' he said. 'I've hit a raw nerve—I didn't mean you specifically.'

'Shall we have some more wine?'

Amy held up the empty bottle, and caught the waiter's eye. He must have noticed her fragile emotional state, for he reappeared with commendable speed with a replacement.

How different Toby was from Dave Carmody, Amy reflected. If Carmody had allowed her to drink at all, he'd have lectured her ad nauseam about the need not to overdo it after a month's abstinence. Undoubtedly, he would have vetoed the second bottle, whereas Toby had pointed out her craziness, and let her roll with it.

'I agree there are rotten apples in the City,' Amy admitted between hiccupping sobs, 'which is why I walked away. I did my best to be a decent person, and I'm well aware I'll suffer for it, without you ramming it down my throat.'

'Of course.' Toby now tried, belatedly, to make amends for his insensitivity. 'What you did was brave—few have the guts to stand up for what's right. And you're not unemployable—there's bound to be a job for you somewhere.'

'Well, I gather IPT are in the market for a Finance Director.' Amy forced a laugh. 'I bet I'd solve the mystery in two minutes.'

'I bet you would too.'

'And if I went in undercover, no one would twig that Crazy Amy, super sleuth, was on the case.' They held eye contact for a smidgeon longer than necessary, their little spat forgotten.

Amy still found him appealing. Much of the bilge he spouted was misguided, but he sincerely believed it and had the courage to stand up to what he saw as a corrupt establishment. And Amy reckoned he felt the spark too, even though he was married to the perfect Celia.

'You know what,' she said. 'I think you'd better take me home—Chiswick's on the way to Acton, after all.'

11

Amy woke with a pounding headache and a powerful urge to vomit. How had a month without alcohol turned her into such a lightweight?

Toby was gone, but no matter—last night had been a one-off, and she was in control. Toby hadn't wanted to be unfaithful—or take advantage of a drunken woman—or use her body. Sure—she understood—it proved he was a decent human being. But even a decent man can succumb to temptation.

For Amy, their fling had concluded unfinished business from the past. She now had an overwhelming sense of having come full circle, of "closure" to use the word so loved at the Priory.

The shower washed away the worst of her hangover. She stood lathering shampoo into her hair, exhilarated by her freedom. If she never heard from Toby again, fine. In fact, she rather hoped she wouldn't, or at least not for another twenty years. Because by then they'd be knocking on the door of old age and able to look back dispassionately on their lives.

Amy tottered downstairs to the luxury kitchen with its granite worktops and sleek white units. A mould-encrusted coffee machine greeted her, reminding her how much time had elapsed since her impromptu departure to the Priory. She eyed the integrated refrigerator with suspicion—unable to recollect what had been in there, but disinclined to check in her nauseous state. Instant black coffee it would be then.

The immaculately restored grandeur of her Victorian house had always terrified Amy. The kitchen was a particular focus of her insecurities, a disquieting symbol of the gulf between the charmed life she craved and her inner feeling of unworthiness. The mega job, the designer wardrobe and the alpha male husband had all been part of the same syndrome.

Now, Amy viewed matters differently. Oddly, Toby's voicing of her worst fears had enabled her to confront and overthrow the dread she'd tried to suppress. So what if she couldn't find another high-flying job—she'd been miserable in it anyway. The house was an emblem of everything rotten, and now superfluous, in her life, and she'd put it on the market without delay.

Her phone rang, shaking her out of her reverie.

Toby.

Typical—you're ambivalent about a guy and he's on the phone before you can blink. Otherwise, you wait, willing him to call, for all eternity.

'Hi there—I trust you're not too fragile this morning,' he said with depressing jollity. But then, he'd drunk vastly less than her. 'We've plenty to do, if it wasn't just the wine talking yesterday evening.'

He neither mentioned the conclusion to the evening, nor thanked her for it. Somehow this mattered more than it should have done.

'I'm not with you.'

Amy was wary, in case her recollection of the evening was less than precise.

'Your brilliant idea—going undercover as finance director in IPT Plc.'

She gave a hearty laugh.

'Um, you do realise I was joking?'

'Well yes, and it would be a tough one to pull off. They'd never hire Amy Robinson and if we put you in undercover, we'd struggle to construct a fake identity robust enough to stand up to scrutiny.'

'Oh well, that's it then,' said Amy, puzzled he'd even bothered to bring it up.

'But it's not—you see I've come up with an even more brilliant idea.'

'What?'

'If you'll have lunch with me, I'll tell you.'

It sounded to Amy like a pretext for something else, and an irrational gratification distracted her from simply asking what the idea was. And by the time she'd arranged to meet him at a Mexican bar and restaurant in Chiswick High Street, the moment to ask him had passed.

12

Toby sat with a Sol beer and a newspaper, waiting for Amy to arrive. Although she was late, he fully expected her to show up.

She'd repeatedly proclaimed that the sex was a one-off, but had she meant it? In many respects, he hoped so, because otherwise he lacked the willpower to resist. Amy had stirred something in him that had lain dormant for many years—and now it had reawakened it would be difficult to control. It wasn't just sexual attraction either—but emotions, potent though only half-understood.

A pang of guilt walloped him as a family walked into the restaurant—shiny happy people, much as the Marchpole family appeared to the rest of the world. No one would guess from the outside how Celia's secrets and his undistinguished career weighed on them.

In many respects, it would be easier if Amy stood him up. He was certain his feelings were reciprocated, whatever she'd said, and they'd end up having a full-blown affair. And it would not be long before Celia, with her finely honed deductive powers, caught on. For all Toby knew, she was of those heartless "one strike and you're out" women, moving with unseemly haste to end their marriages at the merest hint of infidelity. They'd never discussed the matter—there'd never been any need. He didn't want to lose Celia, or to hurt her, but he feared that the passion now ensnaring him would be too powerful to rein in.

He should leave the restaurant now and remove himself from temptation. He would find someone else to help him with IPT. Yes, it made sense.

Too late. Amy strolled through the door, immaculately dressed and coiffured once again. Just the once—bollocks to that.

'Mine's a margarita,' were her opening words.

'Are you sure?'

'Definitely. The sooner I get back to normal drinking levels the better—sobriety really doesn't agree with me.'

'Do you want to eat?'

'Some mini-fajitas might hit the spot—better than drinking on an empty stomach.'

'Any regrets?'

He couldn't resist asking, but despised himself for showing he cared.

She gave him that enigmatic smile of hers he remembered so well, which now exposed the crinkles around her eyes. Amy's face belonged to a woman who'd been unafraid of life, and Toby admired her for that. By contrast, a jumble of absurd fears lay behind the unlined perfection and confident façade of the juice-drinking, near-teetotal Celia.

'No—none whatsoever. How about you?'

'Same.'

His indifferent words belied his inner turmoil, but it could be worse, he supposed—if she had no regrets, she might want more.

'But as I've made clear,' she said, knocking Toby's optimism on the head. 'Last night was strictly a one-off—fun, but never to be repeated.'

So why was she dressed up for him then? Was she taunting him, or did the clothes reveal the lie?

'Fine by me. As long as we're on the same page.'

After they'd ordered the food, Amy turned to the ostensible purpose of their meeting.

'So—what's this brainwave of yours?'

'I checked out other vacancies at IPT—jobs they'll fill without putting the applicants through the Spanish inquisition. And here's what I found.'

He whipped out his iPad and brought an advertisement up on screen.

EA to CEO, IPT Plc—Negotiable to £50K

'No way,' said Amy, with vehemence.

'But it's a golden opportunity. You'd go in undercover and you'd be working for Richard Pedley himself. You'd have access to data at the highest level.'

'No.'

'What's the problem?'

'Why should I help you?'

'Because you want to know.'

She'd said so not once but repeatedly the previous evening—and he trusted that the strength of this motivation would secure her cooperation.

'But I'd never get the job. They're after someone who can type at sixty words per minute, with outstanding skills in Microsoft Office. There'll be tests and there's no way I'd bluff my way through.'

'No problem. The agency who ran the ad will conduct the tests, so we can find someone to do them for you—they'll be none the wiser.'

'But what about my CV? It says they want an experienced EA.'

'You will be. We'll build an entire fake ID with references. I'm sure you can wing it at the screening interview, then impress Pedley on the final selection day.'

'Yes but there's no guarantee that I'll be successful.'

'Why not? You're the tops—you could do it standing on your head. Attention to detail—excellent spelling, grammar and grasp of business English. Organisational ability. Hell—Amy—these are skills you already have.'

'A calm and measured individual?' Amy read out. 'I'm trying not to laugh.'

'Well, that part *might* be a problem,' Toby conceded. 'Although I'm betting you are calm and measured most of the time. And you can pretend, can't you? You're good at that. Compared to your previous job, this will be a doddle.'

'It better had be. They're only paying a measly fifty grand a year tops.'

He'd heard about City fat cats being out of touch with financial reality, but had imagined Amy would be more grounded.

'Fifty thou is a good salary, even in London, Amy. Many people would give their eye teeth to earn that money. You'll still be living a relatively privileged life.'

'Only kidding. Even at PM we employed people on less and they managed to eke out a bare, subsistence-level existence.'

She grinned at him, but he wasn't convinced. A part of her regarded the salary on offer as a pittance, however much she protested.

'But even if I applied,' Amy went on. 'There's still no guarantee I'll be hired.'

'I have a cunning plan to maximise your chances.'

'What?'

'We can use Pedley's ego to our advantage. He has two

main weaknesses. One, he prides himself on his impeccable judgement, and secondly he's susceptible to a pretty girl. So we engineer a chance meeting between you, and he gets to like you, giving you an edge in the recruitment process.'

'How do you know all this?'

'Ah well, I got an inside track from the previous secretary. I wangled her contact details on a pretext and found her very forthcoming. Turns out things didn't end well. She'd been offering very personal services to Pedley until he got bored and fired her. Then she kicked up a huge fuss, filed a complaint against him for harassment and threatened to tell Foxy Roxy.'

'Who?'

'That Chinese bird from IPT's PR agency—Pedley's girlfriend.'

'None of this is encouraging. I've only recently escaped from a psycho, control freak boss, so why should I work for another?'

'Because you need to know what Venner meant. You said so yesterday, many times.'

'Yes,' she agreed. 'I do need to know.'

'So are you in?'

'Only one slight reservation. I'm wondering how risky this is. If Venner was murdered…'

'But you don't believe that, any more than I do.'

'No but…'

'But what? No murder, no danger—nuff said. So are you in or out?'

'OK,' said Amy, after a long pause. 'I'm in.'

Mission accomplished—done and dusted before their lunch had even arrived. If only it was as easy to persuade Amy to develop their relationship.

13

The two Americans sat in the transit pod at Heathrow. The five-minute journey from the car park to the terminal, safe from listening devices, was plenty long enough for their discussion.

'Nice work with Venner,' said Patrick, the older guy. Now in his sixties, he had finally reached the point where he could praise his subordinate without weakening his own position. 'The consensus is you headed off a major international incident.'

Ethan, some thirty years Patrick's junior, suffered from a reputation for impetuosity. He'd decided to eliminate Venner on a whim, without the correct authorisations, and had sweated over the likely consequences. But now he was being lauded for his incisiveness. And while he suspected that his superiors still sought an excuse to criticise him, this deniable covert operation would provide no ammunition.

'Thanks—I wish the media hadn't gotten hold of the story though.'

'Might have helped to do it somewhere a little less public,' observed Patrick with his wry humour.

Typical—he never gave praise without some negative to counterbalance it. But the timing was critical—it had been essential to stop Venner.

'The journalist concerns me,' said Ethan. 'He's been sniffing round for a while now.'

'What—that Marchpole fruitcake?' Patrick replied with a dismissive snort. 'He's one crazy dude who's out to make a quick buck when the stock price falls. He'll never figure it out—heck he's not even looking.'

'But Venner did.'

'Venner was way smarter.'

'We could put him under surveillance,' Ethan said.

'Total waste of our resources.'

Ethan disagreed. Since it had been a pure fluke that they'd stopped Venner in his tracks, it must be tempting fate to ignore Marchpole.

'Or why not take him out as well—to be on the safe side?'

'Ethan—you young guys are far too trigger-happy. And just because you happened to make the right call on Venner doesn't give you a mandate going forward. Is that understood?'

'Plainly. But I still say watch him, for a while at least. And if nothing comes up, we back off. Look at it this way—it may stop me having to make another snap decision. What do you say?'

'I'll give it some thought on the flight home.'

14

'Ash blonde and as short as you like. I'm in the mood for a change.'

The stylist ran her hands through Amy's glossy shoulder-length chestnut hair.

'Are you sure?'

'Positive.'

Whatever happened now, the sleek mane was history—a wig donned to act the part she'd played to perfection for over thirty years.

She'd take her chances with the EA job and see where that led. IPT might well be less than squeaky clean, and no one was better equipped than Amy to dig for the dirt. But besides her quest for the facts, something far more fundamental motivated Amy, which she hadn't mentioned to Toby for fear of ridicule. Her old life lay in tatters, and she'd grown sick of being pitied and shunned as Crazy Amy. The chance to become a different person, unencumbered by all the baggage of the past, was irresistible. And who knew—perhaps by assuming another identity, she might at last find her true self?

The stylist worked in silence, sensing that chitchat would not be well received. She doubtless pigeon-holed Amy as yet another newly divorced woman having all her hair chopped off, and Amy was content to leave her in ignorance. For she could barely understand, let alone convey, the seismic shift in her psyche and the new sanity emerging from her madness like a butterfly from its chrysalis.

***

Two hours later Amy left the salon with a short, sassy blonde crop, and an urgent need to shop for clothes—one of her favourite activities. The Armani suits hanging in the wardrobe at home were well beyond her new price range, and from now on the mainstream high street stores would cater to her needs.

This is how normal people live, she reminded herself as she examined the price tags, people who don't earn half a million quid a year. Wow, a suit for less than £100, and with tailoring far more precise than she'd expected. And a dress for £55, not quite as elegantly cut as Nicole Farhi, but hey— who cared? She would wear it with bravado. And such a stylish blouse—not silk but who would notice?

She scooped up suits, dresses and tops with enthusiasm and bought everything that fitted. Wow—a whole work wardrobe for less than she'd have paid for one suit in her Pearson Malone days.

The jewellery would have to go—EAs didn't wear diamond earrings, or Omega watches. But the high street chains were full of funky little imitation pieces that suited her new persona down to the ground. She'd keep her favourite Tiffany gold earrings though—they were so cute and no one would know their origin. And she'd keep her shoes—painful enough wearing stilettos again after three months without breaking new cheap pairs in.

As a final detail, Amy picked out a clear pair of glasses.

15

'Wow,' said Toby, as he strolled into the pub off Oxford Street. 'When I said you'd have to change your appearance, I didn't have anything so drastic in mind.'

'What—don't I look the part?'

'Did I say that? No—you look tremendous.'

'Not too intellectual?'

'Well you do project a certain aloofness, but perhaps that's no bad thing. It might help Pedley keep his hands off you.'

'Or not hire me more like,' said Amy gloomily as she took the first swig of her gin and tonic.

'I've sorted out your new identity, anyway.'

'Great.'

Toby didn't know it, but she had a Plan B. If Pedley didn't hire her, she would use her alias to slink away incognito somewhere obscure.

'Your new name is Jane Eccles.'

Amy spluttered into her glass.

'*Jane Eccles*! You must be kidding. Don't I get to choose?'

'I'm afraid not.'

This was not at all the name she'd envisaged for herself when shopping for her wardrobe. She'd thought of Emma or Alice, and a distinguished surname with class. Jane Eccles sounded chavvy to Amy's ears.

'Oh, and I need your picture for the passport.'

'Passport?'

'Why yes. You'll have to verify your ID when you join. And

we'll have a driving licence for you, bank accounts, oh yes, and you'll need to rent a flat. That place in Chiswick is way too flash for a secretary—must be worth two and a half mill.'

He'd obviously done his research. That very morning Amy had settled on an asking price of £2,590,000, with a view to accepting a touch less than the sum suggested by Toby. This would leave her upwards of a million pounds to start a new life. In summary, she told herself, whatever happened with Jane, her situation could be a lot worse.

16

The American Bar in the Savoy was one of Amy's old haunts from Pearson Malone days, and therefore a risky venue. But hopefully the dramatic change in hairstyle would lessen the chance of being recognised. According to Toby, Pedley came here when he had no evening engagement. Amy was sceptical at first and then amused—what sort of man treats the Savoy like a local pub?

Amy, or rather Jane, sat strategically positioned to see Pedley arrive. Even though her wardrobe was much reduced, she'd still dithered over choosing her outfit. Eventually she'd settled on a navy dress and jacket, with her fake pearls—safe professional attire.

Toby's intelligence proved to be spot on. Shortly before six, Pedley strolled in, sat down and summoned the waiter, who greeted him effusively.

Pedley was in his early sixties, with a shock of white hair combed rakishly back. He wore the obligatory Savile Row suit and hand-stitched shirt, with a handkerchief in his breast pocket. For no particular reason, Amy recalled her father, dead at forty-two. He'd always been a snappy dresser, fond of sharp tailoring, although never in the market for bespoke suits. He'd always worn a bow tie, she remembered.

Men like Pedley were a dying breed. Mostly alumni of minor public schools, they were relics of a time when an unwritten code of 'gentlemanly' conduct had yet to be supplanted by political correctness and reams of ineffective legislation. Nowadays, it was unusual to find Pedley's sort as a CEO, although there were still plenty of them strutting their stuff in non-executive roles.

Once she'd finished her initial sizing up, Amy drained her glass and approached her prey with the planned opening gambit. She hoped that Toby's information about Pedley being a smoker was accurate; otherwise the conversation would be very short.

'Excuse me, but do you have a light? I'm gasping for a ciggie.'

He gave her a lounge lizard's up and down appraisal. She must have passed the test, because he said, 'Sure, no problem for a beautiful young lady like you.'

Only the most hard-hearted feminist would be offended by his old-fashioned, politically incorrect charm. Amy simpered as he handed her a gold lighter, heavy enough to be the real thing.

'Wow. That must have cost a fortune,' she observed. 'Aren't you afraid I might be a con woman planning to steal it?'

'No,' he said airily. 'I'm familiar with your type. After years of experience, I'm a great judge of people.'

The irony amused Amy.

'I'll be back shortly.'

Pedley displayed no sign of anxiety when she returned minutes later, his trust in her repaid.

'May I buy you a drink?' he asked, with depressing predictability. 'Or are you waiting for someone?'

'Well I am, but unfortunately he's been held up, so yes, a drink would be very welcome. I'll have a gin and tonic please.'

'Large or small?'

'I'll stick with a small one for now,' she replied—for first time in her life.

But this was Jane's life, not Amy's, and Jane was a sensible, sassy woman—moderate in all respects. Amy's role as a Pearson Malone partner had required her to project an air of complete invincibility. Now, to be credible as an EA, Jane must add a smattering of humility and find the perfect pivot point between confidence and modesty.

'I'm Jane,'

At least she'd remembered to use her fake name, which was a start.

'Richard. You're looking very smart, I must say. Are you meeting your boyfriend?'

'Now why do you assume that if I'm dressed nicely, it's for a boyfriend?'

Would Jane pull him up for his comment? Amy didn't know, but it was too late to retract her remarks.

'Isn't that the most natural explanation? Am I wrong?'

'As it happens, yes. I'm here to talk to someone about a job.'

'I would definitely hire you,' Pedley assured her.

If he was surprised by Jane drinking alcohol before a job interview, he didn't say so. But then, in his heyday, before the mineral water brigade had seized control, people weren't so fixated on sobriety as a virtue.

'What job are you applying for?' he asked, perhaps wondering if she was a high-class hooker.

'I'm an executive assistant—and someone very well-known is coming, hopefully to give me the final nod of approval.'

'Executive assistant,' said Richard, rolling the words around. 'My HR people tell me that's the correct term for a secretary these days.'

He looked doubtful, as though he suspected they'd mis-informed him. He probably believed the HR department should be called Personnel.

'Yep—they're doing a good job keeping you up to date with the jargon.'

'I suppose you can't say who this well-known man is.'

'Did I say it was a man?'

'No, but I assumed so. Prickly, aren't we?'

Whoops—a slight misstep there. Men like Pedley could be prickly themselves, and it didn't pay to challenge them too aggressively. The old order was changing fast and they didn't much care for the new, diverse playing field. Sexism and racism still simmered under the cover of political correctness.

'Not prickly, but too argumentative for my own good sometimes.' She gave him a disarming smile. 'But you'll spot him when he comes in.'

'Secretary eh?' he said. 'I'm hiring a secretary at the moment.'

'What a coincidence.'

Amy's eyes-wide-open astonishment was done to absolute perfection.

'Yes, isn't it?' He spoke in a way that made Amy wonder whether he knew she was playing him.

'What company do you work for?'

'I don't work for a company. The company works for me—I own most of it.'

'Oh—most impressive. And would I have heard of your company?'

He took out a gold case and extracted a card with the IPT logo.

'Oh, gosh—I bought my bathroom taps from you guys.'

Amy would have sooner died than install mass-market bathroom accessories. Jane was a different animal though.

'Not surprising,' he said. 'Our retail arm is going from strength to strength. So what time is the mystery man due?'

'Six-fifteen.'

'Ah—he's late. And who did you say he was?'

'I didn't.'

'But can't you tell me, seeing as how I'll recognise him?'

'There's no fooling you is there?'

Amy leaned over and whispered a name in Pedley's ear. She prayed he didn't know him—London was nothing but a big village sometimes.

'I've never seen him here before.'

Amy gave an inscrutable smile, as she pretended to consult her phone.

'Ah—he's emailed—he won't be here until seven.'

'You going to wait?'

'I am. Why—would you tell him to get lost?'

'I might, if I had other irons in the fire. How'd you like to come and work for me?'

It surprised Amy how effortlessly she'd manipulated him. The game plan had been to engage him in pleasant conversation and give herself an advantage at interview—Pedley's suggestion was an unexpected bonus.

'Well I'm hoping everything will pan out with the other job.'

'Sure, but if I upped the offer…'

'You know nothing about me,' Amy laughed as Pedley called the waiter over with an imperious click of the fingers.

'Well let me find out. For a start, where are you working now?'

Amy trotted out her rehearsed CV, soon to be backed up by fake references. Her current position, working for the CEO of a recently taken over company had become redundant, she told him. In fact, the CEO in question was a chum of Toby's—in the picture and prepared to play ball.

'Ah—so you have experience of working with a CEO.'

'Most definitely.'

Many CEOs shared the same characteristics and Amy had seen the worst of them among her entrepreneurial clients. First, they possessed an innate sense of entitlement and required everyone to do their bidding. Second, if their instructions were misguided, their subordinates took the flak. Third, should they fail to issue instructions, mind reading was required. Fourth, the inevitable trail of devastation they left in their wake must be swept away unobtrusively and without humiliating them. There are more narcissists among CEOs than any other section of society, and beneath the suave façade, Pedley could easily be one of them.

'So you understand what's required.'

'I certainly do,' Amy said. 'You need someone loyal who shows initiative.'

'Spot on, but most of these girls lack gumption.'

The "these girls", with its baked-in casual sexism, nearly prompted Amy to suggest he hired a man. But Jane would hold back.

'Although, take it from me, if you fire them for incompetence, they suddenly turn into human dynamos, wheeling out hot shot employment lawyers and threatening to take you to tribunal. And it's odd, because if they'd shown the same energy in the role you wouldn't have sacked them in the first place.'

'That must be *so* annoying,' Amy replied diplomatically.

'You should definitely apply, Jane. There's something about you—you're a real class act.'

'Well I'm very flattered, but in the nicest possible way—no. I'm really keen on the other opening.'

'Of course—I understand. But if it doesn't work out, would you consider it?'

'Yes—why not!'

The waiter arrived with Amy's drink. She'd prearranged for Toby to call her at 6.55pm prompt, pretending to be the prospective boss changing the venue. There was thirty minutes left to kill, but this proved not to be a problem. Pedley's superficial old world charm made conversation effortless, as long as she stuck to non-controversial topics. And it gave Amy the chance to ease her way into the new role.

At the appointed hour, Toby called and Amy gave her excuses. She left wondering whether the meeting had been a little too straightforward.

17

'You,' said Pedley as she walked into the final interview two weeks later. 'What happened to the other job?'

'Well, after the guy switched the venue, he took an hour to arrive, and by then I felt at best lukewarm about the role. And I enjoyed chatting to you tremendously, so I thought well why not apply?'

'I'm glad you're here,' he said, with every appearance of sincerity. 'But be honest with me—they didn't hire you at the other place.'

There seemed little point in denying a fictitious point of detail in a bigger lie. Better to play to Pedley's ego with flattery.

'OK, I'll level with you—I should have realised I couldn't pull the wool over your eyes.'

He shot her a shady City gent's reptilian smile.

'So what went wrong?'

'Truthfully?'

He nodded.

'He wanted a yes-girl, which I'm not. And from what you've told me, I don't think you're looking for one of those either.'

This was true up to a point. Pedley likely wanted an EA who would second guess him, but not outrun him, to hire an "independent mind" who would always boost his ego. What better tribute to his genius than a smart girl who always deferred to him?

'Yes, Jane—you have an inner core of steel. Some men might find it threatening.'

'Not the intelligent ones though,' said Amy, lathering on more of the soft soap.

'In fact, I rather like it,' he agreed.

Although she'd got off to a storming start, it turned out Pedley hadn't been as readily suckered by her bullshit and flattery as she'd imagined. The interview was far from being the perfunctory affair she'd envisaged, and she strained to answer some of the searching questions he posed. She'd assumed far more about Pedley—based on his old-school, sexist, pompous exterior—than he had about her. If he appointed her, she would have to watch her step.

The end of the interview came as something of a relief, particularly when Pedley told her she was hired.

'I should pretend to think about it,' she said, 'but this is exactly my kind of dynamic company, so I've already made my decision. Provided you come up with a sensible financial offer, I'll accept.'

'And how much would be sensible?'

'Fifty,' Amy replied firmly. 'That's what the other guy would have offered and I'm worth it.'

'The other guy didn't hire you,' Pedley shot back. 'But I shan't haggle. Fifty it is, plus a signing on bonus of two thousand.'

They shook hands and as Amy walked out of the building, she wondered what her new life held in store.

18

'You actually like the sleazy old rogue, don't you?' Toby suggested, only half-jokingly, as Amy described her interview.

'God no, he's a creep,' said Amy, with a mock shudder. 'Although I must admit, he's smarter than I expected—he gave me a real going over in the interview.'

'I never said he was dumb, but he's a smooth conman so you'll need to be careful. Don't let him bamboozle you.'

Amy had no intention of being bamboozled by anyone, and Toby's suggestion that she'd been swayed by Pedley's charisma irritated her—particularly as there was a nugget of truth in it.

'Don't worry—I'll be very much on my guard,' she said, in sarcastic tones.

'Impressed that you nailed it though.'

And so he should be—she doubted he would have pulled off such a convincing performance.

'So,' said Toby. 'I've got all the components of Jane's new life here. Passport. You should avoid travelling abroad on it, but it'll do for an ID check.'

Too bad about the passport, thought Amy. Weirdly, now she'd landed the role, solving the mystery suddenly assumed less importance. It seemed much more appealing to slink off somewhere and become Jane Eccles permanently.

'Ditto, driving licence,' he added. 'Try not to get pulled over. Bank account—opened. National Insurance number. And here's the keys to the flat.'

He'd told her the address earlier, but now she focused on the exact location.

'N15,' she said disdainfully. 'Where the heck is it?'

'Seven Sisters.'

Amy googled it on her iPhone.

'It's bloody Tottenham. I'll be murdered walking along the street.'

'No honestly, it's a ten-minute walk from Seven Sisters Tube, but it had to be somewhere commensurate with what you're earning.'

'You don't know what I'm earning.'

'Forty-five?'

'Fifty—top of the scale. I'm a better negotiator than you give me credit for. And a "golden hello" of two thou.'

'It's a nice flat, honest. Two decent sized bedrooms so you can have friends stay over—pleasant leafy road—near the Tube.'

Amy wished she hadn't allowed him to rent the place unseen. And to suggest she might invite friends to stay while being Jane was laughable. Not that she had any friends now anyway—her business acquaintances and former colleagues had scattered to the winds once Crazy Amy hit the self-destruct button.

'The rent's only one thousand five hundred a month, so you should be able to afford it with ease.'

'Well it had better not be a real dump, or else you'll...'

Amy broke off. Once she'd longed to escape from her mother's compulsive hoarding and would have happily lived anywhere, as long as it was clean and tidy. How times changed.

'Or else what?'

'I was just remembering,' she began, 'the night when you ended our relationship.'

'Yes?' Toby sounded wary at her rehashing the events of two decades earlier.

'I still owe you a proper explanation for not letting you use the bathroom.'

'It's been a long time in coming, but better late than never.'

'My mother is a hoarder.'

Five words—tripping glibly off the tongue. The fear and embarrassment that had silenced Amy was now banished, and the big secret overshadowing her life for decades had finally lost its sting.

She'd anticipated the standard reaction—the perplexed expression as he grappled with what it meant, then the questions about why the hell it mattered so much. But Toby's response was different.

'Yes,' he said quietly. 'I knew, or rather I know now—there was no word to describe it then.'

'How?'

'I stole your key from your handbag and let myself in when you and your mother were away.'

Amy felt her cheeks redden. It was one thing to discuss the mess in the abstract, but a different matter entirely to accept that someone had seen and smelled the squalor.

'No! How could you?'

Strangely enough, she remembered the loss of the key with the utmost clarity. Her mother had gone ballistic, filled with fury and paranoia. But Amy had blithely scorned these concerns, because how would anyone know it was the key to their house?

The answer to that question was now evident. It had been stolen, not lost, and the thief had her address.

Logically, she should have suspected Toby when the key mysteriously reappeared in her bag, after she'd searched

every inch of every compartment. All along, she'd been sub-
liminally aware that this didn't stack up. But she'd never
foreseen such an appalling betrayal of trust from someone
who set such great store on ethical behaviour.

'I'm very sorry.'

'Is that all you can say?'

'It was a rotten thing to do, but you wouldn't tell me the truth.'

Amy breathed deeply, trying to rise above the anger.

'And what good came of it?'

'None. I couldn't confront you without owning up.'

'But you judged and condemned me, no doubt.'

'I never blamed you,' he added. 'Your room was the only
normal part of the house, so it obviously wasn't you.'

'How very generous of you to acknowledge that. And will
you also acknowledge how much you've hurt me?'

'Well you hurt me too, with the lies you told, the secrets
you kept. Why didn't you trust me enough to confide in me?'

'I trusted you too much—trusted you not to rifle through
my handbag while my back was turned.'

'Look, I said I'm sorry, but it was such a long time ago.
But I had to do it, because you wouldn't tell the truth.'

'So it's my fault that you stole from me—right?'

Toby's claim of moral superiority was hard to stomach.
He'd taken the key from her handbag. He'd entered her
house without permission. He'd kept her in the dark.
Knowing damned well why he wasn't allowed in her house,
he'd forced her to lie, and then cited her untrustworthiness
as the reason for ending the relationship.

'Of course not. What can I say? I'm truly sorry.'

But being sorry wasn't good enough. What Toby did all
those years ago was unforgivable. And now, his appalling

disclosure shifted her perception of his integrity. A man capable of such dishonesty could be using her to obtain inside information and profit from short-selling IPT's shares.

From now on, she would watch her back.

***

Jane's flat was clean, with inoffensive décor and new furniture from Ikea. Toby had chosen better than she'd feared. Even so, Amy couldn't help but notice the stark contrast with her beautiful house in Chiswick.

No walk-in wardrobe. No wet room, but a tired old shower fitting over the bath with a plastic curtain—like a third-rate motel. A kitchen without integrated appliances or granite worktops.

While the shadow of the hoard darkened her young life, anywhere tidy with working plumbing had seemed luxurious. Now—shaped by a decade or more of prosperity—she viewed the world through a different lens. Somewhere along the line, wet rooms and granite worktops had become absolute necessities. They were not, however, necessities for "normal" people.

Amy had little experience of normal. After being deprived of normality growing up, she'd spent all of her adult life striving for it. Ironically though, she'd ended up with a privileged life in many ways even further from "normal" than the crappy life she'd escaped. Incredible as it seemed, when she'd earned the half a mill a year, she'd been eaten up with jealousy of others earning twice as much. Now she asked herself new questions. How much money does anyone need? How many state of the art features does a house need?

In principle, a simpler life ought to compensate for less luxury. Jane wasn't responsible for the welfare of battalions of people below her in the hierarchy. She had no unattainable sales targets to give her dyspepsia, and was not accountable for a profit and loss account. Had she finally found the freedom she'd sought all her adult life?

19

On the first day, Amy donned a grey trouser suit and pale blue blouse—classic, elegant, safe, but boring. High street stores did an excellent job in churning out conservative clothing for conventional people like Jane. But Amy had grown accustomed to the individual little embellishments common in designer wear—ways of displaying originality without deviating too far from the norm. As a gesture of rebellion against her new persona, she replaced her fake pearl studs with the Tiffany earrings she'd kept.

Although Amy arrived early, Pedley was already at his desk. He'd interviewed 'Jane' in a meeting room, so this was her first glimpse of his office.

The fake décor, with reproductions of old masters hanging on the wall, struck Amy as indicative of deeper deceptions. Only the silver-framed photograph of an attractive Asian woman displayed on the antique replica desk seemed authentic.

'Stunning girl, isn't she?' said Pedley, as he caught Amy looking. 'That's Roxanne, my girlfriend. And she's brainy for a woman too, although it's politically incorrect to say so.'

'Isn't the whole point of political correctness that you *don't* say it?' she asked, wondering if he *really* viewed women as less intelligent than men, or whether it was a wind up.

'That's why it's so silly,' he retorted. 'Because no one can stop me thinking it.'

True enough—Amy had come across plenty of men who paid lip service to PC without adjusting their misogynist, racist mind-sets one iota. But even if they stuck dutifully to the scripts they'd learned in their diversity coaching courses, you always sensed the vibe. In Amy's view, PC only brushed prejudice under the carpet, so you couldn't expose it. Jane might feel differently, though.

'Of course they can't,' came her coy reply. In letting him off the hook she demeaned herself, but so be it—Jane had been demeaned, not Amy.

'How about some coffee?' she suggested.

'During a breathless, whistle-stop briefing, Amy discovered Pedley was a Luddite who required all his emails to be printed out. Ten years earlier, there'd still been a few old dinosaurs at her firm with this modus operandi, but she'd believed the species had become extinct. Pedley handed her two piles prepared by his temporary EA—one where he wished to review the responses before despatch, the other for Amy to both draft and send. In both cases, the illegible notes he'd scribbled in the margin would guide her.

He then showed "Jane" to her workstation, in a kind of antechamber to his office. As well as Jane's desk, it was furnished with two easy chairs and a coffee table, for people to sit in comfort while they waited for an audience with the great man. Filing cabinets lined the walls, and Amy speculated on what incriminating material they might contain.

'Is this OK for you?' he asked.

'Just fine, thanks.' It would have to be, with no alternative available.

Pedley retreated into his office, then emerged a few minutes later with his raincoat and disappeared on an unspecified mission, not mentioned in his diary.

Without any interruptions, the emails would have been easy to deal with. But a succession of incoming phone calls, generating further tasks, broke Amy's concentration. She tried the techniques she'd learnt on the many time management courses she'd attended, but Jane's busyness appeared to be of a radically different nature from Amy's. In addition there were the visitors, of which Roxanne was the first.

In real life, Roxanne was striking but not beautiful. She wore an immaculately tailored red dress, likely Roland Mouret, black peep-toe stilettos and carried a Prada handbag.

'Roxanne Chang,' she announced. 'Magick PR. And you must be Jane, the new EA.'

She spoke with an American accent—cultured, East Coast, and projected herself as every inch the haughty professional.

'Do you have an appointment?' asked Amy, unable to resist goading her.

'I don't need an appointment.'

'Well obviously you do,' Amy retorted. 'Because Richard isn't here.'

'So where is he?'

She eyed Amy suspiciously.

'I'm not sure. There's nothing in his diary.'

'Well then—you should have asked him.'

Roxanne's hawk-like eyes took in every minute detail of Amy's office, as if seeking clues to her personality.

'You have no photographs on your desk,' she observed. 'Have you no family?'

'I prefer to keep work and home life separate,' came Amy's icy reply.

'Children?' she asked.

'No.'

'Husband?'

'Sort of.'

'*Sort of.* Surely either you have a husband or not?'

'We're no longer together.'

Stick to the facts where possible, and don't arouse suspicion.

'And whose fault was that?'

Roxanne ran her finger along the top of the filing cabinets, checking for dust, as if any deficiencies in the office cleaning were Amy's responsibility.

'Nobody's fault—just one of those things.'

'There's an art to keeping a man interested.'

'Yes, so I gather.'

'Ah well, perhaps you'll have better luck with the next husband.'

The door opened and a second visitor arrived, saving Amy from giving a wholly inappropriate withering response.

'Hi, Nelson,' said Roxanne. 'Richard's not here. But I've been talking to Jane. She's the new EA.'

'Nelson Chang,' he said, extending his hand. 'I'm Roxanne's brother and one of the directors. Welcome to IPT, Jane.'

'It's great to be on the team,' Amy replied.

'You must learn to control Richard's diary more effectively, if you plan on lasting long here,' Roxanne chided.

'But it's only my first day.'

'I wouldn't push your luck, if I were you. Nobody likes an upstart.'

Amy reined herself back from a cutting rejoinder. In the past, she'd chewed people up without compunction, but Jane had to work to a higher standard.

'Aw—cut the girl some slack, Roxy.'

'Thank you,' said Amy, forcing her face into a pleasant

expression. 'I do plan to sit down with Richard and review his diary very soon.'

'Never mind. We only dropped by on the off chance—let's schedule a meeting for later,' said Chang.

'Sure,' Amy said. 'No problem.'

As she swept out of the door, Roxanne flashed Amy a final disparaging glance.

Phew—Amy found holding back on the backchat much tougher than she'd envisaged. Though she'd often been oppressed in her previous incarnation, she now understood how senior executives enjoyed more latitude than junior staff. And the role itself was more challenging than she'd foreseen. How did the executive assistants at Pearson Malone stand it? They usually worked for several people, with competing demands, and not shy in vocalising them. Now Amy stung with shame as she recalled how she'd treated them.

Even with the disruptions, Amy finished the emails by late afternoon. She'd eaten no lunch and had not even stopped for coffee, thereby carving out valuable time to nose around.

Her predecessor had kept all Pedley's emails meticulously organised in neat folders, as if she knew this day would come. There was even one helpfully labelled Venner—a logical place to start.

The folder mainly consisted of legal correspondence concerning IPT's purchase of another company. The connection with Venner wasn't clear, until she noticed that Venner owned JV Associates, the company in question. As she skimmed through, her eyes lighted on a draft press release.

IPT Plc has recruited John Venner as its new Finance Director and has bought his firm JV Associates for £1m in cash. He takes over on 1 August. Venner was formerly

a partner in Pearson Malone, and brings a wealth of experience of entrepreneurial businesses to the role.

She checked online—the press release had been issued and the transaction been completed. Toby had missed a trick there, it seemed.

What the hell was this JV Associates? Venner had been employed until May and cruising during June. How had he managed to create a million pound firm from a standing start by the beginning of August?

The simple answer was he hadn't—he'd received a million pound bung—but in return for what? Amy so much wanted to have faith in Venner; she'd hoped with all her heart that Toby was mistaken. Now, with sorrow, she was forced to concede this seemed unlikely. And looking back, there had been some indications of Venner's devious nature. After all, what kind of man stoops to secretly recording a colleague's phone calls?

Amy promptly shut down the window in her browser when she heard Pedley returning.

'So, how are you getting on?'

'Been busy,' said Amy, still reeling from her recent breakthrough.

'Ah, that's what I like to see. Shall we have a quick debrief?'

'OK.'

She followed him into his office and sat down opposite him.

'I've finished all the emails. And here are the responses you wanted to review.'

'You've a very professional turn of phrase,' Pedley observed as he read through the first one.

'Thanks—people do say I've got a way with words,' Amy now wondered if she'd over-engineered the emails.

'Very good, Jane—couldn't have written this better myself.'

Amy flushed with pleasure at this endorsement for a diplomatically worded refusal of an invitation. A boss who gave due credit to his staff had some merit as a human being, whatever his other deficiencies. Smithies had never managed it.

Pedley might, however, be less satisfied with how she'd handled her encounter with his girlfriend, especially once Roxanne put her toxic spin on the story. Tactically, Amy considered it preferable to pre-empt this with her own version of events.

'I met Roxanne today,' she began.

'Ah jolly good.'

'I may have been a bit uppity with her.'

'Oh I wouldn't worry,' Pedley replied. 'I bet she was uppity with you. She's a feisty girl, but she needs to be in that PR job.'

Who controlled their relationship? Amy didn't see Pedley allowing himself to be dominated by a woman. But equally, she found it impossible to imagine Roxanne silently enduring all Pedley's sexist attitudes. There was something about them, as a couple, that didn't quite ring true.

20

'There's something strange about that Eccles girl,' pronounced Roxanne over dinner in Pedley's elegant Kensington town house.

The most pleasing aspect of Roxanne's personality was her ability to switch from tigress at work to pussycat at home. The least pleasing aspect was her unreasonable dislike of his secretaries.

'What makes you think so?'

'I asked her a few simple questions, and she was *so* evasive.'

'I'd be evasive under interrogation by you,' laughed Pedley. 'Actually, she's terrific—smart, reliable, punctual.'

'Not like the last one then,' said Roxanne pointedly.

'No—totally different.'

Pedley had a sneaking suspicion that Roxanne had a detailed knowledge of the harassment claim made by Jane's predecessor, even though they'd never discussed it. But bizarrely she never raised the subject.

He couldn't help it if all these stunning women threw themselves at him. He suspected that even the sensible, uber-professional Jane had the teeniest little crush on him. And, admittedly, Jane fascinated him too. She wasn't, in his view, evasive, but had hidden depths.

Sadly though, he'd have to leave Jane alone. His life was complicated enough already. A longstanding married ladyfriend had suddenly become available and seemed keen to develop their relationship—maybe even marry him. On the whole, this seemed an excellent plan, particularly as she was worth a few million. He'd proved he could pull an exotic younger woman—time to move on before she dumped him. His friends would be pleased—they'd been urging him for a while now to find himself someone "more suitable". In an ideal world, Roxanne might agree to the occasional shag afterwards, but he accepted this was wishful thinking. So, once his friend had prepared the ground with her family, he'd finish with Roxanne and they'd go public. But nothing would stop him enjoying the benefits of Roxanne in the meantime.

'So what's with the Tiffany earrings then?' Roxanne demanded, breaking his train of thought.

'What are you talking about?'

'Her earrings are from Tiffany. I spotted them in the catalogue—they're very distinctive and allegedly inspired by Venice's grand hanging lanterns.'

'Is that a fact?'

'They're nearly two thousand quid—how does an EA afford that?'

'Someone must have bought them for her. Lucky girl.'

'I trust it wasn't you.'

'Roxy,' said Pedley, sipping at his wine. 'I may be a fast mover, but even I take longer than a day to progress to the Tiffany stage.'

'If I find out you're lying…'

'I'm not.'

Well, not about that at any rate…

21

'You still mad at me?' Toby asked tentatively, as he answered Amy's call.

He now bitterly regretted telling her about the key. In retrospect, he'd blundered hugely in an attempt to salve his conscience. He could easily have kept his mouth shut and Amy would have been none the wiser. By his own stupidity, he'd planted seeds of doubt in Amy's mind, when he urgently needed her to trust him. But why should events of so long ago still be significant to her?

Perhaps because they were significant for him. The incident with Amy had convinced him that the pursuit of truth motivated him more than anything, and consequently he'd settled on a career in journalism. Now he saw with startling precision how his life had been at a pivotal point that spring, with many courses open to him. And recognising this, he continually asked himself what if, what if…

Amy's re-entry into his life felt pre-ordained, bridging the gulf between past and present and giving him a chance to deviate from the course he'd chosen, opening up a parallel universe previously closed off. Did Amy share his sense of destiny? He held his breath as he waited for her response.

'I'm not sure. What you did was pretty shabby.'

'I know, and I can't begin to tell you how sorry I am.'

'Well don't then,' she snapped. 'Let's just move on, shall we?'

He'd got off lightly, in all the circumstances.

'So how did today go?' he asked.

***

Amy had checked—JV Associates was a £100 shell company.

'So Venner received a million in cash from IPT in exchange for something worthless?' said Toby.

'In essence, yes—it's a massive fraud on the shareholders.'

'No surprise really—Pedley has a history of these transactions. Did you know IPT has a disused factory in Bermondsey, on contaminated land?'

'No.'

'Pedley bought it for a song from his old company and then sold to IPT at a huge profit. But it's worthless, because the cost of remediation exceeds the development value.'

'Wouldn't the auditors pick up on that?'

'Not if Pedley hires some crook to write a report saying otherwise.'

'I still can't see Venner taking money for nothing. I worked closely with him for six years. Sure, he might put a gloss on some questionable accounting policies, but he'd never do this…'

'Except that he did.'

'Perhaps there's another interpretation…'

'Such as?'

'Perhaps it was a Golden Hello—a signing on fee.'

She had racked her brains for an innocent explanation, and this was her best shot.

'Well in that case it's a fraud against the taxman,' Toby retorted, quick as a flash. 'Signing on fees are taxable. Although you'd be more clued up on that than me, being a tax expert.'

And Venner would have been too.

'Well for all we know, tax *was* deducted.'

'So why dress it up as a company purchase?'

'To stop the remuneration committee or the shareholders from vetoing it?'

'You're clutching at straws. I'll wager the remuneration committee is entirely ignorant of this little arrangement.'

'But why would Venner put his whole professional reputation on the line for something so transparently stupid?'

This, above all, bothered Amy. It seemed so out of character for the man she'd known and worked with. But Toby had his own views on the subject.

'That's crony capitalism for you. People like Pedley and Venner behave as though they're invincible—they're so confident they'll *never* get caught. And the media collude with them. They print the bland supportive PR stuff Foxy Roxy and her cronies put out because it's less effort than upsetting influential people by revealing the facts. Don't you see? That's why I left the *Globe*—couldn't stand my hands being tied.'

'And I left Pearson Malone,' she reminded him. 'You're not the only one to take the moral high ground.'

'Yes, but most people aren't like us—they go along with the status quo. You can't deny it would have been much easier for you to ignore that fraud you uncovered than to stand up and expose it.'

This was undeniably true, and though she was loath to entertain the notion, she accepted it was possible that Venner had chosen the path of least resistance.

22

The next day Amy had another visitor—a woman of a similar age. A good twenty pounds overweight, with hair in a shapeless mousy bob, she wore the standard loser's office uniform—cheap navy skirt, greying white blouse, and scuffed black pumps. Pearson Malone employed plenty of these worthy, frumpy, dumpy girls working in back office roles. They got on with their jobs, kept their heads down and quietly kept the wheels turning.

Even as Amy made this damning initial assessment, she checked herself. She was no longer a big cheese in a toxic world—she was Jane. And Jane was more generous in spirit than Amy.

'Hi,' said the visitor. 'I'm Melanie Cronin, the payroll manager.'

So where did a payroll manager stand in the pecking order with the CEO's EA? Especially as Melanie didn't look particularly managerial, and was maybe bigging herself up. Uh, uh—there she went again—making snap judgements Amy-style. Must try harder.

'How can I help you?' she asked.

'Couple of things. First off, I'm after the paperwork for poor John Venner's final expense claim—someone said it was with you.'

'Sorry—John who?' asked Amy, remembering at the last moment that Jane might not instantly recall who Venner was.

'John Venner—the finance director who passed away.'

'Oh him. I haven't seen anything, but I'll take a look.'

She couldn't even guess at where such paperwork might be, but opened and closed her desk drawers to show willing.

'His widow wants everything tidied up, and the claim was quite large, what with those long haul flights to China and everything.'

'What the heck was he doing in China?' Amy said, thinking out loud.

Melanie eyed her with suspicion.

'What's it to you?'

'Oh nothing,' She now wished she'd kept silent. 'Just being nosy. I'd better have a more thorough search—I've only been here a couple of days.'

'Thanks—there's something else as well.'

'What?'

'There's an issue with your National Insurance number. And I need it before I run the payroll.'

'An issue?'

'It doesn't exist.'

Amy froze.

'Did you key it in right?'

The faintest hint of annoyance clouded Melanie's features.

'Yep—I've checked and double-checked. Maybe you wrote the number down wrong.'

Amy seethed. She was a top accountant, for heaven's sake, who did not write numbers down wrong.

'OK,' said Amy, as calmly as she could. 'I'll check tonight at home.'

She hoped to God there wasn't a problem.

***

Pedley perched on the edge of Melanie's desk.

She might have found this invasion of her space intimidating, but she knew Pedley too well to feel threatened. He had a reputation as a philanderer, but these Lotharios never troubled girls like Mel.

In many ways, Pedley was more like a father to her, which Mel relished, having spent most of her childhood in care. Not that anyone at IPT was aware of her background—why give them the power over her?

It was Pedley who'd encouraged her to study for the payroll exams, given her paid leave and footed the bill for her courses. In due course, her qualifications had allowed her to move into the perfect role. Many millions of pounds a year were processed through IPT's payroll. Who'd have predicted some mediocre little nobody would wind up in charge of all that?

'Saw you talking to my new secretary today, Mel,' said Pedley. 'Any particular reason?'

'Oh mainly trying to track down John Venner's expense claim—someone told me she had it.'

She said it casually, though she'd detested Venner, whose eagle eye had zoomed in on the superficially innocuous and inconspicuous, as if experience told him trouble lurked there. And Mel, cloaked in a mantle of invisibility she'd woven for herself, had been a prime target. She'd been glad to see the back of him.

'I might have it,' said Pedley. 'I'll check for you.'

'Thanks.'

'What do you make of Jane?'

Mel wavered. Jane had got up her nose big style, but she saw no particular merit in sharing her views with Pedley.

'Oh, I only talked to her for a few minutes.'

'But you're good at reading people, so first impressions.'

Mel detected that Pedley didn't anticipate unalloyed praise for his new EA, so reluctantly she said,

'Snooty, a bit up herself.'

'She's a little scary for sure, but do you reckon she has anything to hide?'

What a weird question—all the more weird because Mel was *certain* Jane had something to hide. Because she'd checked with HMRC, and not only was Jane's National Insurance number non-existent, but so, it seemed, was Jane.

'No—why do you ask?'

'There are those who say she's too good to be wholesome.'

And Mel would have bet on Roxanne as the prime mover.

'Well, lots of people have stuff they'd rather keep from their work colleagues.'

'Do they?'

Mel squirmed. There were times when she feared that Pedley had ferreted out all her secrets, and could see deep into the darkness of her soul.

'Perhaps—like personal stuff.'

If he had uncovered her skeletons, Mel had the dirt on Pedley too, stuff no one expected the stupid fat girl to be aware of. If push came to shove, they could cut a deal.

'Well, she's apparently divorced, so maybe that's it.'

'Possibly, yes,' Melanie agreed.

'So you didn't pick up on anything?'

'Definitely not.'

Pedley's visit left Mel uneasy. Her decision to cover for Jane by using another NI number had been calculated rather than benevolent. She disliked the toffee-nosed bitch intensely, but intended to gain some useful leverage for the future.

With hindsight though, perhaps she should have alerted Pedley to the issue. Her whole strategy could rebound spectacularly if he too was suspicious of Jane. But the time had passed to do anything differently, which left her only one course of action.

Find out what Jane's game was before Pedley did.

23

The rest of the Venner email folder was supremely dull. The messages covered tighter checks on employee expenses, strengthening internal controls, a review of accounting policies, implementing a supply chain tax optimisation strategy, and a mock payroll audit. All of these were sensible priorities for a new finance director from a bean counter background.

Although on second thoughts, the mock payroll audit seemed strange. It would involve a team from Pearson Malone checking the correct amount of tax had been paid to HMRC. But with Venner himself up to his neck in a tax avoidance scam, was it wise for him to put his head above the parapet? He must have been utterly confident that the PM work programme wouldn't spot it. Or, somehow there was an innocent explanation. Amy kept cycling back to this possibility, even if she couldn't fathom what it might be.

By Thursday, Amy's new life had fallen into a rhythm. Pedley wasn't the easiest boss to work for. His mysterious absences and need for his EA to be clairvoyant presented some challenges, but nothing too drastic. And Nelson Chang proved to be the perfect antidote to Pedley's politically incorrect vagueness, with his unfailing politeness and grasp of detail—an ideal second in command. Apart from the Venner payment, there was no reason to suspect IPT of being anything other than the vibrant emerging global business it purported to be.

Which made her question Toby's motivations once more.

He must have been aware of Venner's backhander before she'd brought it to his attention. He'd done his due diligence on Venner, and if you merely googled him, the press release on JV Associates came up near the top. Why hadn't Toby told her about it? Amy recalled the scathing comments on Toby's blog suggesting he was shorting IPT shares. Why should she trust him, above John Venner who she'd worked with amicably for years? The bastard had even stolen from her bag.

She had to wonder—what were his real motives for wanting her in here?

24

It transpired that Melanie, or Mel as she now urged Amy to call her, had indeed input Jane's National Insurance number incorrectly. She stopped by on the Thursday afternoon to apologise.

Thank God. Amy had been so fearful that Toby had screwed up, especially when her concerned messages to him had gone unanswered.

'Oh don't worry,' she said breezily, simultaneously trying to hide her relief and avoid sounding condescending. 'We all make mistakes.'

By way of an olive branch, Mel asked Amy if she'd have a drink with her that Friday evening.

In Amy's world, people invited her out because they wanted something from her—careers counselling, free tax advice, free drinks even. But it was Jane, not Amy, who'd been asked, and the apology sounded thin as a motivation. Whatever Mel's true reasons, Amy figured she might well be a useful source, especially if primed with a few drinks. So—after taking several seconds too long to decide—Amy accepted. The worst that could happen would be she'd have to suffer a tedious evening.

***

The early signs were not promising.

A crummy chain pub compared unfavourably with Amy's usual upmarket haunts. Surely Mel could afford somewhere classier than this two for a fiver dive?

As a nod to the occasion, Mel wore sparkly eyeshadow and a navy dress, which was limply and unflatteringly draped over her ample body. Mel had evidently bought into the myth about loose clothes being slimming on fat girls.

Mel ordered something called a Jägerbomb and Amy followed suit. The carpet felt sticky underfoot as Amy wandered back from the bar and the cocktails, such as they were, tasted as disgusting as they looked. If this was the only form of alcohol available, Amy could take it or leave it.

'So, how are you settling in, Jane?' Mel asked, as if she genuinely cared.

Guilt stabbed at Amy. Once again, her thoughts were bitchy and critical. Only since being Jane had she become aware of how "Amy with the Big Important Job" viewed people through a negative filter. It was a knee-jerk reaction—a defence against a hostile environment—a destructive habit that had to stop, even when she'd done being Jane. Thinking the best of someone did not diminish her own status.

'It's OK—although Pedley isn't around much and it's manic trying to keep up with him.'

'He's a bugger for that,' Mel replied. 'And I should know—I worked as his EA once.'

'You did?'

'On a temporary basis—he told me I wasn't glam enough to be "front of house".'

Unkind, even by Amy's standards, although she would never have said it out loud. In truth, she'd been no better than the men she disparaged—politically correct in her statements, but not in her mind.

'And he didn't offend you by saying that?'

She gave a nonchalant little smile.

'Well look at me.'

'So why hire you then?' asked Amy.

'Oh I was just filling in for someone. He took me on as a dogsbody when the company started up, so I've been in loads of different roles.'

'Like what?'

'Started off as general gofer, then an accounts payable clerk, then marketing, then payroll, and Pedley paid for me to study for those payroll exams. Now I'm payroll manager for a Plc. Not bad for a girl from a council flat in Barnet with two GCSEs is it?'

Amy listened as Mel burbled on. An hour in and after three cocktails, she'd gained an encyclopaedic knowledge of Mel's life. She described in detail her childhood with loving, hardworking but impecunious parents and two brothers. Her educational qualifications appeared to have been a matter for rejoicing rather than embarrassment, and her father had advised her to seek a job where she'd be trained.

She hadn't heeded her dad's advice—not to begin with—and she'd drifted from job to job until her late twenties. But then she'd joined the fledgling IPT, a tiny company with huge ambitions, and she'd grown with it. Now she was thirty-three, she told Amy proudly, and see where she'd got to. To Mel, payroll manager represented the pinnacle of human achievement.

Amy suppressed the knee-jerk reaction to despise Mel and feel smug about her own success. Instead, she processed Mel's story through Jane's ears. And, with a twinge of envy, she grasped what Mel enjoyed and which had eluded Amy all her life—self-satisfaction.

'It was kind of Pedley to support your studies.'

He couldn't be all bad, Amy reflected, not for the first time.

'Yes, he's a nice guy, even if he does sail close to the wind sometimes.'

Although intrigued, Amy resisted the temptation to press Mel.

'That girlfriend of his, Roxanne, is horrible though.'

'I agree—I don't trust her an inch. She struts around like she owns the place, all dolled up in her slinky outfits, but who knows what's going on in her head? People say she's got designs on marrying Pedley, but I'm not so sure. She looks like her own woman to me.'

And she did to Amy too. In fact it beat her why Roxanne bothered with Pedley—a successful PR professional had no need of a sugar daddy.

'Her brother seems OK though.'

'Yes, Nelson's a real gent, as smart as a whip, and with a very devious mind.'

'They both sound American.'

'Yes, they were born in Boston—Chinese father, American mother. The father was one of the first Chinese students to be allowed to study abroad in 1979 and he got his US citizenship by marrying their mother.'

'So what are they doing in the UK?'

'The whole family's been here twenty years or so—since their dad was hired by some big corporation in London.'

'If Chang's so smart, why's he content playing second fiddle to Pedley? You'd think he'd want to run the show.'

'Oh, I'm sure he does,' Mel said. 'But he's only my age, so time's on his side. But he's ruthless and devious too, so maybe he's playing a long game and waiting for Pedley to drop off his perch. Who can say? I don't see so much of him since he's been a main board director and I've been in payroll. But in Accounts Payable, he'd come in with a bunch of invoices from our Chinese supplier regular as clockwork every month.'

'What happened to Pedley's wife?'

'Divorced him four years ago, and came out of it with a huge financial settlement. Good for her, I say, because he's a cheater. Still you needn't be concerned on that score.'

Amy was hit by a sudden and irrational insecurity, which she failed to hide.

'Why not—I'm not exactly ugly?'

'No but he told me you were scary. He never shags the women he's scared of.'

'Odd that—would have said that Roxanne was pretty scary.'

'Yes, she's scary all right, but he doesn't get it. He believes he can control her, and she's happy to let him think so. You mark my words, she'll be off once she's got what she wants from him.'

'And what does she want?'

'Who knows,' Mel replied. 'But, in my opinion, she definitely has her own agenda.'

'Incidentally,' said Amy. 'You never told me. Did you find that paperwork you needed?'

She'd been trying to manoeuvre the discussion onto Venner, and this was her best shot.

'Oh yes—would you credit it? Pedley was sitting on it all the time?'

'That doesn't surprise me,' Amy laughed. 'His office is a terrible mess—tidy enough on the surface but cupboards and drawers all stuffed with crap—some of it goes back years. I must have a good tidy up someday when he's out.'

And a good nose, as well.

Leading on from there, she asked, as naturally as possible, 'Did you work very closely with that Venner guy?'

'Why do you want to know?'

Amy detected a trace of apprehension, although she might have been mistaken.

'Just wondering if you missed him?'

'Well, we didn't work together very long, and I know it sounds horrible, but I shed no tears when he died.'

'Why not?' Amy asked.

'He was an interfering busybody.'

'How so?'

'Well, he was dead keen to have an audit of the payroll done—like he didn't trust me or something.'

'How awful,' Amy sympathised. 'It's terrible working for control freaks, isn't it?'

She left it there, not wanting to arouse Mel's suspicions—she could always return to the topic later.

'Same again?' she asked, raising her glass. After three rounds, she'd warmed to the Jägerbombs. It was like the old joke about martinis—one is perfect, two is too many, three is not enough.

'So tell me about you,' said Mel, when she'd returned from the bar.

If you're lying, it's best to be as truthful as possible. Therefore Jane's background was an idealised version of Amy's—the widowed teacher mother who had always done her best for her (clearly, that bit stuck in the craw), and the pebble-dashed semi in Croydon. After letting it all hang out in the Priory, it felt strange to revert to fiction, but old habits die hard and Amy fibbed as fluently as ever.

'Surprising you didn't end up at uni and some high-flying

job,' said Mel, zooming in on the flaw in Jane's back story with remarkable prescience.

'Didn't do enough work at school—too much hanging out with boys and smoking behind the bike shed. Got five GCSEs though.'

Amy been a slacker at school too, but still wound up with ten—all top grades. But then, she was way smarter than Jane.

'More than I managed, but you don't need exams when you're posh, do you?'

Posh—people often called her that. Funny how she'd grown up in the worst squalor and still people considered her socially superior.

'Let's just say I got lucky.'

Amy's fake work history had been well-rehearsed, but if Melanie chose to google Jane Eccles, she'd find nothing but a sparse LinkedIn account. Surprisingly, her meagre social media profile hadn't been raised during the recruitment process. But Amy guessed that Mel was the kind of person who'd check, and considered it best to pre-empt this.

'Although not so lucky with the husband,' she added.

'Oh—I didn't know you'd been married.'

Amy wasn't sure why Mel sounded so shocked, but didn't care to ask.

'Yes, but not for long. Unfortunately he's violent—I can't even use social media in case he tracks me down.'

'Ooh,' said Mel. 'How terrible. Was he always like that?'

'No,' replied Amy truthfully. 'He was fine until the end, but he always used to say, "Amy, you always trust the wrong people". And boy, how true that turned out to be.'

Aghast, Amy realised she'd let her real name slip. She tensed, but Melanie gave no sign that she'd picked up on the gaffe.

'Have you ever been married, Mel?' Amy asked, in an effort to move the conversation on.

'Never—men are overrated.'

'What—you mean you're gay?' asked Amy, sounding more alarmed than she'd meant to.

'No—don't be silly. Some bad experiences when I was younger proper put me off. I mean, if you want a shag, you can have a shag, but the emotional shit that goes with it—not my cup of tea.'

'Yes,' said Amy, with Toby, Dave, and ex-husband Greg all very much in mind. 'I get all that. They complicate your life, don't they?'

They clinked glasses in a moment of true understanding.

Amy would have been up for a fifth drink, if only to blur Mel's memory of her misstep, but Mel said she had to be up early to visit her brother Joey in Kent.

As they left the pub, Amy caught sight of Dave Carmody in the distance, utterly absorbed by his statuesque blonde companion as they strolled down the road arm in arm. A dart of jealousy stabbed at Amy, although rationally there was no reason to object. His preoccupation with his lady friend virtually guaranteed he wouldn't spot her, but she steered Mel across the road to make sure.

The Victoria line was out of action so, in a fit of extravagance, they hailed a taxi, and dropped Melanie off en route to Seven Sisters. Amy nearly asked on autopilot for her address in Chiswick, but corrected herself before the words came out.

Afterwards, as she reflected on the evening, she concluded that leaving aside the two tiny slips, her first social performance as Jane had been a resounding success.

***

So, thought Mel, *her real name is Amy.*

This snippet didn't seem helpful, until she woke at three am with a pounding headache, her body crying out for water. And as she settled back to sleep, it dawned on her.

'Tell Amy.'

Oh God, she couldn't be.

Melanie grabbed her phone to view the pictures of Amy that had appeared in the media. Even on the small screen and with Amy's drastic change of hairstyle, there was no mistaking those elfin, slightly asymmetric features.

All those lies—bigger than her own lies.

Mel replayed their earlier conversation in her head. Now she understood why Amy had shown such an interest in Venner—she'd been fishing. But why was she pretending to be Jane? Only one answer presented itself to Mel's fevered mind. For some inexplicable reason, Amy had picked up the baton from Venner. But why? Not at Pedley's instigation for sure, because he too was wary of "Jane". And what about the NI number? Surely it wouldn't have beyond the wit of someone as smart as Amy to use a legitimate number? Unless that had been part of her game, and Mel had walked into a trap by fixing it.

As Mel devoured the press coverage of Amy, she began to hope she was only up against a flaky woman, who'd been thoroughly discredited. But the stories of Amy uncovering a fraud at a client were disturbing. Was she an avenging angel hell-bent on exposing white-collar crime? Or under-cover for HMRC?

Of course, Mel might not be the target of Amy's inves-tigations. God only knew, there were enough other scams going on at IPT. But even so, it would be prudent for Mel to assume the worst, because there were too many unanswered questions for comfort.

When Venner had begun his witch-hunt, she'd never been sure whether he had evidence, or was merely suspicious. Either way, she'd laid contingency plans to move on somewhere she'd never be found. She'd assumed that with Venner out of the way, the doubts would die down, but now this seemed foolish, reckless even. Fortunately, her scheme remained just as viable in the new circumstances.

Thanks to Amy's slip-up, she was still ahead of the game. And she firmly intended to stay there.

25

Amy's doorbell rang before eight the next morning, sending her into a paroxysm of paranoia. Years of living in a hoarder's house had left her with numerous neuroses, and even now she still dreaded unexpected visitors. She peeked out of the bedroom window.

Toby.

Amy pulled on jeans and a sweater before buzzing him up. She suspected that despite everything, he still had the hots for her, and answering the door in nightwear would give wholly the wrong signals.

'Jesus, you look rough,' he said, taking in her dishevelled state.

'Charming—that's guaranteed to boost a girl's ego.'

'Any chance of a cup of coffee, having made it so far?'

'I suppose so. What are you doing here anyway?'

'Just passing.'

Unlikely—Seven Sisters was not en route to any plausible destination.

Perhaps sensing her scepticism, he added, 'Plus I wanted to tell you that I checked out that NI number with my mate and it's one hundred per cent kosher.'

Which he could have dealt with over the phone.

'You're too late. Mel the payroll manager already told me she typed the number in wrong.'

He pursued her into the kitchen, triggering another of her hang-ups. Occasionally, before her mother's hoarding became too entrenched, friends were allowed in certain rooms of the house, but had to be excluded from others, notably the kitchen. The strain of managing wayward houseguests had left Amy with a lifelong fear of people wandering around in her home.

'She apologised very nicely and we went out drinking together last night.'

'Ah—that's why you're a bit fragile. Good evening?'

'It was OK. I might even get to like her if you doubled her IQ and halved her dress size.'

'Miaow—that's catty,' said Toby.

Oh dear—she'd done it again—making her contemptuous judgements, even though she'd vowed to stop it. In her account of the evening, she carefully avoided sneering at the venue, the drinks or Mel's taste in clothes. See—she could be a nice person if she tried.

'So did you find out anything useful?'

'She didn't like Venner—said he was a control freak. Oh yes, and she says Pedley sails close to the wind. So she may well know more than she's telling.'

'Possibly a useful source,' Toby agreed. 'Any more in the emails?'

'I've been through thousands of the bloody things this week, and nothing of interest, apart from the ones dealing with Venner's sweetener.'

Toby circled his arms round Amy's waist as she prepared the coffee. She could feel his erection as he snuggled up to her, and had correctly assessed his intentions in visiting her.

'Any problems with Pedley coming on to you?' he asked, apparently oblivious to Amy's discomfort with his own advances.

'No.'

'Mmm—you smell good. Pedley doesn't know what he's missing.'

She turned and pushed him away. He had no intention of disrupting his life with the perfect Celia—he'd said so repeatedly that first night. But now that he'd had a taste of easy sex, he must have decided being unfaithful wasn't such a big deal, and he wanted more. She'd only ever be his bit on the side, and she deserved better.

'Toby—I told you—just the once. I meant it.'

'But what's the difference between once and twice?'

'The same as the difference between twice and three times and a hundred times. I refuse to be your mistress.'

He looked as though he was on the verge of saying something profound, but had thought better of it.

'Sorry,' he said, after a long interval. 'Out of order—though you can't blame me for trying.'

But Amy did blame him for trying. It showed a lack of respect, as did stealing the key from her handbag.

'You seem off with me this morning,' Toby observed, as they settled in the lounge with their coffee.

'Oh, well spotted,'

'What is it now?' he said with weary resignation.

'You haven't been honest with me—again.'

'How?'

'You knew about Venner's million pound bung before I brought it to your attention, didn't you?'

The long silence told its own story.

'Or if not, you're stunningly incompetent. If you google Venner, that story's on the first page.'

Another pause, then a sigh.

'OK, I'll admit it. But there was a reason I kept quiet.'

There was always a reason with Toby. He took considerable trouble to justify his actions, especially the morally questionable ones. Preservation of his self-image as a 'good' person was paramount.

'What?'

'Well, you seemed very loyal to Venner.'

'Yes.'

'And it seemed best if you came to it in your own time, otherwise…'

He broke off, perhaps afraid to disclose what the otherwise was.

'Otherwise I might not have come on board—right?'

Toby nodded sheepishly.

'So the truth is important to you, Toby?'

'Well yes but…'

'Except when it's inconvenient?'

'For example?'

'I just gave you an example. And if you want another, there's the business with my house key.'

'Oh you're not still on about *that*, are you? You were the one who said we should move on.'

'But I did move on, and you've pulled the same stunt again. Frankly, even if I had new info on IPT I'd be wary of sharing it with you.'

'What do you mean by that?' he demanded.

'Well, there are people who say you make money by shorting the market after you've published your crap. That's bordering on market abuse, if not over the line. And now I'm left wondering what your game is. Are you trying to expose a big fraud or line your pockets by tapping me for inside knowledge?'

'That's crazy. I never take positions in the shares, except a small holding to get me into an AGM. Look—we have to trust each other.'

'I agree, and you omitting to tell me key facts makes it impossible.'

'You know what—I'd say you've gone native at IPT.'

'That's ridiculous.'

'I bet you're like putty in Pedley's hands, letting him schmooze up to you. If anyone isn't being trustworthy, it's you.'

'OK—you're right about one thing—mutual trust is essential if we're going to work together. I don't trust you, and you don't trust me. So there we are—it stands to reason—no working relationship.'

He seemed agitated, but possibly only because he'd been thwarted in his true objectives.

'But I paid to set you up with that fake ID.'

'Fine,' said Amy. 'It's only money. If it bothers you, I'll reimburse you, so I'm under no obligation.'

'But what will you do?'

'Carry on without you.'

'Carry on my arse,' said Toby. 'You'll just stick around playing at being Jane, because it's easier being Jane than Amy.'

He had more understanding of what made her tick than she'd expected.

'And what about us, as friends?'

'There is no us—we shake hands and say goodbye.'

'How about an occasional coffee and catch up?'

'Not a great idea.'

She thought, for a moment, he would cry, but he rapidly composed himself.

'Are you very angry with me?'

'More disappointed than angry.'

She'd hoped he'd be a better person—better than her, in particular. Now she saw they were equally imperfect, though in different ways.

'Well,' he said, 'I'm sorry you feel that way. But don't you worry—I'll find some other way to expose those bastards.'

'I'm not worried,' Amy replied.

And then he was gone—his coffee still untouched on the table. From the window, Amy watched him walk down the street, empty except for a man a few yards behind him.

Toby stopped.

My God—he's coming back. He's coming to tell me he's sorry he's been a knob. Well no dice—my mind is made up. No—merely consulting his phone, perhaps to check for an Uber cab. The man behind stopped too, checking his own phone. Toby started up again, and so did he.

Was it a coincidence, or was Toby being followed?

26

'Coffee for four please, Jane, in Meeting Room 5,' came Pedley's voice on the telephone minutes after Amy's arrival on Monday morning.

Typical—Pedley had no meeting scheduled.

If she was to carry on acting as his EA, she would have to seize control of his diary. Still, at least making coffee and arranging biscuits artistically on a plate was an easy start to the week. Armed with the beverage trolley, she pushed open the meeting room door.

'Ah, Jane—that was quick,' Pedley said.

Panic swept over Amy like the rush from a drug. Sitting round the table with Pedley and Nelson Chang was her toxic ex-boss Smithies, and a junior sidekick Amy vaguely remembered. Her last meeting with Smithies, at Venner's funeral, had been disagreeable enough, but at least then she hadn't been masquerading as someone else and in fear of exposure. She had two options—bolt, or brazen it out and pray they didn't twig. Neither choice appealed. To flee would attract unnecessary attention, but staying to pour out the coffee was no less risky.

Smithies' whining tones dominated the room. The mere sound of him used to send Amy into a tailspin of fear, but now her dread of being outed as an imposter dwarfed all other anxieties.

'Undoubtedly,' Smithies opined, 'we have to consider the reputational risk of implementing the scheme, particularly now you're moving onto the main market.'

'Ah,' said Pedley, lowering his voice. 'In strictest confidence—because we haven't announced it yet—the listing won't be happening. The regulators have rejected our application.'

Amy nearly dropped the flask of coffee. It was the first she'd heard of it.

'Oh dear—why?'

'I'm afraid we've been victims of our own success,' said Pedley smoothly. 'They've turned us down because they claim there's been a significant change in our scale of operations. It's all those acquisitions we've been doing, and Venner's death hasn't helped. But it's not over yet—we can consider various options—hey, we might list in the US.'

'Oh well, not all doom and gloom then,' said Smithies, stating the obvious.

'So does that change your view on the reputational risk?' asked Pedley.

'Well it's difficult to assess precisely. That's why it's a risk. HMRC's attitude to tax schemes is constantly shifting, and what's a sensible planning strategy today may be tomorrow's unacceptable avoidance.'

'But what is it today?'

'Today, it's intelligent planning,' put in Smithies with a winning smile. 'Otherwise, we wouldn't recommend it. And at least now we're no longer auditors, there are no conflict issues.'

Three months ago, Amy had engaged clients in such discussions. Now she saw the arse-covering, disingenuous underlying motives in stark clarity. Pearson Malone wanted the best of both worlds—to sell a potentially ineffective product while avoiding a lawsuit.

Amy relaxed as they all took their coffee without showing the slightest interest in her. She should have known, for not only had her appearance been altered, but her status too. Amy, a prominent professional whose judgement people valued, had become Jane, the girl who served the coffee—invisible and insignificant to pompous jerks like Smithies.

'Now moving on to the next agenda item—do you still intend to go ahead with that mock payroll audit?'

'Wouldn't it be sensible to leave it until the new finance director's on board?' Pedley suggested. 'I always thought poor old Venner was barking up the wrong tree there.'

'Oh I do agree,' said Chang.

Amy sat back down at her desk, her heart pounding. She took several minutes to recover her poise sufficiently to home in on the key point.

The listing was off.

Admittedly, she'd paid little attention to the mechanics of the listing, but now she noticed a flurry of emails had arrived over the weekend. Amy had written reams of professional gobbledygook during her career, and was therefore well-qualified to read between the lines. As she skimmed through, it was plain that the reporting accountants had concerns. This impression was reinforced by an email from one of IPT's two brokers—a key advisor—resigning with a month's notice.

That nailed it—something was very wrong.

***

By the evening, following IPT's official announcement, there were eight missed calls from Toby, and four voice messages.

The first message condemned her roundly for not sharing the news.

'I know you've refused to work with me, but you could have given an old friend the heads up on something huge like this. I'm really pissed off with you.'

Why? She'd told him she wouldn't leak confidential data.

Ten minutes later, he'd plainly calculated that antagonising her would be counterproductive.

'Hi again—sorry if I was a bit off just then. I totally get where you're coming from on the price-sensitive information. Be nice to catch up sometime—if you can bear it.'

After another fifteen minutes, he proffered a more comprehensive apology.

'Hi—I don't want you to think I'm hassling you, but you're right. I understand why you can't trust me. I've behaved like a real shit. Sorry for everything.'

Amy laughed—if he didn't want her to think he was hassling her, he should stop doing it.

And finally—a heartfelt plea.

'Amy, I'm so, so sorry and well, obviously I can't apologise to you properly in a voicemail. I'd give anything to hear your voice one last time. Then I'll be out of your life forever—I promise. Please, please call me.'

Amy accessed Pedley's email from her home computer and pored over the reports. There were concerns about IPT's complex web of acquisitions and their "innovative" accounting policies. They'd also queried IPT's dependence on their main Chinese supplier, Plumb Enterprises. But intriguingly, they had glossed over the central points on profits and inventory that Toby had raised at the outset. And they had not directly questioned the payment to Venner.

The mention of Plumb Enterprises sparked a memory. On their evening out, Mel had mentioned Chang bringing her the invoices every month. Why would he do that? And why were the invoices addressed to him?

As she recalled her previous experiences, Amy began to have a hunch about what might be amiss.

***

Toby found himself choked by regrets. He'd lost Amy forever, entirely through his own stupidity. Not only had he forfeited her trust, but he'd leched after her as though she was an animal on heat, rather than trying to communicate his complex and evolving passion for her. Now he'd squandered the opportunity of even a platonic working relationship—and he'd have settled for that, just to see her occasionally.

Toby wished he could erase the voicemail messages he'd left, not only the first one when he'd been mad at her, but also the last one where he'd sounded desperate. He wouldn't leave any further messages, as hoping in vain for an answer was torture.

Just one final call.

To his amazement, Amy answered straight away.

'Toby.'

She sounded neither hostile nor surprised, nor, he had to concede, too chummy.

'Hi,' he said, launching into his pitch for mercy. 'I'm so, so sorry. And…'

'OK—you can cut the crap. I get it, although frankly I don't much care. Glad you called, because I was about to ring you.'

'You were?'

'Yes. I'm giving you another chance.'

Toby could scarcely believe it—she'd been adamant on Saturday.

'What brought this on?'

'It'll be safer for both of us if we join forces, even if I can't entirely trust you.'

'What do you mean—safer?'

Toby had to admit, safe was not a word often associated with him.

'If you come over tonight, I'll explain.'

He longed to, particularly as she sounded agitated, but it would be impossible.

'Sorry—Celia's at a chambers dinner and I'm on babysitting duty.'

'OK—I'll come over to you.'

He shuddered at the notion of Amy's Coco scent lingering when Celia returned to cross-examine him.

'Not a good plan.'

'Why not. Is Celia a secret hoarder?'

Toby laughed.

'No, but she's suspicious of you.'

And justifiably so. Somehow she identified Amy as a threat to the family, if only in Toby's mind.

'OK—if we can't meet up tonight, I'll go it alone.'

Her stance lacked logic and felt manipulative to Toby—still he wasn't in a strong bargaining position.

At a push, he could leave the kids overnight with Celia's friend Marilyn, and lie to Celia about the reason. There would be recriminations, cold criticism, and suspicion, but inviting Amy to his house would be a transgression never to be forgiven.

'No, wait—I can sort something out with the kids. It'll be an hour before I can reach you though.'

'I'll be here. Oh—and you told me you had Chinese shipping records.'

She'd an accurate memory—he'd only mentioned them in passing.

'Are they just for IPT?'

'No—their main suppliers too.'

'And do they show the names of the companies in Chinese?'

'Yes.'

'Bring them with you.'

Keen to see Amy, and curious to discover what was afoot, Toby bundled his sleepy-eyed toddlers into the car, scribbled a hasty note to Celia, and set off into the night.

27

En route, the irrational half of Toby's brain decided that Amy must have something extra in mind, on top of discussing IPT. Well, a guy must be allowed his illusions.

Amy abruptly shattered those illusions when she answered the door sober and dressed in sweatpants and a baggy sweater. The outfit sent a powerful signal—watch your step, Marchpole.

'Coffee?'

'OK.'

'Right—stay in the lounge while I make it.'

He accepted her keeping him at an emotional and physical distance, because a day ago he hadn't any hope of meeting her again, so any contact was a bonus.

Amy returned a few minutes later with two mugs—no biscuits.

'So what's happened?'

'OK—here goes. But first off—here's the deal. I still don't trust you, and if there's any more of your double-dealing, lying by omission, or anything else that hacks me off, including unwanted physical contact, our agreement is cancelled.'

'There won't be,' Toby promised. Her hard-nosed approach surprised him, until he remembered that in her high-flying job, she would have habitually been assertive and direct in articulating her demands. It was a facet of Amy he hadn't seen before, and he admired it.

'Although if I'm such a piece of shit, it beats me why you think you'll be safer working with me,' he added.

'Yes well, I'll explain more in a moment. But first, I agree there's definitely something fishy going on at IPT.'

Hallelujah, thought Toby, but said nothing.

'And you're right—they are manipulating the profits.'

Yes!

'So why the light bulb moment—what did you find?'

He prayed whatever it was would be worth all the trouble with Celia.

'Well, I've read all the reports and the regulators are antsy as anything, but the reasons they gave are mere padding. Seems like they can't quite put their finger on the problem. But I can.'

'What?'

'OK—here goes. I reckon Plumb Enterprises, IPT's biggest supplier, is secretly linked to IPT. In fact, I'm close to proving it's controlled by Nelson Chang.'

As Toby evaluated this suggestion, he saw the possibilities. With a captive supplier billing what they wanted, when they wanted, IPT could show whatever profit they chose.

'Are you certain?'

'Pretty much—Mel said something that sparked off an idea.'

'What—the silly payroll clerk?'

'Payroll manager,' Amy corrected him, before repeating what Mel had told her about the invoices.

Toby's spirits sank. Had he really been lured over here by the passing remark of a girl too stupid to type accurately? Wonderful as it was be with Amy, it would be a shame to incur Celia's wrath over a wild goose chase.

'So why did you ask for the shipping records?'

'Plumb Enterprises seems to be an unofficial English name of the company. I've probably tracked it down, but I need the Chinese version to be sure.'

'You brought me over here for *that*?'

'Why, what else would I have in mind?' she replied, with a suggestive grin.

He almost blurted out that he loved her. But what would be the point? She was only toying with him—why give her the power?

'I thought you were in danger,' he said. 'All your dire warnings about it being safer working together.'

'We might both be in danger.'

'How so?'

'For a start, you're being followed.'

'Bollocks—if I was being followed, I'd know.'

'The point is—you didn't.'

His disbelief turned to dismay as she related Saturday morning's strange incident.

'Why didn't you say something earlier? For heaven's sake— they must know I'm here now. You should have warned me—I could have shaken them off.'

'It's too late. They already realise we're in contact.'

'So why hasn't IPT fired Jane without a reference?'

'Not sure, but I've a terrible feeling it's not the IPT crew. Which is why it's so sinister, because we may have unknown enemies.'

Amy leafed through the documents as they conversed.

'Look. It's the same company!' she exclaimed triumphantly.

Toby peered at the indecipherable characters on the print out and then at the equivalent on Amy's screen.

'It looks similar.'

'Glad you agree.'

She tapped away at the keyboard.

'What are you doing now?'

'I'm emailing my contact in Pearson Malone's Beijing office. He's standing by to carry out a full company search.'

'But it's four am in Beijing.'

'Yep, I know—he owes me a big favour.'

'No related party disclosure in IPT's accounts, I assume,' said Toby.

'Don't be silly—I checked straight away—they're hiding it.'

'Or you're mistaken,'

'Well we'll see—that pickle I'm not allowed to talk about concerned a string of secret connected companies, and it didn't end well.'

How long before she understood how her pointless her silence on this subject was? She'd talk then, and he would wait.

'And you expect me to stay here until the stuff comes through?'

He remembered Celia. That wouldn't end well either, but she'd be more amenable if he arrived home first.

'Yes, so you can help me evaluate it. Fancy another coffee?'

Actually, he fancied her, but feared jeopardising their détente by saying so, even though she'd bent the rules with her lascivious smile.

The half hour delay before the data arrived felt like eternity. The air crackled with sexual energy as they laboured over their conversation. Finally, Amy's computer pinged, and she skim-read the email.

'OK, first off, Chang definitely owns it. And here are the accounts.'

Amy printed the attachment and they pored through them.

'It's making next to no money,' Amy pronounced. 'Looks like it's selling on the inventory to IPT at a tiny margin.'

'That accounts for the high profits in IPT. How much does Plumb Enterprises turn over?'

'Around fifty million sterling. On the face of it, it's a huge operation, supplying a third of IPT's stock.'

'Yet according to the address, it's run out of Room 202 of a hotel.'

They used Google Earth to zoom into the street view of a shabby, rundown building in what looked suspiciously like a red light area.

'Hardly premier office accommodation, is it?' Toby observed. 'And definitely no storage facilities.'

'From memory, most of the inventory is held on consignment at IPT's new central distribution centre near Beijing,' said Amy.

'*If* it exists. After all, we know those goons in Pearson Malone can't be relied upon to conduct a proper audit.'

'They're not *that* bad.'

Toby was staggered by the loyalty she showed to PM after everything, but wisely kept quiet.

'But would they really be arsed to go all the way to China for a stocktake?'

'They would ask the Beijing office to check, you idiot. It's too large a proportion of the inventory for them to ignore.'

'But just because the gear is there, it doesn't follow that IPT's been billed. Plumb Enterprises might make a big delivery immediately before the year end, and hold off billing until the auditors have signed the accounts. A good old-fashioned inventory fraud.'

'The audit work programme should pick that up too,' said Amy coldly.

'But clearly it didn't.'

'I wonder what benefit Chang is deriving from the arrangement? He must get a payback somewhere down the line.'

'Without a doubt,' Toby agreed. 'And I'm sure we'll figure out how before too long.'

Amy seemed pensive.

'What's up?'

'Does this affect the Venner situation? Because he'd just returned from China when he died. Could he have been a potential whistleblower as I originally suggested?'

Amy's determination to stick by Venner was as incomprehensible to Toby as her loyalty to the firm that shafted her. Maybe one day she would explain.

'No. Venner got paid a million pounds—most likely to buy his complicity.'

'OK—to be fair, he would put the best gloss on the listing application, and push the boundaries with accounting policies—bean counter bad behaviour. But I can't see him ignoring an inventory scam.'

'You're kidding yourself, Amy. But irrespective of Venner's involvement, this needs further research. Plus, if it's not IPT following me, there's another dimension to this we're not understanding.'

'So what should we do?'

'I haven't decided yet—I'll think about it. But meanwhile,' Toby said, checking his watch, 'I'd better get back home before I turn into a pumpkin.'

Amy saw him to the front door.

'If you are being tailed,' she said. 'Let's feed them disinformation on why you came.'

And though the street appeared empty, she insisted on giving Toby a tantalising, lingering kiss that left him aching for more.

28

'How's Marchpole doing?' Patrick asked Ethan at their weekly debrief.

'Oh—OK, although our guy's not the only one keeping tabs on him.'

'Now that is interesting.'

'Not really. Seems like he's playing away and his wife has set a private eye on him.'

'Who's the other woman?'

'No one we know.'

'Talking of other women, how are you getting along with Michelle?'

There was an innuendo in Patrick's voice, which Ethan didn't much care for.

'You must be kidding me,' Ethan said. Although physically attractive, his new colleague was a tough old bird, a seasoned agent ten years his senior—drafted in, Ethan suspected, to keep an eye on him and curb his youthful excesses. 'She'd have me by the balls if I made a move on her—besides, someone told me she's gay.'

'I'm saying nothing,' Patrick replied.

'What you don't mean...?'

Ethan sounded surprised, although it seemed plausible. A hard-nosed bitch like Michelle would have no compunction about sleeping her way up the ranks, with men or women.

'You suffer from an overactive imagination, young man.

But going back to Marchpole—anything other than his extramarital activities?'

'Nothing. If it wasn't for his mistress, he'd lead a dull life, and he doesn't seem at all interested in the Chinese angle.'

'See—I told you—waste of our resources. Call off the surveillance right now—we've more important targets in our sights.'

29

Before recent tumultuous events, Amy had rarely thought of death. After all, a thirty-something woman might reasonably assume that she had more life ahead of her than behind her. But now, following a couple of close shaves, Amy viewed her mortality through a different prism, and had taken certain precautions.

Death itself didn't scare her—life was overrated and arguably a quick demise beat expiring in hospital attached to a bunch of tubes. But picturing her hoarder mother squandering her way through a seven-figure inheritance chilled her to the marrow, so she'd made a will.

There was also Smithies. She cast her mind back to the recordings that tied him to the big fraud. Just in case he'd any designs on doing away with her, she'd locked away the incriminating CD at her lawyers with strict instructions for it to be handed the police if she died. Clichéd? Yes. Paranoid? Yes. And utterly useless.

Now as her personal danger levels edged up once more, it seemed a pity to miss the exposure of Smithies' misdeeds. But then again, if the CD's contents were revealed now, he'd rebuild his empire before long. Hell—politicians and businessmen rehabilitated themselves after much worse. And Smithies was as skilled as anyone at spinning stories his way.

Much more enjoyable to make him sweat.

So far she'd failed miserably on that score, because the slime-ball had assumed she'd never rat on him. While this had annoyed her ever since Venner's funeral, seeing Smithies the previous morning, as cocksure as ever, had stiffened her resolve to act. Now, the answer was clear—if she wanted him to sweat she must raise the temperature.

30

Mel refused to panic over "Jane's" true identity.

Being regarded as a dimwit conferred many advantages. Amy would likely assume Mel was too dumb or drunk to have noticed her slip, and therefore wouldn't anticipate Mel's escape. And even if her position was more dire than she supposed, panicking wouldn't help anyway, as decisions were best taken by a mind uncluttered by emotion. She'd enjoyed a fantastic few years, but nothing lasts forever. She would have preferred to choose when to quit, but still had the upper hand.

So, keeping very calm, Mel implemented the first step of her plan. She processed leaver's paperwork for the five fictitious employees on the payroll, one set each day of the week. Then on the Friday, she informed everyone that her brother had fallen gravely ill, obliging her to take indefinite leave of absence. For obvious reasons, "everyone" did not include Amy. The outpouring of sympathy and kindness from her colleagues almost prompted a pang of conscience, but she suppressed it. Those crooks royally deserved to be ripped off.

Afterwards, proving the scam would be an undemanding task for a competent professional. But Mel would be gone and unreachable by then, denying Amy the satisfaction of seeing justice done.

As she finished packing up the last of her possessions, Mel noticed she had a visitor.

'Can we have a quick word?'

She gulped. Were they on to her, even as she executed her escape?

'Sure.'

'Sorry to hear about your brother.'

Phew—only friendly concern.

'Thanks—it's such an anxious time.'

'I came to thank you for your contribution to the company and wish you all the best. Of course, it goes without saying—you're welcome back at any time.

How touching that a bigwig like him had bothered.

'Thanks so much—I'll miss you all and thanks for everything you guys have done for me.'

Including the hefty financial contribution to the Mel Cronin Benevolent Fund.

'Before you go, may I ask a small favour?'

'Sure,' Mel replied, intrigued. 'No problem.'

31

Eric Bailey, CEO of Pearson Malone, was mystified to receive a CD accompanied by an anonymous note.

'Ask Ed Smithies what this means—I never make idle threats.'

Oddly, when he'd worked out a way of listening to the wretched thing, he found the disk was blank.

Smithies came straight away when summoned—his usual sycophantic self.

'Eric—great to see you, buddy—how's it going?'

Eric detected a level of nervousness beneath the bonhomie, as though Smithies feared he'd somehow fallen out of favour. His uneasiness pleased Eric. Far from allaying these anxieties, he would stoke them, because it paid to keep upstarts like Smithies on their toes.

'Good, thanks,' he replied.

'So what can I do for you?'

'Shed some light on this, I hope.'

Bailey produced the CD with a dramatic flourish.

For an instant, Smithies registered a look of horror, before rapidly regrouping.

'Oh yes?'

The tone was light, in contrast with Smithies' tense body language.

'I received it in the post this morning.'

'What is it?' Smithies asked, trying to sound nonchalant.

'You tell me,' said Eric, turning the screws.

'No idea.'

Smithies sat back in his chair, his arms folded behind his head. The beads of sweat on his forehead and damp ovals under his armpits belied his confident posture.

'Strange, because whoever sent it suggested you might know.'

'Who, *me*?'

He was way overacting. Most of these younger partners would benefit from a spell at drama school as part of their training, thought Bailey.

'And said they didn't make idle threats.'

'What do they mean, *threats*? Have you listened to it?'

'Yes.'

'And what's on it?'

Tactically, Bailey saw no reason to disclose that the disk was empty.

'Surely you know?'

'No clue at all.'

With Smithies on red alert, an infinitesimal movement of the eyebrow was all Bailey needed to hint at his scepticism.

'Oh come on, Eric—cut the crap.' Smithies could no longer keep the anxiety and frustration from his voice.

'Let's put it this way,' said Bailey. 'It's something you'd rather I wasn't aware of.'

'Oh dear me, I can't imagine what.'

More ham acting, and Smithies was sweating profusely now.

'Well one thing's for sure. Whoever sent this isn't a fully paid up member of the Ed Smithies fan club.'

'I'm still in the dark, although obviously intrigued to hear it. Perhaps if I borrowed it.'

'Oh no. That wouldn't be appropriate at all.'

'Why not?'

'Because, Ed, sometimes it's better not to know. And sometimes it's better to pretend not to. You get my meaning?'

Smithies nodded, like an obedient puppy dog.

'I'll be guided by you, Eric. Shall destroy it for you?'

'No—that won't be necessary. I'll see to it, Ed.'

***

Smithies' brain whirred frantically as he left Bailey's office. He hadn't expected Amy to rat on him, but evidently his grasp of events had been way off. Bailey would inevitably use the contents of the disk against him in the future, even if for some reason he was holding off now.

But amid Smithies' panic, came a calmer inner voice. Various aspects of the conversation with Bailey jarred with his knowledge of the man's character. For example, why hadn't Bailey discussed the recordings with him, probed for additional details, asked about the context? He'd been strangely uncurious, in the circumstances. Moreover, he hadn't allowed Smithies to hear the recording. And though Bailey had waved a disk at him, was it necessarily *the* CD? Could Bailey, wily bugger that he was, have got wind of the CD's existence, and be pretending he had it either to rattle him or extract information? If so he, Ed, had played the meeting egg-zackly right—a masterly piece of blustering, during which he'd given nothing away.

Or was Bailey playing a more elaborate mind game? Had he been trying to convince Smithies that he possessed even more damaging revelations? Or, worst of all, was there in fact another disk in circulation more damning than Amy's?

The uncertainty was excruciating. He had to know for sure.

32

Celia exasperated Toby more than ever. He understood her fury at him parking the kids overnight, but several days had now elapsed with no indication of an early ceasefire. At a guess, the real issue was Amy. He'd been unfaithful—once—and Celia, as prosecuting QC, had no proof. But this didn't stop her wild accusations.

Toby reacted by withdrawing from the battlefield, even staying up into the small hours to avoid lying next to Celia. He spent all Friday night hunched over his computer, less troubled by a sleep deficit than the prospect of interacting with his wife.

Undoubtedly, his intense passion for Amy was a symptom of a deeper malaise in their marriage, but it suited Celia to pin all the blame on Toby. In truth, they were not well matched. Celia didn't need an alpha male who earned shed loads of money, but he often felt she coveted one, to parade round as a fashionable accessory. But alpha males don't marry neurotic women, and Celia had enough baggage for a world cruise. So she'd ended up with Toby.

Toby had tried to be sympathetic and tolerant of Celia's issues. He'd always anticipated that with his help she'd overcome the trauma of her past, but nearly two decades later he'd made little impact, and was close to admitting defeat. Meanwhile, Celia's high-powered establishment chums knew nothing of his endeavours, regarding him as a figure of fun to be mildly ridiculed. And he'd grown tired of being an unsung hero and the butt of everyone's jokes.

Worst of all was the more general credibility issues Toby suffered. Frankly, no one cared about rooting out fraud in the City of London. The big players had a vested interest in allowing the gravy train to continue to the next station, the small investors were deluded, the mainstream media were in cahoots with the fraudsters and nobody else gave a shit.

He'd been caught in this rut for far too long, and stuck with Celia for years after the ego boost of attracting a beautiful, clever partner had worn off. He kidded himself that he stayed out of loyalty, and because of the kids. But now Amy had accused him of avoiding the truth when it suited him, he was forced to confront an uglier motive for his inaction. Celia earned the money, thus allowing him to do what he loved. And though it gutted him to admit it, he was hooked on the lifestyle.

At times, when he got his teeth into a particularly juicy case like this one, the trade-off was worth it. The toothless, gutless, Financial Conduct Authority often declined to act, but he loved turning the screws on these rogue CEOs, and watching them squirm. But otherwise, he found his life meaningless and unsatisfying.

Celia greeted him with an icy, 'Good morning,' as she came downstairs.

When would be the right time to mention he'd booked a flight to China departing the next day? He'd been waiting for relations to thaw a little before breaking the news, but little chance of that happening before he ran out of time.

'Good morning. Did you sleep well?'

'No—I've had a crap night.'

He could think of no suitable response, especially as he was about to ruin her day.

'I'm sorry to spring it on you, but I have to pop over Beijing tomorrow for a few days.'

'For what purpose?' she asked, scrutinising him in "cross-examination" mode.

'I need more ammo on a fraud investigation.'

'You can't just *pop over* to Beijing—don't you need a visa?'

'All sorted—one of those express services. Apologies for the short notice.'

'This isn't very convenient.'

Those four words conveyed so much. She must have worked out that Toby's principal motivation was to grab a break from her, especially as she often employed the same tactics. He'd suspected for several years that Celia was as stifled by the marriage as him. What were her reasons for staying? Perhaps he should ask her.

'Yes—I'm sorry, but I'm back Wednesday and I'm sure Marilyn will take care of the kids and I'll make it up to you…'

'Marilyn,' she said, with gritted teeth, 'is furious with you, and the other night was the last straw. You have responsibilities, Toby, to your children. Instead you go gallivanting around like a hyperactive toddler yourself.'

'Yes, I'm so sorry but these are exceptional times.'

'And you have obligations to me too. Now tell me straight—is that crazy bitch Amy going with you?'

Ah—here we go again, thought Toby.

'This has nothing to do with Amy.'

'It's got everything to do with Amy. I check your phone and it's all calls to and from her—emails too.'

'You shouldn't be checking my emails and phone.'

'And as an investigative journalist you should cover your tracks.'

'But there's no *need* to cover my tracks because it's all completely innocent.'

He wished he had the guts to tell Celia how he craved contact with Amy as an addict craves a fix. And it was all the sillier to lie when Celia had perhaps guessed the truth.

'All that's required is a simple yes or no answer—is she going with you?'

'No—certainly not.'

She rolled her eyes—their partnership had deteriorated so far that she disbelieved him irrespective of what he said.

'What gets my goat is you can't even choose someone normal to shag. Amy Robinson is dangerous. I was chatting to a senior partner in a law firm the other day who's a buddy of PM's CEO. And he told me she's seriously crazy, a total fruit loop. Not that I was surprised—she was nuts even when we were at school. I mean she once pretended she lived in my house—why in the world would she do that?'

Toby now earnestly wished he'd never mentioned this strange little episode to Celia when they'd first got together. But he'd recognised the house and had naturally asked Celia if she knew Amy. Out of loyalty to Amy, he hadn't shared her very cogent reasons for misleading him. But bizarre as Amy's antics must have seemed to Celia without this clarification, something else bothered her more. And her questions, dormant for many years, had re-erupted since Amy's reappearance in his life.

'She let herself in to *my* house with a key hidden in the shoe in the porch.'

'Yes, she did.' Toby anticipated what was coming.

'How did she know about the key? I never told her.'

Celia's precise recall of the details twenty plus years later puzzled Toby. Why was this so important to her?

'Someone else must have mentioned it to her,' he suggested.

'But who?'

'Can't help you there, and I'm sorry—I have to shoot off now.'

'To meet her, no doubt.'

Toby neither confirmed nor denied, but picked up his jacket and made a beeline for the door.

In the distance, he heard her shout,

'Ask her about the fucking key.'

33

They ate brunch at a brasserie in Chiswick, both ordering coffee, a fruit bowl and Eggs Benedict.

'Have you visited China before?' Amy asked.

'Never.'

'But according to your blog most of the Chinese companies on AIM are shams.'

'They are, but on the whole they're so smelly you can sniff them out without setting foot outside the UK.'

'If it's so widespread, shouldn't the authorities stamp on them?'

Toby laughed hollowly.

'Why should they?'

'I don't understand.'

'Self-interest. The reality is they're encouraging *more* Chinese companies to list on AIM, because each one generates more money for the fat cats to skim off.'

'Must admit, I can't see why you're off to China now. I mean, we already know Chang owns Plumb Enterprises, which operates out of a poxy hotel.'

'I'm missing whatever Venner spotted, that's why—the final link in the chain.'

'How Chang's making his money?' she suggested.

'No—I've cracked that already. The Plumb Enterprises' margin is irrelevant because Chang's making a killing through trading IPT shares.'

'No kidding?'

'Look.'

Toby fished out a wad of papers from his rucksack, and walked Amy through his intricate logic, linking Chang to a Jersey trust with a sizeable holding in IPT.

'Impressive,' said Amy.

'Predictably there's no disclosure of his beneficial interest in those shares. Hardly surprising, since they've gone to considerable lengths to hide it.'

'So,' Amy summarised, 'IPT massages its profits. The punters love it and the share price soars. And Chang's sitting on a gold mine.'

'You got it—Pearson Malone could have done with you in their audit department rather than dispensing dodgy tax advice.'

'My tax advice was all perfectly legal and above board.'

'But morally questionable all the same.'

Once Toby's needling would have riled Amy, but now she shrugged it off. For years she'd regarded herself as a highly skilled and ethical professional, while Toby saw her riding a corrupt money merry-go-round. But Jane viewed the world differently and might even concede he had a valid point.

'These frauds never end well,' Amy said. 'If they're advancing profits, then they have to keep on doing it, more and more each year—so the deficit between the real balance sheet and the fictitious one keeps increasing. They'll probably get away with it if the business keeps expanding. But once there's a downturn, the finances will implode and they'll go bust.'

'That's precisely what happened to Pedley's previous venture. Went down the pan owing creditors right left and centre. Remember?'

'Yes, it was another PM client and we lost millions in unpaid fees. The partner in charge of the account got fired, which seemed a tad harsh. But there was no fraud there, only poor cash management.'

'If you say so,' said Toby.

'Venner used to act for that company too,' Amy recalled. 'But he handed it over to the other partner shortly before the shit hit the fan. Venner always was Mr Teflon Man.'

'By the way, I'm meeting Pedley straight after I fly back—the American Bar in the Savoy again.'

'You're meeting Pedley,' echoed Amy, astonished.

'You're obviously not on top of his diary,' Toby chided her. 'That is, unless he's keeping it secret.'

'Who instigated this?'

'He did. Says he wants to put a stop to all the lies I'm writing once and for all. Should be a fun meeting, especially with the pieces in the Chinese puzzle.'

Their eggs arrived and they ate in silence. Amy fancied that Toby had something else on his mind, and was proven right when he said, eventually,

'Can I ask you a question?'

'Don't ask whether you can ask—spit it out.'

She hoped it wasn't another come-on.

'Celia wants me to ask. Do you remember the time you pretended you lived in her house?'

Amy's heart sank.

'How the hell does she know what I did?'

'I told her—years ago, because I remembered the house.'

'Please tell me you didn't mention the hoarding.'

'No—I didn't.'

'I'm amazed she even remembers.'

'Oh, it's been a constant theme since you reappeared. And what she's asking is this. You let yourself in with a key they kept in the porch. How did you know it was there?'

Amy's stomach tightened, and she pushed her remaining food aside.

'She's concerned about *that*?'

'She does seem to be,' said Toby. 'She's adamant she didn't tell you.'

Amy remembered vividly how she'd learned of the key's location. She kept the knowledge in a tightly sealed compartment of her mind, inaccessible even to prying therapists at the Priory. But to throw Toby off the scent she pretended to comb the deeper recesses of her memory.

'I can't recall,' she lied, after a suitable interval. 'It was so long ago. I do remember how much I envied Celia though, in that perfect house, so that's why I must have pretended to live there. You know—I sometimes ask myself what my life would have been like if I'd enjoyed Celia's idyllic childhood.'

Toby laughed, although Amy couldn't see the joke.

'You have no clue about Celia's childhood. Just because a person lives in a nice house doesn't mean they're happy. And why do you assume you were the only one with secrets? For all you know, Celia might have envied you.'

Amy's first impulse was to dismiss this unlikely suggestion, but then it hit her. Celia's dark suspicions about the key signified a deeper anxiety. And in a sickening moment of clarity, Amy grasped how Celia's childhood had been imperfect, though she would never discuss it with Toby.

'Celia must have let it slip in an unguarded moment, whatever she says.'

'Sure,' said Toby. 'That's what I thought too.'

As they parted company, Amy kissed Toby again, because he looked so hopeful, like a puppy dog starved of affection. If he hadn't been married, she might have been tempted by his offer of no-strings sex—there was reassurance in finding continuity in her broken life.

34

Each day, Amy checked her real iPhone, kept hidden in Jane's flat.

So far she'd received few messages, but on her return from meeting Toby she found a voicemail from Smithies asking her to call him urgently.

Amy chuckled to herself—no doubt about the subject matter. She toyed with ignoring the message, but decided she'd derive far more entertainment from speaking to him.

He answered on the first ring.

'Hi, Ed, just picked up your message. How are you?'

'Great thanks, and you?'

'All good,' she replied.

'What are you up to these days?'

'Oh this and that—exploring some interesting opportunities.'

'I see,' said Ed, in a tone conveying his scepticism.

'So why the urgent message? Is it a client issue?'

'Not egg-zackly,' he said carefully. 'But can you answer a simple question?'

'Fire away.'

Smithies, the master strategist, must be distraught, thought Amy. Loath to admit to any weakness, he'd have agonised long and hard before dialling her number.

'Did you send the CD to Eric Bailey?'

'What? The one you referred to as "highly ambiguous" when we last met?'

'Possibly.'

'But surely,' said Amy, savouring the moment as she twisted the knife. 'If it's so ambiguous, why are you bothered?'

'I didn't say I was bothered,' Smithies snapped back.

'Did he listen to it?'

'Apparently, yes.'

'Interesting. But he didn't discuss the contents with you?'

'No—he didn't.'

It was hilarious to picture Smithies and Bailey jousting over the blank CD, each trying to gain the upper hand.

'So did you send it?'

Amy paused for dramatic effect.

'I sent *a* CD, yes. But it was blank.'

There was a long silence—very long. Amy pictured him frenziedly assessing how much he'd given away to Bailey, and how he might now turn events to his advantage.

'Why?'

'Because you pissed me off at Venner's funeral.'

'It seems rather vindictive,' he said, in a whiny little-boy voice. 'All I said…'

'I heard what you said. And how is it vindictive to send a blank CD—what harm have I done you?'

But she had harmed him. She'd shaken his confidence, which had been her aim all along.

'Oh none at all.' He laughed nervously. 'I can see it's a little joke. And even if it had been the real disk, as I said before, you're overestimating the importance of…'

'Ah, there you go again. Shall I send Bailey the real thing and let him decide?'

'You wouldn't do it.'

'Don't count on it. And, for the avoidance of doubt,' she added, using one of Smithies' favourite phrases. 'I've lodged copies with my lawyer and if anything happens to me they'll be sent to DCI Carmody, Bailey and the BBC.'

'That sounds like your paranoia rearing its ugly head again.'

'You reckon?'

'Now surely,' said Ed, putting on his most reasonable voice. 'We can compromise on this. I mean we always got on well, didn't we?'

'No,' said Amy. 'We did not. There'll be no deal. And hey—I'm so unstable I might even wake up randomly one morning and do the dirty. You'll never know.'

'But…'

'Bye, Ed—have a great weekend!'

What a bitch she was. It had been fun, though.

35

Monday morning brought fresh revelations.

Amy hadn't told Toby about IPT's broker resigning. There'd been no public announcement and she still feared he'd be tempted to misuse the knowledge. Besides, it seemed an unimportant detail compared to Plumb Enterprises' ownership. But now, amid a burst of emails detailing some very odd transactions, it suddenly seemed vastly more relevant.

IPT's shares had already fallen on the news of the failed listing, though the positive spin Pedley and Magick PR put on it had limited the damage. But once the broker's resignation was announced, the downward spiral would pick up pace.

Clearly, Pedley wanted to extract value before the shares fell further, but a director selling shares would knock market confidence, precipitating further declines.

Enter Dodge Equity, an aptly named US company, who offered an innovative solution to Pedley's dilemma.

The arrangements encompassed a loan to Pedley with his shares held as security. In isolation, the loan was fine, but there was a clever twist. If the shares tanked, as looked likely, Pedley could keep the cash and walk away, leaving Dodge Equity with their security. Meanwhile Dodge wouldn't lose either, because nothing stopped them from effectively selling before the price fell. If both parties knew that the shares would fall in value, this was blatant market abuse.

Amy dithered over whether to tell Toby, because if he was careless, any leak would be easily traced back to her. But ultimately she'd have to choose either to trust him or walk away, and now seemed as good a time as any to make that decision. This latest development was huge.

36

From the instant he stepped off the aeroplane, Toby knew he was on a different continent. Beijing smelled like nowhere he'd been before.

Stunned by the crowds and the noise, he forced his way through the jostling throng of people and made for the official taxi rank. At least there were signs in English, thank God. Less than an hour later, after a nerve-wracking journey, he arrived at his destination.

The Imperial Hotel boasted a five-star ranking, but not in the same constellation as European hotels. In dire need of refurbishment, and infused with ancient cigarette smoke, its aura of faded splendour was weirdly comforting. Despite its deficiencies, the hotel was adequate for a fleeting visit, and the vast bed, in particular, looked inviting. However, Toby had no time to rest—he was on the trail of Chang's secret company.

The Zhou Quan Hotel, allegedly the headquarters of Plumb Enterprises, was many rungs down from the Imperial in the hotel hierarchy. Toby struggled to imagine why anyone would choose to stay in such an inaccessible and menacing area of the city.

A weary desk clerk informed Toby in semi-comprehensible English that the building currently had a restaurant on the first floor, a Karaoke bar on the second and a hotel on the third. All offices had moved out of the building the previous year and though she had worked at the hotel before the change, she was not familiar with the company he mentioned. When Toby asked if he might visit Room 202, the clerk shrugged and pointed towards the elevator.

The decoration on the door of 202 had been disturbed, as if a small plaque or something similar had been removed. Toby tried the handle, but the room was locked.

His next port of call was the address in the Shi Yu apartment building, which turned out to be an equally down-at-heel hotel. The desk receptionist here was at least familiar with the company's name and directed him to the office building of the same name two doors away. In the lobby, a sign listed various companies including Plumb Enterprises. Room 304 had no nameplate, and Toby faced another locked door. However, similar unlocked rooms down the corridor contained only a desk, a few chairs and a shelf. Even though the goods were physically despatched from elsewhere, neither address could be described as fitting premises for IPT's largest supplier.

On his way out, Toby studied the nameplates in the lobby, and noted that a second company, TMT Materials, shared the same office as Plumb Enterprises. The desk clerk said the two companies were linked, though he wasn't sure how. Toby photographed the board for future reference, before returning to the Imperial, all too aware how little the expedition had added to his knowledge.

After two moderately priced beers in the hotel bar, Toby retired to his massive bed wishing Amy was with him, and reflecting once more on the unsatisfactory nature of his life. He'd striven mightily to have a proper relationship with Celia, but without success. Her frosty aloofness seemed her only defence against the chaos in her head, and slowly but surely her coldness was freezing his own heart. Meanwhile, Celia and her circle treated him like a pet cockatoo who'd picked up bad language but was cute enough to be tolerated in polite company.

Amy, by contrast, was utterly bonkers, as she always had been, but she'd played all of her many roles with a warm heart. Even when lying through her teeth she conveyed a fundamental authenticity. And he felt confident that in a little corner of her soul, she reciprocated his passion.

It was odd how he'd attracted these two women, both traumatised in their own ways. Perhaps their choices revealed something about him. And moreover, both had a curious obsession with the other, out of all proportion to their limited acquaintance, as though recognising common ground.

His iPhone ringing interrupted his musing.

Amy—psychic or what?

'Hope I haven't woken you.'

'Not at all. Been enjoying a few beers in the bar, and just turning in—it's been a long day.'

'How's it going?'

'So—so. Like we thought, there's little substance to Plumb Enterprises.'

He considered jazzing up the pitiful amount of knowledge he'd gleaned during the day, but rejected the idea. She'd surely find out later he was exaggerating.

'It's a long way to go to confirm something you knew already.' Amy said, pointedly. 'Meanwhile I've had a hugely more productive day in London.'

Toby hung on to her every word as she outlined the mysterious share transactions. He'd come across similar smoke-screens before, but none as flagrant as this.

'How the hell can Pedley think it doesn't require disclosure as a change in directors' shareholdings?'

'Search me. Even worse, he's telling the press that he's borrowing money to purchase *more* shares, because they're such a great buy. But in reality he's buying nowhere near as many as he's effectively selling.'

'This is dynamite,' said Toby, fired up. 'And once I've got the lowdown on the China connection, we'll hit 'em with everything at the same time.'

'When do you get back?'

'Wednesday afternoon.'

'So what's the plan for tomorrow?'

'Trip to the distribution centre.'

'Well maybe that'll be more useful for you.'

She sounded like she was humouring him, but he couldn't be sure.

'Maybe,' he said, without optimism. 'But I've still got plenty of material to discuss with Pedley anyway.'

'I wish you'd leave this new stuff out of it. He's bound to wonder how you got onto it.'

'Don't worry,' Toby reassured her. 'I never reveal my sources.' But he suspected she already regretted confiding in him.

'Should we debrief after you've seen Pedley?'

'Let's do that—say eight?'

'Same place?'

'Better not—in case he hangs around afterwards. There's the pub down the road—the Coal Hole—that'll do. Anyway, I'll call you when I land to confirm.'

'Be safe,' said Amy, suddenly anxious for no reason she could pinpoint.

'Don't be silly. Of course I will,' Toby replied. 'Ciao.'

He drifted off, and slept until nine in the morning.

37

Organising the trip to IPT's distribution centre, a hundred kilometres from Beijing, proved to be challenging. Toby had originally intended to hire a car, but was dissuaded by red tape and the antics of local drivers. Eventually, however, the hotel had come up trumps and provided Toby with an English-speaking driver at an unexpectedly modest cost.

As they headed out of town, the chauffeur zigzagged skilfully through the traffic. He deftly avoided the hordes of cyclists, simultaneously phoning, smoking and holding umbrellas as they meandered erratically from lane to lane. In this mayhem, it was a while before Toby noticed the black Mercedes. It dogged them along all the twists and turns of their route, before sitting stubbornly behind them on the expressway.

'See the car behind,' said Toby to the driver.

'Yes, sir.'

'I think they're on our tail.'

The driver neither seemed surprised, nor disagreed.

'You want me to lose him, sir?'

'If you can yes.'

'No problem.'

The driver exited the expressway and after ducking and diving round side streets, the Mercedes was no longer visible. Toby relaxed as he chatted about his work and expounded on the inherent dangers of fraud in an emerging economy. He was under no illusions—the driver was doubtless bored silly, but his professional politeness ensured a semblance of respect, and Toby was grateful even for the pretence. A man could only endure so much derision, and Toby had been nearing his limit.

The distribution centre, allegedly the cause of IPT's high inventory levels, was an anonymous giant-sized Nissen hut in the middle of nowhere. The majority of IPT's goods intended for distribution in the Asian and US markets were held there. A proportion of the inventory in the centre was technically owned by Plumb Enterprises but held by IPT "on consignment". To Toby's mind, such arrangements lent themselves to all manner of fudging and obfuscation.

There was little to see. Security was surprisingly tight for a warehouse full of plastic pipes and plumbing components, and it proved impossible to get close to the building. Nonetheless, Toby managed to snap some zoomed-in shots of lorries leaving and the armed guards protecting it.

They set off back to Beijing, both recognising, though not acknowledging, the futility of the excursion. But before long, their shadow showed up again in the rear view mirror.

'I thought you'd lost the Merc,' Toby observed.

'I did, sir,' came the driver's sanguine reply, 'but perhaps they anticipated where we were going.'

On reflection, Toby concluded that he was probably correct.

Ahead, in the distance, an identical black Mercedes was stationed at the roadside. It pulled out in front of them, before halting abruptly and blocking the narrow road. The car tailing them pulled up behind, sandwiching them between the two.

'Trouble,' said the driver—an understatement if ever there was one.

A thickset guy emerged from the front car and approached theirs. He whipped out a small revolver, which he pointed at the chauffeur.

'Out of the car, now.'

They had little choice but to surrender.

'What are you doing here?' he asked in English. 'This is a private road.'

'We're headed for a meeting in—what's the name of the town again?' Toby looked to his driver for support. 'And we're lost.'

How proud Amy would be to hear his dissembling, Toby thought.

The chauffeur fired off a rapid stream of Chinese invective, prompting two other men, also armed, to step out of the rear car.

'Your phones please, and your wallets.' said one.

Toby weighed the options. Non-compliance would guarantee certain death, although realistically, they were done for anyway. Grudgingly, he handed the items over, as did the driver. And now, they'd be frogmarched into the forest and shot.

It surprised Toby to be viewing imminent death so dispassionately—shouldn't he be hysterical? Randomly, he remembered Amy conjecturing twenty years earlier that despair was easier to endure than hope. Now, as he stood in a foreign country, reconciled to his own death, he fully understood her argument. And his only regret, from a life peppered with mistakes, was that he'd never told Amy he loved her.

'Don't try to follow us,' said the thickset guy, returning to the Mercedes, while still pointing his firearm towards them.

Then the hope kicked in, making Toby queasy to the pit of his stomach. Was it possible they would survive?

He blinked in the bright sunshine as their assailants drove off. The world had never seemed more beautiful—the cloudless blue sky, the lush green of the forest, a rabbit bolting across the road. He inhaled deeply, hyper-aware of every breath. Losing his phone and wallet had been a small price to pay for his life, plus he'd even had the foresight to leave cash and a credit card at his hotel. And at least they hadn't been carjacked.

'This happens,' said the chauffeur in his laconic style.

***

Toby tossed and turned. The Chinese firewater he'd swilled down with the driver to celebrate their safe return to Beijing had packed a powerful punch, and now its toxic residue robbed him of sleep. His dreams replayed the near-death experience in a repeating loop, and he woke each time in the clammy grip of a fear that had been absent in real life.

Drained by the cycle of wake—nightmare—wake, Toby pulled himself out of bed and sat in the armchair, willing his eyes to remain open. This proved easy enough, for now a multiplicity of questions assailed his wakeful mind. Who had followed him, and why hadn't they killed him? Why had they wanted his phone?

The answer to the final question was clear—to deprive him of the photographs he'd taken. But why? He'd been too far from the building to capture anything significant, although sadly he couldn't check now.

Except…

iCloud.

If he fired up his Mac computer, in principle his pictures should be backed up there. Ha—they wouldn't have anticipated that—he was too clever by half. He drummed his fingers impatiently as he waited for the internet connection, slowed by the VPN service he used to bypass the Great Firewall of China.

Damn—they were shrewder than he'd imagined. They'd deleted the pictures from his iPhone, and hence from iCloud.

Track iPhone?

Nothing—they'd somehow disabled it.

What had they been seeking to hide? Why the elaborate security precautions? As Toby turned these questions over in his mind, he became convinced that something other than plumbing components was being stored in the warehouse. He remembered TMT Materials, based in the same hotel as Plumb Enterprises, and potentially connected with it. This was the only unexplored avenue, and since he still had the previous day's pictures on his Mac, Toby could google the name.

The results of the search astounded him.

38

Toby's hotel landline rang.

It was four-thirty am Beijing time, although he was still awake, his mind racing with all the extraordinary material he'd amassed. And with the help of a journalist chum in London, he'd discovered without a doubt the stunning secret that had likely cost Venner his life.

He predicted the caller would be Amy, as he'd tried to reach her earlier with his news and a warning to be careful.

'Hi, Amy,' he said. 'You'll never guess what I've found. It's sensational…'

'Actually, it's me,' came Celia's frosty tones from across the globe.

Celia was the last person he needed to converse with. What on earth did she want?

'You realise what time it is here?'

'Didn't seem to bother you when you thought Amy was on the line.'

Which was different, because he'd told Amy to call at any time.

'I've been thinking,' she announced, evidently assuming she had free rein to vocalise her ideas at this uncivilised hour.

'What?'

'You're with Amy, aren't you?'

'Is that why you're calling—to check up on me?' said Toby. 'Isn't it obvious Amy's not here?'

'You're quite capable of trying to mislead me.'

Toby sighed.

'Look—I've had a shitty old day. My phone and wallet were snatched at gunpoint—I thought they would kill me.'

'A likely story.'

In three words she had dismissed his experiences. Did this woman not even care whether he lived or died?

'It's true. Would I lie to you?'

'That is what I'm trying to establish,' said Celia, in her best prosecuting QC voice. 'And I'm putting my foot down. Now be honest, are you two having an affair?'

Toby was sick of all the futile lies. And Celia didn't even trust him when he told the truth. But to explain the complexities of his feelings for Amy would take forever, and he barely had it straight in his own mind. So a half-truth, which he could expand on later, seemed the best tactic at this point.

'OK—I'll tell you. I slept with her once.'

Silence. He felt certain she sensed that his attachment to Amy ran much deeper.

'It was an error of judgement,' he added by way of mollification. 'I'm so sorry.'

'I don't believe you.'

'What, that I'm sorry or it was a mistake?'

'Neither, and I bet you screwed her more than once.'

'Can we discuss this when I get back?'

'I want to discuss it now. Do you want a divorce?'

Yes, yes, screamed out an inner voice he'd suppressed for years. But the rational part of him knew that he would have to break it to her gently, and not now.

'No, of course not,' he replied.

'OK—well I'm prepared to give you a second chance.'

He couldn't bring himself express the required gratitude—

he only wished she was a "one strike and you're out" woman, because then she would make the decision for him, absolving him of all responsibility.

'I see.'

'But only on condition you'll never see or contact her again.'

'OK, I'll speak to her,' he lied. 'And I truly am sorry.'

And he truly was—not for sleeping with Amy, but for the uncontrollable emotions that engulfed him and threatened to destabilise their whole lives.

But Celia had hung up already.

39

Toby boarded his flight with a stinking headache and his mind in turmoil. The British Airways complimentary champagne dulled the worst of the hangover, but did little to address his mental anguish.

On the plus side, what he'd learned was remarkable. It justified the whole trip, and was enough to annihilate the crooked, murderous scumbag Pedley. But the chaos of his emotions blunted the pleasure of his achievement.

In that twilight moment in the forest when he'd hovered between life and death, Amy, not Celia had come to mind. Which told him everything.

He had to at least try to win Amy round. She hadn't rejected Toby Marchpole per se, but refused to be his mistress. He sensed he'd got under her skin, just as the crazy bitch had got under his. And if he disentangled himself from Celia, Amy might be more receptive to developing their relationship.

He shuddered as he pictured the scenes in the divorce courts. Celia would adroitly manoeuvre through the process, humiliating him financially and emotionally, using the children as pawns. She would cite not his adultery, but the more dishonourable unreasonable behaviour as grounds for divorce. And Amy might still reject him in the end. Was he really prepared to put himself through the wringer for an uncertain outcome?

And there was the lifestyle. Shouldn't his near-death experience have given him a new perspective, so that these were no longer important? Well it hadn't—maybe because at heart he was as corrupt and materialistic as those he condemned.

His mind swirled over and over the same ground, without resolution, though more slowly as lack of sleep and the champagne caught up with him. Eventually, his eyelids closed and by the time he woke, the plane was descending into Heathrow.

40

Amy's afternoon was dragging.

She'd checked online that Toby's flight had landed on time, but there was still no word. And when she'd tried to ring him, his phone had gone straight to voicemail. Then she'd missed a call, bizarrely from Toby's home landline, while she'd been stuck with Pedley, but the message he'd left was as brief as it was uninformative. He would meet her in the pub, as arranged.

Bugger.

She consulted her watch—still over three hours until she would learn what Toby's "sensational" breakthrough was.

On a whim, Amy dialled Mel's extension to ask if she fancied a quick drink after work. It would nicely fill the time until she met with Toby.

Mel's assistant answered.

'Mel's on indefinite leave. Hadn't you heard?'

Amy had not heard and was shocked by the news.

'Since when?'

'Last Friday.'

'Wow—that was sudden.'

'They let her go straight away. Her brother's gravely ill.'

'Goodness—how dreadful—I must call her and see how she's doing.'

Her conversation with Mel flashed through Amy's mind. Although she'd talked ad nauseam about her family, at no stage had she mentioned her brother being sick. Too bad for Mel, being forced to quit the job she loved. Amy understood how it felt to have your life upended without warning and could sympathise.

She rang Mel's mobile, but there was no reply.

***

Pedley left the office on the dot of five-thirty and Amy bade him goodnight as usual. As she'd pointed out to Toby, he'd put nothing in his diary. Given his haphazard approach to such matters, this may or may not have been significant. But instinct told her Pedley was keen to keep the meeting under wraps.

With two hours still to kill, Amy caught up with Jane's in-tray. Funny how the work ethic was written into her DNA—who else would strive to be an over-achiever in a fake job? Irrespective of Toby's breakthrough her work at IPT must be almost finished, which saddened her, because in a strange way she'd enjoyed being Jane.

She would miss Pedley's politically incorrect banter, his old world charm, his diary muddles, and the smell of his aftershave, along with Chang's legendary politeness and attention to detail. Rationally, she ought not to care about a pair of fraudsters, but it was impossible not to form some attachment to people you saw every day. She'd even miss Mel, who'd offered her friendship in her own clumsy way. Roxanne, however, was a bitch—and good riddance to her. But most of all she would miss Jane, and her simpler, less jaundiced view of the world.

As Amy worked, her mind wandered. What had Toby learned? He'd used the word sensational, which even allowing for journalistic exaggeration, must mean significant. She was all the more intrigued because realistically she hadn't expected the trip to be productive and neither, she suspected, had he. By half-past seven, she could contain herself no longer. She sprayed on a liberal quantity of Coco Chanel, applied her lipstick and dashed off to the Underground.

When she arrived at Embankment Tube Station, there was a tremendous commotion up the street, with a large area cordoned off and many police officers attending the scene. A tent had been erected and crews of TV reporters hovered like vultures outside the police barriers.

'What's going on?' she asked a cameraman.

'Some poor bugger's been shot.'

'Really—in the West End? What's the world coming to?'

In the bar, she ordered a large gin and slimline, and occupied herself with the *Telegraph* crossword.

One Across

"Collector finding it more difficult to hold nothing"

Seven letters.

Answer—HOARDER—how ironic!

Fifteen minutes later, she'd finished the crossword and drained her drink. And Toby was late. She tried calling again, but no answer. Perhaps his meeting with Pedley had overrun, or there was a problem with his phone.

Another twenty minutes passed and Amy had by now completed two Sudokus. She tried to suppress the ghastly intuition gnawing at her stomach, moved onto the code word puzzle and ordered another gin.

By eight-forty-five, Amy was on her fourth drink and onto the killer Sudoku. The optimist in her still hoped Toby would walk through the door, with a half-cock explanation for being late. It was the same fragment of her soul that yearned for her mother to conquer the compulsive hoarding.

'God, Amy,' he'd say. 'You didn't seriously think someone had killed me, did you? Well, you always were one for melodrama.'

And the joke would be on her.

On the giant wall-mounted TV, breaking news dominated the screen.

VICTIM OF WEST END SHOOTING NAMED.

Amy's stomach heaved as her old foe DCI Carmody appeared, looking a hundred times more self-assured than during his last TV performance. They'd no doubt forced him to retake the media training course for a third time, and he'd finally passed. He wore an inappropriately smug facial expression, but then for Carmody a new murder enquiry was merely a tool to resurrect his promotion.

'I can confirm that the victim has been identified as Toby Marchpole, a freelance journalist and blogger aged forty. At present, we have no steer on possible motives for the killing.'

But Amy had.

She hurried out of the bar; afraid a tsunami of emotion might swallow her up. Her heart thumped and rivulets of cold sweat ran down her face.

Outside in the street, she vomited into a drain.

***

When the call came, Dave Carmody sprang into action without delay.

Only as he raced over to the scene in the squad car did he remember who Marchpole was. And though he'd detested the little shit, no one should end up like this. Still, on the plus side, it looked like his period in the wilderness had ended.

Marchpole's body lay in a crumpled heap on the pavement. Initial observation indicated a single shot to the head at close range. From the front, the only visible blemish was a small dark circle on Marchpole's forehead, but the exit wound at the back would have blown away most of his skull. Marchpole's face showed no sign of suffering, only mild surprise, but in Carmody's experience this was not unusual.

Fact was, Marchpole had not expected to die.

41

Unable to face the challenge of public transport, Amy hailed a taxi in the Strand. As the cab passed all the familiar London landmarks, she reflected that Toby would see none of this again. No one dealt better than Amy with sudden death, or was more conscious of the fragility of our hold on life, but the brutality of Toby's passing had shaken her to the core. Once safely behind the front door of Jane's little flat Amy collapsed on the floor of the hallway, convulsed by a devastating cocktail of anxiety and shock.

After some minutes, she crawled into the lounge and switched on the television. The coverage would be agonising but compelling viewing. As an image of Toby appeared, an aching hollowness hit her full on in the solar plexus as it struck her she'd never see his lopsided grin again.

He was gone, like her father, like Venner. But this was worse—much worse. Toby had known her from way back, before she'd become Amy Robinson, mega important businesswoman. He represented a link to the past, a thread of continuity in the tatters of her life, which had now been cruelly broken.

Amy slept fitfully on the sofa, dreaming of her mother's house full of junk and Toby inside it, struggling to escape.

'Why couldn't you be honest with me? Things could have been different—I would have loved you whatever.'

She woke, agitated and drenched in sweat—caught in a churning vortex of emotion as fear kicked in. She must be next. She wasn't safe here. She wasn't safe anywhere.

As she watched the morning news, Amy saw that events hadn't moved on in any meaningful way overnight. However there was now speculation that Toby may have been killed because of a story he was working on.

Not half.

The killing, said the Sky reporter, bore the hallmarks of an experienced assassin's work. IPT wasn't named, but they mentioned Toby had returned from a trip to China on the afternoon of his death. To support the latest theories, they wheeled out a former colleague from the *Daily Globe* to pay tribute to Marchpole.

'Even at the risk of his own safety, Toby couldn't let anything lie,' said the journalist. 'It wasn't in his nature. He always had to expose the truth, however unpalatable.'

What should she do now? Back in her heyday at Pearson Malone, before they'd set out to undermine her, they'd prized Amy's incisive decision-making and cool head. Boy—she needed that hard-nosed woman now.

Deep breaths—come on, Amy, you can get through this—use your brain. Point one—you're still alive—so your cover hasn't been blown. Point two—running away creates suspicion, assuming there's none already. So—what to do?

Should she report her suspicions about Pedley? And if so, should Amy or Jane come forward? She didn't fancy justifying her undercover assignment to Carmody, or indeed any police officer. And besides, what could she add? Carmody already knew of Marchpole's connection to IPT. She looked at her watch—half past seven.

Scary as it was, only one course of action remained.

42

'You screwed up, Ethan,' said Patrick, his annoyance evident even over the secure telephone line.

Ethan would gain nothing from reminding his boss that he'd instructed him to cancel the surveillance on Marchpole, so he allowed the diatribe to continue.

'You've been asleep at the switch and this is a mess. Have you even figured out who killed him yet?'

'Someone hired by the IPT guy.'

'That asshole's becoming a nuisance. Do we know why?'

'Marchpole found out what Venner had latched onto.'

'Did he talk to anyone before he died?'

'Already covered off. We've had access to the telephone records from the hotel—for once the Chinese are cooperating fully. He called his mistress—but the call was so short, I'm confident he told her nothing. And he spoke to another journalist, but the guy died peacefully in his sleep last night. No questions will be asked.'

'Well done,' said Patrick, awestruck, before delivering the customary dilution of his praise. 'Let's pray *he* didn't spread the word any further.'

Ethan held his tongue. He had yet to deliver the best news of all.

'What baffles me,' Patrick continued, 'is why he didn't eliminate Marchpole in China? That would have been much tidier.'

'It baffles me too. It wasn't like with Venner, where we didn't become aware of the danger until he was back in the

UK. According to Marchpole's driver, they were robbed after they visited the warehouse—for their photographs, I guess.'

'You mean the shipments are still ongoing? Holy shit—has he no brains?'

'Seems not—it's possible he didn't want *us* to find out, so he took matters into his own hands with Marchpole.'

'In this business, you get a nose for when things don't add up,' said Patrick, 'and there's something here we're not comprehending, like their guy's got his own agenda and we have no clue what it is.'

'But we can find out.'

'How?'

Now Ethan played his ace.

'We know who Chang hired. There's enough on him to see him behind bars for life—so we turn him, and offer him immunity. He'll talk.'

'Ethan,' said his boss. 'Gotta say—you've got this buttoned down better than I thought.'

'Why thank you, sir—that means a lot to me.'

43

Facing Marchpole's likely murderer had Amy quaking. Her makeup disguised the evidence of her crying jag and sleepless night, so all she needed to do was hold herself together. But this was easier said than done.

Pedley breezed in, his normal unruffled self, or almost.

'Jane,' he began. 'This is awkward.'

Uh, uh—sounded ominous.

'May I ask a minor favour?'

Perhaps not so ominous.

'Yes—no problem.'

She forced a rictal smile.

'The chap who was shot yesterday evening…'

Amy didn't flinch. He might be toying with her, to see if she cracked. But she was stronger than he knew.

'Terrible, isn't it? What is the world coming to?'

There—aced it—as relaxed as anything. She eyeballed him, but he didn't blink.

'You know who it is, don't you?'

'No—should I?'

'Maybe not, but it's that jumped up little blogger who's been writing all those lies to drive our share price down.'

'Gosh—really?'

Her surprise sounded overdone, even to her own ears.

'Dreadful thing to happen,' he said. 'But I won't be shedding any tears.'

Chilling. How he could be so calm? Was he a psychopath

as well as a fraudster?

'Shame for the wife and kids though,' said Amy, mainly because it seemed a Jane-like sentiment. Though to her chagrin, she'd been so wrapped up in her own emotions, she hadn't given Toby's family a second thought.

'Well he should have considered the consequences before he started raking up non-existent scandals.'

'Oh undoubtedly,' said Amy, willing Pedley to come to the point.

'It's rather awkward,' Pedley repeated.

'What is?'

'If you check my diary, you'll see I was due to meet March-pole after work yesterday.'

'I hadn't noticed.'

Principally because it wasn't there.

'Obviously he didn't show.'

'Obviously.'

'Thing is, I'd appreciate it if you kept quiet about it.'

'Why?'

More deep breaths—doing well, considering everything.

'Because he was shot near our meeting place.'

'Oh,' said Amy, wide-eyed. 'Surely no one thinks you're implicated.'

'Of course not,' he laughed. 'I'm being a silly old man, but with the bad blood between me and Marchpole I'm afraid it might look suspicious.'

Amy ostentatiously checked the diary, before popping back in to confirm what she knew already.

'Well, you're in luck—there's nothing in your diary,' she said, with a sangfroid she didn't feel. 'So no need for deletions, and who's to know?'

'Thank you so much.'

On an intellectual level, Amy feared Pedley was playing some Machiavellian game, though her guts told her not.

'Why meet him if you dislike him so much?' she asked, mainly because Jane would definitely be curious.

'I called him to tell him to stop libelling us, or else we'd sue. And rather to my surprise, he offered to discuss his findings.'

This was entirely consistent with Toby's account.

'Said I wouldn't like them though,' Pedley added.

'So it's convenient for you that he's dead.'

'Not at all,' Pedley retorted. 'I can't sue him for libel now.'

He retreated into his office, leaving Amy utterly bewildered. Either Pedley was completely innocent, or a fine actor. But whatever his misdemeanours, a man whose theatrical talents put Amy's into the shade was downright dangerous.

***

Sometimes people fail miserably to anticipate future developments, and wonder afterwards how they missed the obvious. This seldom happened to Amy, making the call from reception all the more shocking.

A DCI Carmody wished to see Richard Pedley.

Adrenaline surged through her. How could she have been so foolish as to presume she had a choice over contacting the police?

'I'll arrange for them to use one of the conference rooms,' Amy said, calculating that if she avoided Carmody, all would be well.

'Oh, no worries, I've already sent him up,' came the cheerful rejoinder. 'Can you meet him outside the lift?'

The receptionist had no authority to direct visitors off her own bat, but rebuking her was pointless now. Amy burst into Richard's office, in a blind panic she couldn't for the moment conceal.

'There's a policeman on his way up,' she blurted out.

'Well calm down, dear—it's not wholly unexpected. And remember what we agreed.'

It seemed an eternity as the lift climbed to the 29th floor. Then the doors opened and Carmody stepped out.

Bravely, Amy moved forward.

'DCI Carmody—I'm Jane, Richard Pedley's EA. How do you do?' She extended her hand to shake his.

'Pleased to meet you, Jane.'

Class—he played it beautifully—not a flicker of surprise. Another loss to the stage.

44

Carmody did a double take as the lift doors parted, but even with the hairstyle and the prissy glasses, he never doubted Amy's identity. But, boy, she'd startled him.

He'd almost asked her what she was playing at, but she'd stepped in so rapidly with her introduction that he felt compelled to play along with the fiction she'd woven. Even so, it took all his willpower not to rapid-fire a series of questions at her in the corridor.

For someone who'd come perilously close to being exposed, Amy seemed oddly un-rattled as she led Carmody through to Pedley. And although the girl needed someone like Carmody to save her from her own flakiness, there was no denying her inner grit.

'This is purely a routine visit, sir,' Carmody began, parking his maelstrom of thoughts. 'I'm here to ask some questions about Toby Marchpole.'

'I expected you chaps to show up sooner or later,' Pedley said, with disarming candour. 'How may I help you?'

He appeared no more tense than the last time they'd spoken, Carmody noted.

'How well acquainted were you with Mr Marchpole?'

'I mainly know of him. As you're aware, he wrote some defamatory pieces on IPT in recent weeks.'

'How many times have you met him?'

Pedley paused for a fraction of a second.

'Never—except when he gate-crashed our AGM. He's

not the kind of chap who moves in my circles.'

'Quite a coincidence, two people in such close proximity to you at the AGM being dead.'

'Coincidences happen,' Pedley pointed out. 'And Venner died from natural causes.'

'But not Marchpole.'

Pedley's courteous manner didn't sway Carmody one way or another—he'd met his type before. And as they both knew, either the deaths were a fluky coincidence, or strongly linked—there was no middle course. Carmody now feared his hasty closure of the Venner enquiry might come back to bite him. For there'd been developments on that score which he'd hoped to keep under wraps. Fat chance of that now.

'I imagine Marchpole's death has made life simpler for you,' Carmody said, hoping to break through Pedley's veneer of politeness.

'Is that supposed to give me a motive?'

'It *is* a motive, from where I'm sitting.'

'Sorry to disappoint you, but his death is actually rather inconvenient,' Pedley confided. 'My lawyers were preparing a libel case against him.'

'Can't they still sue the estate?'

'I'm told it's complicated,' he replied, leaving Carmody wondering what kind of man would consult his lawyers so promptly on such a matter.

'So to get to the nitty gritty,' said Carmody. 'Can I ask about your movements between five and six pm yesterday?'

'Well, I left the office at five-thirty, as my secretary Jane will confirm. Then I went straight home in a taxi, arriving half an hour later, as my girlfriend Roxanne will testify. But I fail to understand how these questions help you, Chief

Inspector, unless you're suggesting I pulled the trigger myself.'

With no evidence against Pedley, the primary aim of the interview was to rattle him. But Pedley, either through innocence or arrogance—impossible to tell which—proved to be unflappable.

'As I said, sir, these are routine enquiries at this stage.'

The phrase "at this stage" introduced a hint of menace not lost on Pedley.

'But I am, I presume, the prime suspect.'

'Oh, I wouldn't say that, sir. Marchpole crossed a number of people recently.'

'That doesn't surprise me at all. Now, I'm a very busy man, Chief Inspector, so unless there's anything else I can help with…?'

'That's all for the moment, sir. I appreciate your assistance and we'll be in touch if we need anything else.'

Twenty years in the force had made Carmody a pragmatist. Unless Pedley had been idiotic enough to leave a financial trail, they would struggle to incriminate him. Realistically, their best chance of solving the crime was to locate the hired assassin and work backwards. There was usually someone in the criminal underworld prepared to talk, at a price.

'Oh, and while I'm here,' said Carmody, ostensibly as an afterthought 'May I have a quick word with your secretary—Jane, isn't it?'

He noted a perceptible reticence, before Pedley said, with the utmost charm, 'Sure, no problem, but she hasn't been working for me long.'

'But she can confirm what time you left the office,' Carmody reminded him.

'Yes—so she can.'

***

Alone with Amy, Carmody put his fingers to his lips, before bringing out his notebook.

'Room may be bugged,' he scribbled.

'You're kidding,' she scribbled back.

Nevertheless, for the benefit of the bugs, if any, Carmody conducted a "proper" interview.

Amy gave deadpan answers to the phony queries—how long she'd been working for IPT, Pedley's whereabouts the previous day, and so forth. But the big questions remained both unasked and unanswered.

Finally he jotted something on his notepad and showed it to Amy.

'Daly's at seven tonight?'

As Amy gave him the thumbs up, the rush of emotion startled him. Perhaps he was not so much of a cold fish as he professed to be.

45

Daly's wine bar was one of Amy's old haunts from Pearson Malone days, and also the venue of her first disastrous meeting with Carmody. It therefore held unhappy memories for them both, making Amy question the wisdom of his choice. Her day spent in the company of Marchpole's probable murderer had taken its toll. Accordingly, she lacked the energy for an interrogation, but calculated that a refusal to join Carmody would be unhelpful to her cause.

When she arrived, intentionally five minutes late, Carmody was already sitting in the same booth they'd occupied on that fateful evening. Provided he avoided the temptation to lecture her on the legalities of impersonation and false documents, the outcome this time might be better.

'Amy—thank God.'

He rose from his seat and flung his arms around her. Drained by events, she allowed him to hold her close for a few moments, relishing the safety of his embrace.

'I did intend to come forward, honestly,' she said, anticipating his concerns about withholding information.

'It's OK—relax. Let me get you a drink. A soft one, I assume.'

'You assume wrong—it's been one hell of a day and I'm done with rehab.'

'Fine with me.' He ordered a bottle of New Zealand Sauvignon Blanc, suppressing whatever judgmental observation he doubtless had in mind. Maybe he'd learnt a few lessons from Toby.

'I love the hair,' he said. 'It's so you.'

Amy ran her fingers through the short spikes. After more than a month she'd grown accustomed to her naked neck, and the blonde stranger in the mirror appeared friendlier by the day. She'd already had the roots retouched and a trim.

'That's ironic, considering it's a disguise. But I know what you mean—this should have been my hair all along, if only I'd had the guts.'

'Why didn't you?'

'I desperately wanted to look normal, and a punky short cut didn't do the biz.'

'Are you telling me your mother's hoarding even affected your choice of hairstyle?'

It was a perceptive comment, which stymied Amy momentarily.

'I never considered it before, but maybe so.'

'Anyway,' he said. 'We didn't come here to psychoanalyse your hairstyle. I'm in listening mode. Tell me everything.'

And she did, leaving out only her seduction of Marchpole, which would poke Carmody's green-eyed monster while adding nothing to the story.

'So, to be clear. Why did you agree to help him?'

She could have lied, told him she wished to exonerate Venner, but Carmody deserved a more meaningful explanation.

'Mainly I wanted to stop being Crazy Amy—to do something useful. And seeing Toby after decades—with his passion for exposing corruption—stirred something in me. Especially after all the other business.'

'Hm,' said Carmody. 'While I hate to speak ill of the dead, there are those who regarded Marchpole as a trouble-making little shit.'

Although Amy still had her doubts, she sprung to Toby's defence.

'That's a tad harsh.'

'And you passed him evidence…'

Ah—the first whiff of disapproval—delayed rather than eradicated.

'I can see where you're headed, but hear me out. He didn't publish anything I told him and he had no position in the shares.'

She hoped to God this was true.

'So what did you find?'

'Loads. John Venner got a bung of a million pounds when he was appointed. They're into complex loan transactions to make it appear Pedley's buying shares rather than selling, and they purchase inventory from a secret connected Chinese company to inflate profits.'

'Sounds like a case study in fraud.'

'You bet—but there's more. Toby travelled to China to gather further data, and he told me he'd discovered something sensational, but I never established what because…'

The realisation that she'd never see Toby again hit her anew, like a missile finding its target.

'I'm sorry,' she sobbed, berating herself for her vulnerability. 'This has upset me more than I realised.'

Carmody passed her his handkerchief.

'It's OK,' he said tenderly, like a different person. 'Take your time.'

The wine arrived and Carmody poured them both a glass.

'I've spent all day with that man. It's creepy, because he's acting perfectly normally.'

'Maybe he's innocent?'

'I doubt it. He begged me not to mention it, but Pedley was meeting Marchpole at six pm round the corner from where Toby was killed.'

Carmody sat bolt upright, figuring this might be the first building block in the case against Pedley.

'What for?'

'To ask him to stop slagging off IPT on his blog.'

Carmody sipped at his wine.

'Why do you think he asked you to keep quiet?'

'He claimed to be anxious about you guys jumping to the wrong conclusion.'

'Or the right one.'

'You said he was innocent a moment ago,' Amy reminded him.

'I'm keeping an open mind. Now—when did you plan to step out from the shadows and reveal all?'

Amy chose to regard this as a sensible question rather than whiff of disapproval number two.

'Oh—very soon. To be honest, I was so shell-shocked this morning I just went into work as normal.'

'Weren't you scared?'

'Yes, a bit, but I reckoned I'd be dead already if my cover was blown. Was that not a rational assumption?'

'Perhaps a little foolhardy.'

Carmody sounded gentle and supportive, even though he probably disapproved of her actions. This made Amy wonder if she'd previously been too hypersensitive to his criticism.

'By the way,' said Amy, for it had been puzzling her all day. 'What made you think the room was bugged earlier?'

'Oh it's a scenario that concerns me a lot these days.'

'Why?'

'According to your old pal Ed Smithies, industrial espionage is rife. He has his office swept for bugs on a regular basis. It wasn't something that troubled me before, but once you're alive to the possibility, you start imagining listening devices everywhere.'

Smithies' anxiety secretly pleased Amy. Clearly, the recording had perturbed him more than she'd expected.

'How interesting.'

'We'll need a formal statement from you tomorrow.'

'From Jane or from Amy?'

'That is rather awkward,' Carmody agreed.

'I don't want to get into trouble.'

'Don't worry—we can head it off. Though you should quit the job.'

'Why? They haven't worked out who I am yet.'

'It's too risky. Consider this. Venner went to China, now he's dead. Marchpole retraced his steps and he's dead too. Doesn't that worry you?'

'But according to you, Venner died of natural causes.'

'Well Marchpole didn't.'

'And we can't be sure the two deaths are linked.'

'You can't risk it, Amy—you have to leave now.'

His voice had taken on a hectoring tone, and although more scared than she'd admit, Amy bristled at being bossed around. What right did Carmody have, even with his policeman's helmet on, to force his opinions on her?

Picking up on her resistance, Carmody softened his tone.

'Look, Amy—I know you're an independent spirit, but I'm concerned about you. I care for you very much and I want you to be safe.'

Put like that, his suggestion sounded much more palatable.

'OK, but an orderly exit would arouse less suspicion. I'll go in tomorrow and resign on some spurious grounds or other, and with luck I won't have to work my notice.'

'Fine,' said Carmody, pouring out more of the wine. 'Tell me, were you close to Marchpole?'

Amy faltered—how could she answer? It was tough enough to analyse how she felt, let alone articulate it.

'You're upset in a way I can't fathom,' he added.

This was worse than a Priory therapy session. And Carmody's inevitable jealousy, whatever words she used, only added to the difficulty of summing up her complex emotions.

'He's someone I knew from a long time ago, before Amy Robinson with the big important job existed. He was the only link to my real self.'

'Were you in love with him?'

She wasn't clear whether Carmody meant past or present, allowing her the opportunity of a semi-truthful answer.

'No—never. We dated for a while, but nothing happened between us.'

Amy now recognised there'd only ever been person who'd triggered a rush of emotion that people called love, and he was sitting opposite her. She'd fought and denied it, but even on their first handshake she'd sensed his rootless energy, the perfect complement to her legacy of shame. She'd pushed him away time and time again, but he still kept hoping, not for a quick fumble behind someone else's back Toby-style, but a meaningful relationship. He wanted to look after her, save her from herself. And if that frightened Amy, mightn't the fear stem from her own insecurities?

Sure, Carmody was a fallible human being, but so was she, and he accepted that. Though he could be judgmental and self-obsessed, he'd made a sterling effort to behave tonight and moreover, he was no worse than her. Ultimately he accepted her, warts and all—shouldn't she afford him the same tolerance? He would protect her, so she didn't have to battle on alone. Now—in her darkest hour, wasn't this the ideal moment to give him a chance to prove his worth?

She leaned across the table and kissed him lightly on the cheek.

'Hey,' he said, his wide enquiring eyes full of hope. 'What's that for?'

'Last time we came here, everything unravelled before we'd even begun. Is that why you subconsciously chose to come here, to rewind?'

'Do you *want* to rewind?'

'Yes—I do.'

'But you said we couldn't ever...'

'Dave, I've said a lot of stuff in my life. Some of it was lies, some I thought I meant, but didn't, and some stuff I really did mean, then realised later I was wrong.'

'And which is this?'

'Tick all the above that apply—but you understand what I'm saying.'

'Yes,' Carmody said. 'I believe I do.'

46

It felt so natural, being together. Why hadn't she seen the light before? She'd been alone forever, even when married. Greg had been part of the charade—the dream man who'd been so deeply flawed—an accessory to the mirage of the perfect life she'd craved. Both of them had merely acted out their roles in a mutual confidence trick—there'd been no passion between them.

By contrast, Toby represented the thread joining past and present, which would never have stretched far into the future, even if he'd survived.

Dave was the future. He'd seen her at her worst, been privy to all her innermost secrets and he still adored her. They talked long into the night, not only about Amy's hang-ups, but his too. He confided with eloquence how he'd been like a rudderless ship at sea, as he'd used all his detective skills to track down the woman who'd abandoned him as a baby. At one point, he'd been convinced he was onto something, only to find his train of impeccable logic had led him down a blind alley.

Dave feared a crazy gene somewhere in him—Amy was certain of hers. Their imperfections, known and conjectured, were perfectly balanced.

In the morning she assembled her clothes, strewn on the living room floor, and took in her surroundings with pleasure. She'd been a stranger in her own house for years, yet had settled in Carmody's flat within minutes of arrival. It wasn't *quite* in Camden, as he'd claimed, but still reasonably central. And though Jane's similar-sized accommodation seemed cramped and depressing, here every one of the six hundred square feet was impeccably organised and presented—nothing lacking, and nothing surplus.

Amy had always craved space, or so she thought. Now she questioned whether on some level the vast empty rooms in the Chiswick house had intimidated her. Perhaps growing up in a house navigable only via goat trails had somehow affected her visuospatial perception.

'How much did you pay for this place?' she asked.

'A shade under three hundred in 2012—not bad for Zone 2, eh? Why do you ask?'

'I'd like to live somewhere like this, when I've got myself sorted out.'

'You can move in here with me.'

This brought Amy up short. He had to be kidding—OK, they'd spent the night together and the omens were promising, but...

'Seriously?'

'Why are you so surprised?'

'It's so soon.'

A dart of foreboding pricked her euphoria, but she pushed it aside.

'Is that a no then?'

'I'll think about it.'

'Breakfast?'

'A piece of toast will do fine.'

'Meant to ask before,' said Amy, as Dave put the bread in the toaster and loaded up the coffee machine. 'How's Marchpole's wife bearing up?'

'Terrible—they've sedated her, but she's in no fit state to be interviewed.'

'How dreadful.' Amy hated her inner bitch for being pleased, but decades of accumulated envy didn't shift overnight.

'You knew her at school, didn't you? Was she your friend?'

'No, she was right out of my league—head girl, sporty, clever, beautiful. You get the picture.'

'I do—I'll bet you were green with envy.'

'Yep—you nailed it in one.'

'With luck, we'll interview her today.'

'All the best with that. And I must go to work and resign, or rather Jane must.'

'Then good luck to you as well. Hope it goes smoothly.'

A quick mirror check convinced Amy that she looked presentable. She wouldn't even bother going home to change. So what if people noticed her wearing the same clothes two days running? She'd be out of there soon.

47

By mid-morning, Celia Holland had recovered sufficiently to be interviewed.

She wore a black cashmere sweater, pearls and immaculate white jeans which hugged her slender figure. Not a hair was out of place, although her skilfully applied makeup failed to disguise her red, swollen eyes. And her fragile calmness bore all the hallmarks of being chemically induced.

Here was a woman accustomed to putting on an act, and still trying to pull it off in the most appalling circumstances. She reminded him of Amy.

Carmody noticed a large glass of white wine on the table beside Celia. It was virtually untouched, and probably just as well—Carmody doubted if her tranquillisers were compatible with alcohol.

'Can I offer you some Chablis, Chief Inspector?'

'Not while I'm on duty.'

'I rarely drink—normally, I'm a health freak. But hey—your life can be snuffed out in an instant, so what the heck.'

She snapped her fingers to emphasise the point.

It had shocked Carmody when Celia had collapsed in screaming hysterics as she viewed her husband's body. He'd assumed she'd be more composed than most, given her profession, and the sight had not even been unusually gruesome. But perhaps the experience was different with your spouse lying on the mortuary slab.

'Chief Inspector,' she began. 'So sorry to delay your enquiries—this has been a terrible shock.'

'Yes, I'm sure.'

'I'm much more level-headed today.'

Or at least she was striving to simulate being level-headed, in between dabbing at her eyes with a well-used handkerchief.

They cantered through some basic questions, before getting to the key issues. She claimed not to know much about the story Toby had been working on, as he never discussed his work with her in detail. Toby's alternative angle on life was sometimes embarrassing in their social circles, she explained, although thank God his stupid little blog didn't have a wide readership.

Until Venner's death went viral, thought Carmody

'Do you believe Venner died a natural death?'

He kept cycling back to this point with everyone—seeking to validate a conclusion he now mistrusted.

'From what Toby told me, definitely. Some fruit loops even crazier than Toby thought otherwise, but he said Venner was a coronary waiting to happen.'

'Were you aware Venner also visited China immediately before he died?'

Clearly not, to judge from her surprised expression.

'Are you saying there's a connection with Toby?'

'We're looking at all the angles, Ms Holland. Did you have any contact with your husband while he was in China?'

'I spoke to him Tuesday.'

'How was he?'

Inexplicably, this question prompted Celia to break down in a fit of sobbing.

'We argued,' she said. 'It was our last conversation…'

Carmody didn't press her, and let her compose herself.

'He told me he'd been robbed and his phone and wallet stolen.'

This might account for the lack of phone on his body, thought Carmody, mentally crossing off the question from his list.

'He said he thought they would kill him. I didn't take it seriously…'

She broke off, as if reflecting on whether she'd missed an opportunity to avert the ensuing tragedy.

'I felt positive he was with her,'

'Who?' asked Carmody softly.

'We haven't been getting along too well lately. He was having an affair.'

More sobs and dabbing at the eyes.

'Oh, I see.'

'Some crazy lunatic woman he used to date when he was at school.'

Carmody didn't bat an eyelid, but his stomach lurched.

'Her name?' he asked, trying to suppress a bubbling cauldron of emotion.

Nothing happened between us…

'Amy Robinson.'

'Are you sure about the affair?'

She nodded.

'And was he with her?'

'No, but he finally admitted they'd slept together—only once, although he was probably lying.'

The force of Amy's treachery hit Carmody like a thunderclap destroying a perfect summer afternoon. How dare she lie to him?

'Is this relevant to your husband's death?' he asked as calmly as possible, while sincerely hoping not.

'It's highly relevant. See what came through my letter box this morning.'

She reached over to the side table and produced a grainy photograph of Toby and Amy kissing, accompanied by a typed note.

BLAME THIS WOMAN FOR YOUR HUSBAND'S MURDER.

48

Amy planned to resign on the grounds of a grave but vague female medical problem—the perfect excuse, as Pedley would be far too embarrassed to probe for details.

But events had overtaken her. Pedley called her into his office on arrival, and he didn't mince his words.

'You, young lady, are fired.'

Amy gulped—there was only one possible explanation. Yet still she played dumb.

'Why—is my performance not up to scratch?'

'What aspect of your performance do you mean, Jane, or should I say Amy? Your work here, or snooping around for that degenerate hack Toby Marchpole?'

'You've got it all wrong,' Amy insisted.

'No—I've got it all right. You're Amy Robinson, a crazy head case who stirred up a whole pile of shit in Pearson Malone and then, for reasons best known to yourself, joined forces with that piece of human excrement to destroy me. You wheedled your way into the job, into my trust. And you have the gall to stand there with those innocent blue eyes and deny it. But I have absolute proof, because I've seen a photograph of you together.'

Amy now saw a different side to Pedley. He could be curt and impatient, but only now did she glimpse his capacity for egotistical rage.

His reaction to being duped did not particularly surprise her. Men of Pedley's ilk were, as a breed, full of repressed anger. The old order was changing fast—old boy networks busted by young upstarts, ethnic minorities and women—with no respect for traditional values. Underneath a wafer-thin façade of political correctness, such men often mistrusted women more than anyone else. They were acceptable as secretaries, tea ladies, mistresses and wives—but not as serious players who challenged the status quo. And on no account must they humiliate the boss.

Amy stood, absorbing the rant. Something didn't add up. If Pedley was behind Marchpole's murder, and he'd rumbled her connection to Toby, why hadn't he killed her too? With some trepidation, she decided to test the water.

'OK—I confess—I'm Amy, but you're wrong about my motives. Truth is, I was John Venner's friend.'

'Yes—the one Venner wanted told. Which makes it doubly disloyal.'

'Not at all. You see, I wasn't working *with* Marchpole, but to clear Venner's name, to prove to Marchpole he had it all wrong.'

He looked doubtful for an instant, but then stiffened his resolve.

'I don't buy it. If that was your intention, you could have talked to me instead of going through all this rigmarole.'

'Yes,' Amy conceded. 'I guess I could.'

'And why would you give any credence to his ridiculous blog? Everybody knows he spews out total bilge for his own financial gain. Have you seen a word against us in the mainstream press?'

'No. But…'

Of course, Toby had his own explanation for this.

'You know, I'm sick of women like you. You consider yourself to be intelligent, but you're not. Roxanne is way smarter. She spotted your Tiffany earrings on the very first day and had doubts from the off that you weren't who you claimed to be. In fact, she was so suspicious she put a private eye onto you.'

Damn those earrings—they'd been a huge blunder, although having her tailed seemed a disproportionate response.

'And more fool me, I stood up for you. Now take your belongings and get out. And don't think this is the end of it either, because I shall personally ensure that you never work in the City again.'

And I, thought Amy, *will reciprocate.*

49

Jealousy tightened its grip on Carmody.

Amy had lied. This time, he'd believed she genuinely cared about him—but no. All he'd been to her was a quick roll around on the rebound after Marchpole, and her dishonesty disgusted him as much as her loose morals. In the past, he'd wasted so much time berating himself for not prioritising Amy, but underneath he'd known all along. She was little more than a whore, unworthy of any sacrifices he might make on her behalf.

'Any idea who might have sent this?' he asked Celia, trying valiantly to suppress his emotions.

'No.'

'Or why?'

'Well, the implication is plain.'

However unlikely Amy's involvement seemed, the prospect of having to follow up filled Carmody with dread. He would have to declare a personal interest and hand over the case to another officer. He would become a laughing stock among his colleagues.

'And, in your opinion, could she be responsible?'

'She had a motive.'

'Yes?'

'I told Toby he must stop seeing her, and he agreed. I mean, that's not unreasonable is it? Some women wouldn't give their husbands a second chance. Oh… my… a second chance… not now…'

Carmody waited until her sobbing had abated. He wished now he'd accepted the offer of wine.

'And how does that give her a motive?' he asked once she'd calmed down again.

Suddenly, Celia became more animated.

'Amy has a history of mental instability—need I say more? She might have flipped out—if she couldn't have him, no one would. And she has plenty of money to hire someone.'

The force with which Celia presented this flimsy argument was compelling. Not for nothing had she become a top QC.

'But you surely don't buy that?'

'It's a very weak prosecution case, but obviously you're obliged to consider it.'

It would be a brave man who ignored the views of a leading criminal QC in deciding whether to pursue a particular line of enquiry. They would have to at least pay lip service to it.

'We shall cover *all* the angles,' Carmody replied. 'Including Ms Robinson.'

Although, Lord knows, he thought, *it puts me in an impossible position.*

50

Amy sensed trouble as soon as Carmody answered the door. The tenderness and openness of the previous night had vanished, replaced by that cold and penetrating gaze of his which never boded well. What could have precipitated the dramatic shift in mood?

'What's wrong?' she asked.

'We have a problem.'

'What?'

'Sit down.' He pointed at the sofa, but she vacillated.

'I said, sit down.'

Amy perched on the edge of the seat, bracing herself for what might come next.

'OK—what's happened?'

'You lied to me.'

'Lied—about what?'

'Nothing happened with Marchpole, you said. But you were having an affair.'

'No!'

'I'll save you the embarrassment of denying it. I've seen a photo of the two of you together—kissing—outside Jane's flat by the looks of it.'

Realisation dawned. Was this a picture taken by Roxanne's private eye, possibly the same one Pedley saw? But how had Carmody obtained it?

'So, we kissed. Do I have to disclose a detailed lifetime history of kisses?'

'But it wasn't just a kiss.'

His tone sounded bullying and accusatory.

'What makes you say that?'

'Because I interviewed Marchpole's wife this morning. She handed me the photograph and told me Toby had confessed to an affair.'

Interesting, and surprising—perhaps Toby's passion for the truth hadn't been as selective as she'd assumed. But more to the point, how did Celia come to have the snapshot?

'Well she did seem suspicious of me and Toby.'

'And with good reason,' said Carmody bitterly.

She could keep stonewalling. Marchpole was dead and Celia might be lying. But denials were pointless because Carmody had already decided.

'Yes, OK, we did have sex—just the once though.'

'You lied—*again*,' he said, stony-faced, and referring to an earlier incident in the disastrous trajectory of their relationship. 'I gave you a pass before, but I should have seen the writing on the wall. Exactly how many men have you slept with?'

'You have no right to ask.'

'Tell me.' He shoved her back on the sofa and cut a menacing figure as he stood leaning over her.

'I bet they were mostly one night stands, because you're such a slag.'

'It was before us.'

'It was after we met.'

'It was before we got together.'

But Amy's appeals for logic fell on deaf ears, as Carmody's tirade continued in full flow.

'I bet you screwed around when you were married didn't you? Christ—no wonder your ex ended up how he did. You know what—I actually pity the poor bugger.'

His anger and irrationality frightened her. They represented the flip side of his intense passion, of asking her to move in with him after one night. It seemed to Amy like he needed to own her past, present and future.

'I repeat—it's none of your business.'

'I disagree. Apart from anything else, did it not occur to you that sexual contact with the murder victim might be relevant to the enquiry?'

'Well, obviously if I'd known in advance he'd be murdered…'

'Don't get funny with me.'

He screwed his hand up in a fist, as if straining every sinew not to hit her.

'I can complain about this—it's called police harassment.'

'You'll be batting on a sticky wicket if you do.'

'Oh yes?'

'The photo I mentioned was delivered to Celia this morning, together with a note suggesting you were responsible for Marchpole's death.'

Amy had accepted the possibility of being next on the hit list, but being a suspect? She hadn't seen that one coming at all.

'*What?* But that's outrageous! Let me see it.'

'You can't—it's been taken as evidence.'

'But I don't understand. Surely you don't…'

'We have to pursue all lines of enquiry.'

This unofficial interrogation had taken on a Kafkaesque quality. Carmody's voice sounded cold, as though he didn't care what became of her now she'd "betrayed" him.

'You surely can't think…'

'My opinion is irrelevant, because now we must eliminate you from the enquiry.'

'Eliminate me—why?'

'Because according to Celia you have a motive. She told Toby to finish with you, and therefore you might…'

The enormity of Carmody's accusation began to dawn on Amy.

'So purely on that bitch's say so, I'm a murder suspect?'

Because the bitch was an important QC and people listened, even if she was talking rubbish. Whereas people didn't listen to Crazy Amy, even when she talked sense.

'You're not hearing me, Amy,' Carmody replied. 'No one is implying you were in any way involved, but we have to check out the facts.'

'Terrific. Is putting that spin on it meant to make me feel better?'

'This is exceptionally awkward for me.'

He had calmed down appreciably, but by contrast an uncontrollable rage welled up inside Amy. After treating her appallingly, Carmody's first priority was himself.

'Awkward for *you*!'

'Well I'm now connected to the case and I'll have to step aside. Frankly, it's improper for you to be here.'

'This is about your bloody promotion AGAIN, isn't it?'

The déjà vu was horrendous, but she'd be damned if she'd put up with this nonsense a second time, or let him treat her like a cheap whore. Two angry men in one day was two too many.

'No, no—I don't care about that at all. I just want everything to be right between us.'

'Well, you're going a funny way about it.'

'Look, I'm sorry I lost it—once I've calmed down, I expect I'll forgive you for lying.'

Amy's rage now simmered up to boiling point. So—he apologised as an afterthought and still considered she was the one who needed forgiveness.

'Well *I* won't forgive *you*.'

'For what?'

'For being an arsehole.'

'But surely you understand the difficult position I'm in.'

'Whereas you have no interest in my difficulties.'

'What?'

'I didn't get to give my resignation speech because Pedley, the man you should be investigating over Toby's murder, knows my true identity. And you say you're in a difficult position.'

'Amy—I'm sorry—it came across wrong. And forgive me for not asking about your day.'

'Forget your false apologies, and let me make it easier for you. There is no personal connection between us—you and I are finished—forever.'

He took it calmly, like he didn't believe she meant it. And this hardened Amy's heart all the more.

***

Shit. What the hell had come over him?

Even as the front door slammed, Carmody recognised that he'd screwed up on multiple levels. He'd called Amy a slag, pushed her, and come within a hair's breadth of hitting her. He loved her so much that he simply couldn't bear to picture her with another man, but this didn't excuse his vile behaviour—nothing did.

In the past, he'd dealt with domestic abuse cases and had always despised the perpetrators. Was this the hideous genetic legacy he'd always feared—that he was a monster, unable to control his anger and jealousy?

He rushed out after Amy, only to see the lift doors close— ran down the fire escape, only to see her hop into a black cab, disappearing out of his life forever. Deflated and dejected, he returned to his flat and dialled her number, but she'd forestalled him not only by switching off her phone, but deactivating her voicemail.

And to top off his misery, now Carmody had to square up to an awkward conversation with his immediate boss.

51

Amy awoke clammy and fearful in the small hours, longing for the sanctuary of the Priory. There she'd kept her emotions under tight control, but now a whole host of unmanageable feelings bubbled up to the surface, not helped by the gin she'd knocked back.

She was almost as angry with herself as with Carmody. She should have fought back when he'd called her a slag. And what about the woman that evening with Mel? Faced with proof of his double standards, she'd failed to challenge him. And how had she not called him out on his anger—which no apology could ever absolve? All her instincts about his control-freakery had been proven correct, but she'd switched off her instincts for the night. She'd allowed him to catch her at a low ebb, to wrap her in his tentacles, and she'd had a lucky escape.

At least the scales had fallen from her eyes before any real harm was done. Far less painful to spend one night with him and to be reminded what a self-centred, jealous creep he was, than to suffer him chipping away slowly at her self-esteem over months or years, then maybe losing control altogether.

On the minus side, however, it appeared she was now a murder suspect. This development would be laughable, except it meant Carmody and Co would waste time going down a blind alley while the true killer continued untroubled with his life. Not to mention the small yet disturbing chance that they might never realise their mistake.

Her first instinct was to call Toby—then it hit her afresh—Toby was gone. Christ—how her life had spiralled out of control in the three weeks since starting her undercover job. But she was still alive, and kept coming back to this basic point. If Pedley had masterminded Marchpole's death, why had she been spared? And if not, then who was the culprit?

52

Monday morning, Amy received a message from a Detective Sergeant Allen asking her to come in for a formal interview.

Amy seethed. How typical of Carmody to subcontract out his dirty work to a subordinate. And she'd bet any money he hadn't stepped aside from the case, and wouldn't do so unless compelled to. Well, she would force his hand, if necessary by making a formal complaint. Let him try to shrug off allegations of improper sexual contact with and intimidation of a suspect. He could wave bye-bye to his precious promotion.

But Carmody was nowhere to be seen, his place usurped by a pudgy guy with a sweaty handshake who introduced himself as DCI Bligh and his sidekick as DS Allen. He informed her in a matter-of-fact way that he had taken over the case from DCI Carmody, carefully avoiding mentioning why.

Amy felt a twinge of disappointment—she wanted to spar with Carmody, not this charmless moron. And Carmody stepping aside undercut her grounds for complaint, as he'd misbehaved in a personal capacity rather than a professional one.

Bligh waffled on about attending voluntarily, and being free to terminate the interview at any time. He could have saved his breath—she'd heard this crap before. And for all his reassurances, Amy knew she might still end up being arrested and charged.

'Following our interview with Celia Holland,' Bligh began, 'we've been following up a few loose ends. And, if possible, we'd like your help in tying them down.'

Amy had no intention of being conciliatory. *Loose ends, my arse*, she thought. This cretin would take everything at face value, and if he was allowed his formal statement, then so was she.

'Before you begin, I should tell you I intend to seek legal advice—in fact, if time permitted, I would have brought my lawyer with me today. I'm astounded to find you've launched an enquiry against me on the basis of Celia Holland's ridiculous and vindictive allegations.'

'Now let's get this straight,' said Bligh, visibly annoyed by her combative attitude. 'Ms Holland has made no allegations—she's reported the facts, which we are investigating. No one is accusing you of anything. In fact, we're hoping to clear you of any involvement.'

'OK—that's good. But if I get a sniff of any intimidation, I shall end the interview.'

'Ms Robinson—it's your right to do so, as I already explained.'

On that basis they began, with Bligh leading the charge and his DS following behind.

Amy expanded on how she came to be masquerading as Jane Eccles. She was unsure whether using a fake identity was in itself a criminal offence, but with no legal advice on tap, she'd have to live with the risk. Neither Bligh nor his colleague showed any disapproval and so, encouraged, she outlined the financial shenanigans they were aware of so far.

'This sounds like one for the City boys' fraud section,' said the DS to Bligh, but the glance he gave to his superior officer suggested the detail had floated way over their heads.

'Talking of financial matters,' said Bligh. 'As part of our enquiries, we've been examining your bank accounts.'

'Oh—don't you need my permission to do that?'

'We don't actually,' said DS Allen.

'Perhaps you can tell us, Ms Robinson,' Bligh continued, 'why you withdrew fifteen thousand pounds in cash from your bank the day before Toby Marchpole's murder.'

That had Amy poleaxed.

'The Amy Robinson account?'

'Yes.'

'But I haven't used that account for a while.'

'According to the bank, you withdrew the money from the counter by signing a cheque, because you couldn't remember the PIN number for your debit card due to mental health issues. They were suspicious and asked for ID, and you showed your driving licence.'

'But it's impossible. My chequebook and driving licence are at home—I mean my real home in Chiswick. I've not been anywhere near the bank. And I most certainly *can* remember my pin number.'

'So what's your explanation?'

'Isn't it obvious? I've been robbed! Someone else made the withdrawal. What the hell were the bank staff doing?'

'You can ask them—but they told us you had a recent history of large cash withdrawals, which reassured them.'

'*Reassured them*!' said Amy, aghast. 'Do they know what I did with the first lot?'

'As I said, you'll have to discuss it with them.'

'Have no fear—I intend to.'

They'd been shamefully negligent, considering the grief they'd given Amy over the cash for the trip to St Paul's. And paradoxically, doing something loony with the first tranche of cash appeared to have made it *easier* to access more.

'And for our part,' said DS Allen, 'if you didn't withdraw that money, rest assured we'll find who did. So if you could try to calm down, we'll continue the interview.'

'Calm down! How would you feel being accused of hiring a killer, which I assume is what you're implying? In fact *I'm* the victim of a crime here. Someone's been into my home, taken my documents and stolen my money.'

'I repeat—nobody's accusing you,' said Bligh, but Amy drew no comfort from his words.

'And if I wanted to hire a killer, don't you think I'd manage to do it without leaving clues the size of elephant's footprints?'

'We appreciate how distressing this must be for you,' Bligh said, without answering Amy's question. 'Please be assured we're doing everything we can to solve this. For a start, we're trying to obtain a CCTV photograph from the bank, which should hopefully bring the whole matter to a speedy conclusion.'

Unlikely, thought Amy gloomily.

'Now, in the meantime, who else has keys to your house?'

***

'What do you think?' DS Allen asked Bligh.

'Either she's a brilliant actress, or she knows nothing about the money.'

'She did seem shocked, I'll admit. Plus Pedley's finger-prints were on the photograph, and on the note. So, I'll wager once we find out who took the cash, the trail will lead us right back to Pedley.'

And Bligh had to agree, it did look that way.

53

Amy left the interview seized by a need for urgent action, and with a focus for her anger.

That someone had sneaked into her home, stolen her documents and plundered her bank account was beyond disturbing. And with little confidence in Bligh to investigate promptly, she set off back to Chiswick to begin her own enquiries.

In comparison with Jane's Seven Sisters shoebox, Amy's house was a picture of opulence. Yet as soon as she entered, she noticed that the air hung heavy with a musty odour of disappointment and frustrated ambition. And perhaps potential purchasers picked up on the negative atmosphere, for although the property was priced competitively, with plenty of viewings, no offers had materialised.

Amy's identity papers were inside the desk drawer, exactly where she'd left them. All the same, her intuition told her someone had been in there poking around. And the only other keys were with the estate agent.

Amy's visit to the agent took Paul, the branch manager, unawares.

'Ah, Ms Robinson, what an unexpected pleasure,' he began. He was a caricature of a West London estate agent, whose superficial polish concealed a sourness at his inability to afford any of the properties on the books. His bitterness became more thinly disguised as Amy calmly levelled her accusations of incompetence.

'The viewings were supervised at all times,' he assured her.

'Well, someone got in and you guys have the only other set of keys.'

'Are you absolutely certain someone couldn't have got hold of your keys, madam?'

'*Absolutely* certain,' Amy said firmly. Her key ring was kept hidden underneath a loose floorboard in the Seven Sisters flat, beyond the reach of even the most determined burglar. 'And as there are no other keys, it follows that the thief used yours to let themselves in.'

'It's impossible. Our security procedures are second to none. And we would never give out the keys except on your explicit instructions.'

'But the fact remains, someone got into my house.'

Paul was a grinning sycophant with not a lot between the ears. But his brain seemed now to be whirring away at top speed.

'What about the cleaner?' he asked.

There was, of course, no cleaner.

'Ha,' said Amy. 'I knew it.'

'But she showed us a letter of authority from you,' said Paul, a touch defensively. 'And we checked your signature, plus her identity. She brought the keys back when she'd finished.'

As if that made any difference.

'Can I see the letter please?'

The signature on the letter authorising a Miss Sylvia Menezes to collect the keys was the work of a professional. If Amy hadn't known otherwise, she would have said it was her own. But she didn't wish to give Paul any justification for accepting it. He should, in any case, have called her to check.

'It's a clear forgery,' she pronounced. 'Thanks to your incompetence, fifteen grand has gone from my bank.'

Paul might be slow to catch on, but now the full enormity of his position hit him.

'It would have been helpful if you'd had the burglar alarm repaired as we suggested,' he said, losing no time in looking for ways to pass the blame back to Amy.

'The burglar alarm is intended as a defence against people who break in, not those who have keys,' she retorted.

'Well, in any event, perhaps we'd better contact the police,' he suggested.

'They're aware already, and they'll be in touch in their own sweet time. Meanwhile, be in no doubt—I'll sue your firm for compensation. Your procedures for checking who has access to properties are woefully lacking.'

***

After an equally strident exchange with her bank, Amy called DCI Bligh to turn the screws on him.

'So tell me what you've done so far,' she demanded.

'Our enquiries are ongoing,' he said vaguely, leading Amy to conclude there had been no action.

'So are mine, and I've already established how the woman gained access to my account.'

'Ah yes, we've been approaching matters from the other direction,' Bligh said, as though this justified their inactivity with the estate agent. 'Your bank has tracked down the CCTV image, which we'd like you to examine.'

An hour later, a female police officer arrived armed with the still from the CCTV.

The picture was grainy and blurred, but Amy gasped as she instantly identified the woman. The bank clearly hadn't inspected the photographic ID provided very thoroughly.

'I believe that's Melanie Cronin, who used to be the payroll manager at IPT,' she said.

54

Melanie ordered a second mojito in the hotel bar, while reflecting on what a bitch Amy was. How sneaky of her to act all friendly while plotting Mel's downfall. Well, the drinks were on Amy—she utterly deserved to be swindled and anyway, it wasn't like the rich cow couldn't afford it.

Those five fictitious staff on the payroll had been easy money until Venner started bleating about weak internal controls. She'd never been sure whether he'd suspected her, or if it was merely a theoretical concern—but it had been alarming either way. With Venner safely gone, she'd naively assumed that she was in the clear, until Amy had showed her hand.

Still, she'd enjoyed a cracking run and had never expected to carry on forever. The fifteen grand was useful for sure, providing her with a handy reserve fund, although it puzzled her why they'd asked her to take, and keep, the money. What did they gain from the exercise? Mel's early experiences had made her cynical about anything sounding too good to be true, and this was a prime example. Would they want something in return from her later, perhaps?

Her one advantage was that they underrated her intelligence. As far as they were concerned, she was still the stupid fat girl, even though they knew she'd duped them out of a shed load of money. But the stupid fat girl had already formulated a contingency plan—a new untraceable identity, which would be ready in a few days.

In the meantime, she would chill and drink Amy's money. She raised her glass in a silent toast to absent "friends".

55

Amy's mind whirred with questions.

First—how the devil had Mel discovered her true identity? Yes, she'd inadvertently revealed her real first name—but how would Mel deduce anything from that?

Second, was the cash withdrawal linked to Marchpole's murder, or some hideous coincidence? Mel hadn't struck her as a likely criminal, but then seeming probity was probably a key competence for fraudsters.

Third, if the two events were linked, could Mel be behind Marchpole's death? Or behind Venner's?

After several days of being fobbed off by police assurances about "exploring all avenues", Amy resolved to take matters into her own hands. She remembered where the taxi had dropped Mel off on their night out, and Mel's flat seemed a logical place to start. The house was divided into two and Amy recalled seeing Melanie enter through the left-hand door. So far, so good.

She rang the bell.

Dawn, Mel's flatmate, answered, and rolled her eyes when Amy introduced herself as a friend.

'Mel doesn't have friends. She uses you and dumps you in the shit, like she did to me. Not a word of warning—just took off while I was out one evening, leaving a note saying sorry with her share of next month's rent in cash.'

'Could be worse,' Amy pointed out. 'She might not have left the rent.'

'I suppose, but I've still got to find another subtenant in the next month though.'

'You don't know why or where she went?'

'No, do you?'

'Well they told me she resigned from work because of her sick brother.'

'Sick brother eh—she said she was an only child. But no doubt she lied about everything.'

Rather like me, thought Amy.

'No forwarding address then?'

'Only a PO Box. I might get round to sending on her mail, if she's lucky.' Dawn gestured towards a pile on the hall table.

'Well, now I put my mind to it,' Amy lied, 'I have an idea where she is, so if you'd like me to pass those on…'

Dawn didn't hesitate—what did she care whether Amy was genuine or not?

'You're welcome and good luck. And if you do find her, tell her I'm extremely pissed off.'

***

Once home, Amy tore open the envelopes.

First a credit card statement, with no transactions after Mel's final day at IPT, meaning she was either using another account or, more likely, the cash. A review of earlier entries yielded little of interest, except a debit card payment for £28.00 at a pub in Whitstable, the day after their night out. So perhaps Mel really did have a brother in Kent.

A statement for Mel's current account showed salary in and normal outgoings. The salary seemed on the low side for a payroll manager, Amy noticed.

The next envelope looked like a mailshot, but contained a receipt from The Larches care home, again in Whitstable, for the care of 'Joseph Cronin'. Did that mean it was true about the brother being sick? On checking out the facility online, Amy learned that the home provided residential care for young adults with learning and physical disabilities. One detail jumped out at Amy—The Larches cost four thousand for the month, way more than Mel's salary.

56

Amy considered contacting Bligh, but concluded she'd be better off continuing alone. Apparently "exploring all avenues" did not entail making the most basic enquiries.

It took Amy over three hours to reach Whitstable in the heavy Friday evening traffic. At least she wasn't wasting her time, though, because she'd called The Larches on a pretext, in case Mel had already spirited Joey away. If she had the nous to skim Amy's account, Mel would foresee the efforts to track her down. But Joey was still there, and hopefully she wouldn't abandon her brother.

Amy checked in to a Premier Inn, several miles from the care home. She ate a sandwich bought from a Tesco en route, washed down with three cans of ready mixed gin and tonic. For the first time since Toby's death she slept soundly and woke refreshed to face the new day.

She parked outside The Larches with the front door in full view and waited.

And waited…

Patience wasn't one of Amy's virtues. She worried that she'd be staking out the place for weeks before Mel visited Joey. And if Mel was lying low, she might not come at all. Now Amy wished she'd worked the timing of Mel's visits into her telephone conversation. But not all was lost—she could call them again or, better still, check the place out for herself.

Amy had once advised a client who ran care homes—unpleasant, impersonal places smelling of urine and over-cooked cabbage. But The Larches was in a different league, and while not up to five-star hotel standard, it compared favourably to the Premier Inn.

'I've come to visit Joey Cronin,' she announced to the receptionist. 'I'm a friend of his sister Mel. I was passing through and decided to stop by and say hi.'

'How thoughtful—he's in the recreation room.'

'Does he get many visitors?'

'No—not too many. Mel comes every Saturday or Sunday, but otherwise there's only the woman from those do-gooders at the church, and he doesn't like her much, says she smells funny. So it'll be nice for him to have a change.'

'Is Mel coming today then?' Amy asked. 'She didn't say.'

'No—she called and told us she'd be here tomorrow.'

Amy didn't see how to avoid visiting Joey for real, especially knowing he'd welcome her visit. So she scrawled Lisa Carter, the name of an ex-colleague, in the visitors' book and asked for directions to the recreation room.

There, a solitary figure sat disconsolately in a wheelchair by the window, hugging the radiator for warmth. On hearing Amy come in, he looked up and grinned, exposing a mouthful of stained, twisted teeth. She gave a weak smile back and sought to see beyond the grotesque, asymmetric facial features to the person beneath.

'Hi, Joey,' she said. 'How are you today?'

'Not so good. My knee hurts really bad, my head hurts a lot, my teeth hurt—everything.'

'Oh dear—I'm sorry. I'm Lisa—Mel's friend.'

'That's not your name,' he replied in a flash.

'How do you know?'

He laughed and pointed his finger at her and asked warily, 'Where's Mel?'

Gobbets of saliva shot out of his mouth and landed on Amy's face. She wiped them away in haste, as though they were contaminated, then felt a pang of shame.

'Mel's coming tomorrow,' she said.

Gently, he took a Tiffany earring between finger and thumb and swung it to and fro.

'Nice. You earned lots of money. But they sacked you.'

'I resigned,' said Amy indignantly, rattled by his astute observations.

'My sister earns loads of money too.'

'Does she?' *Not honestly, though.*

'How's your boyfriend?'

'I don't have one now.'

'Why not?'

Wow, they could use him as a therapist at the Priory, to phrase in stark terms all the probing questions they pussy-footed around. And God only knew how he had homed in on all these important issues.

After half an hour, Amy emerged feeling as if she'd been gone over by a trained interrogator.

'He asks a lot of questions, doesn't he?' she remarked to the receptionist as she signed out.

'He sure does. And he doesn't hold back with his opinions either. And you'd better be careful, because he remembers everything you say, so it's no good fobbing him off.'

'He seemed to know a lot about me.'

'Ah yes, that too. He notices tiny details no one else does, a bit like Sherlock Holmes.'

Yes indeed, thought Amy.

'I sometimes wonder,' the receptionist continued, 'what he might have achieved with his amazing memory and infrared eyesight if he didn't have all his other problems.'

'What's wrong with him?'

'Nobody really knows. His mother was an alcoholic and drug addict—so something she used while pregnant must have caused it—selfish bitch.'

In the evening, Amy walked to a local bar and downed four double gins in quick succession. Her encounter with Joey had rattled her, exposing in sharp relief the eugenic arrogance at the root of her reluctance to start a family. She'd feared her hoarder mother's crazy genes would skew the odds of having a perfect child, yet any "defect" would have jarred with her idyllic life. No doubt Amy appalled others—the rich bitch who'd made a pile in the City—but sometimes she even appalled herself. Being Jane had opened her eyes, and now it was impossible to shut them.

***

Sunday dawned, as it often did, with a hangover.

Amy predicted Mel would visit Joey in the afternoon, but to be on the safe side she stationed herself with sandwiches in the car from early morning. She'd brought water too, but although her body screamed out for rehydration, she shrank from drinking it since toilet breaks would be tricky.

At around three pm, a Ford Fiesta parked directly behind Amy's Mercedes and Mel stepped out. She didn't notice Amy lurking.

Fifteen minutes later she came out of the care home wheeling Joey, who spotted Amy instantly and waved at her.

Melanie looked up.

'Bloody hell—you,' she said.

57

'Joey's taken to you, anyway,' Mel observed as they sat in a pub, trying to make sense of everything. 'Strange—his judgement is normally spot on.'

Mel's aggression perplexed Amy. A casual observer would have guessed that Amy had robbed Mel rather than the other way around. Still, she'd grudgingly accepted Amy's offer of a drink for her and Joey. Amy's wine was so vinegary she grimaced at the first mouthful, but it didn't seem to bother Mel.

'Mel doesn't like you,' said Joey, sensitive to the vibes ricocheting back and forth. 'You lied to me—you're not her friend.'

Blimey, he's worse than Dave Carmody, thought Amy.

'And you lied about your name,' he added. 'Telling fibs is naughty, isn't it, Mel?'

'Yes it is.' She turned to Amy. 'How did you find me?'

'Dropped by your flat and opened your post.'

'Bloody cheek.'

'Bloody cheek,' echoed Joey.

'Not as much of a bloody cheek as emptying my bank account.'

'How did you figure out it was me?'

She evidently saw no point in denying it.

'The police have a CCTV picture of you in the bank.'

'Oh—shit. And of course you've grassed me up to them.'

'I told them who you were, but not your location—yet.'

'But you will?'

'We'll see. For the moment I just want to know why you did it.'

'Well it's not like you can't afford it, is it?'

'Amy's got lots of money,' whooped Joey.

'That's not a reason. Anyway, it's not the money—it's the betrayal.'

'You would know all about that,' she said, cryptically.

'So how did you work out that I'm Amy Robinson?'

'Because you're not as clever as you think. Your kind never are. If you must know, your dodgy NI number set the ball rolling.'

'But you told me you keyed it in wrong.'

And more to the point, Marchpole had confirmed it was kosher so had either been lying, or more likely, lied to by his mate.

'And you swallowed that hook, line and sinker, didn't you? Only too willing to blame the stupid fat girl for making an error. Well let me tell you something, lady—I don't make errors. But I fixed yours for you and kept quiet.'

'Why would you do that?'

'Because I liked you?'

'Hardly.'

'She doesn't like you. I told you already,' Joey piped up.

'I was intrigued about you and what your game was, which is why I suggested the drink. Then you blurted out your real name when you were pissed—dumb or what? I bet you thought I'd be too thick to pick up on it.'

Amy didn't comment, but Joey chipped in.

'Thick—like me.'

'But there's lots of women called Amy.'

'Aw, come on. You couldn't fool me. All those questions about John Venner—it was obvious. "Tell Amy".'

'Tell Amy what?' asked Joey.

'About me,' Mel replied.

'Yes, tell Amy who pays the four grand a month for Joey.'

'Whee—Amy can pay,' whooped Joey.

'I can't talk in front of him,' hissed Mel. 'He understands more than you'd think.'

'I can guess, anyway, and I bet he can too,' Amy replied. 'Ghosts on the payroll?'

Mel nodded and her eyes filled with tears.

'Everything I did, I did for Joey.'

'For me,' Joey repeated, with pride.

'But wouldn't social services pay?' Amy queried. 'Isn't that the purpose of the welfare state?'

Mel regarded her with scorn.

'The purpose of the welfare state is so rich bastards like you don't feel guilty,' was her withering response. 'He used to live in sheltered accommodation, but he got worse physically and they chucked him out. But apparently he's not eligible for residential care. He was caught in the middle of a system that doesn't give a shit about anyone with disabilities. I'd have been forced to quit my job and be his full time carer. That's the reality of life, so don't you fucking dare come here and look down your snobby nose at me.'

Joey covered his ears with his hands.

'Eee—swearing, shouting, nasty—don't like it.'

Meanwhile, the ferocity of the attack left Amy reeling.

'That's unfair. I'd gladly pay more taxes to help those less fortunate than me.'

'A likely story. Remind me, Amy, what was your job again? Helping people reduce their tax bills—ripping off the government.'

Once Amy would have launched into a well-rehearsed self-justification, but Jane knew she was guilty as charged.

'You're in no position to make moral judgements. And I'm still waiting to hear why you robbed me.'

Mel remained silent.

'Although I can imagine. It all got a bit hairy, the net was closing, and escaping—at my expense—seemed like a sensible plan.'

'Why the hell not? The kind of money you earned is disgusting—half a mill a year the papers said. But that's not the worst of it—to act all friendly while you were working undercover to investigate me.'

'*What?*'

Amy drew back, shocked.

'Has Mel been naughty?' asked Joey.

'Very naughty,' Amy replied. 'But she's wrong—I wasn't investigating *her*.'

'You have no concept of what it's like to be me, and how I grew up,' said Mel, continuing on her rant.

'I repeat,' Amy shouted. 'I was not investigating you.'

'You weren't?'

'No, and besides, you told me you enjoyed your childhood.'

'I lied—right. I mostly grew up in care. My mum and dad were drug-addled alcoholic pieces of shit. See what my mum did to Joey. And all the while you lived in your pebble-dashed semi in Croydon, preparing yourself for your glittering career in finance.'

Amy laughed at this false picture of her childhood. Joey laughed too, somehow picking up on the absurdity of the situation.

'What's so funny?'

'Only that I lied too. True, I lived in a Croydon semi, but my mum started hoarding compulsively after my dad died, and the house gradually filled with crap. The plumbing broke and was never fixed, because she was convinced that if anyone saw the mess she'd be carted away by men in white coats. I couldn't have friends over, or anything approaching a normal life. Heck, *I'm* used to envying other people their childhoods and being bitter, not the other way round.'

Mel took a few moments to absorb this new disclosure.

'Seriously? Your mum's like the people on the *Hoarders* TV show?'

'Yep. I haven't spoken to her in ten years because I hate her so much for what she put me through.'

'This isn't some kind of joke?'

'I can show you pictures if you like.'

'But you still earned that huge salary,' Mel pointed out, striving to reconcile the picture she'd built up in her mind with Amy's confession.

'Yes I did, but your childhood leaves a mark, Mel, as you know.'

Interestingly, Mel bypassed the standard ritual of suggesting that growing up in a messy house wasn't such a big deal and generally making light the trauma. Perhaps people made similar remarks about a childhood in care. All the same, Amy's confession seemed to have softened Mel's attitude, and made her more disposed to trust her.

'And you honestly weren't there to investigate me?'

'No. What on earth made you think so?'

'All those questions you asked about Venner—why else would you be interested? And someone else confirmed my suspicions. Now I'm confused. If you weren't spying on me, why the false name?'

'I was working with Toby Marchpole, the journalist who was killed about a week ago, to expose Pedley as a crook.'

She contemplated the implications of this, and then said quietly, 'That figures—Pedley *is* a crook. They've been ripping off everyone right, left and centre. Why shouldn't they pay for Joey?'

While Amy couldn't quite bring herself to condone Mel's actions, she did sympathise. It was easy to be ethical with a million quid in the bank.

'You still haven't told me why you robbed my account.'

'It was just as you said. I thought you were onto me, and well—why shouldn't you foot the bill for me clearing out? Now I know the score, I *will* repay you…'

'The money isn't important, but I'll get it back. I can sue the bank and the agency, and they'll settle out of court because it's embarrassing. Hey—perhaps I'll receive double compensation.'

'Oh shit—you've told the police it was me.' Mel's face fell as she remembered.

'Sorry,' said Amy. 'It's more complicated than you realise. The timing of your cash withdrawal was unfortunate, because now I'm a suspect for Marchpole's murder. They believe I used the cash to pay a hit man, so I had to tell the truth. Anyway, at least I'm giving you the heads up. If I can find you, so can the cops. I'd get out of here sharpish.'

Unaccountably, the colour drained from Mel's face.

'Joey,' said Mel. 'Amy and I are popping to the toilet. Stay here.'

Amy nearly said she didn't need to go, then twigged that Mel wanted to tell her something in private. Once in the Ladies' room, she began.

'I'm so sorry. I never meant to set you up for a murder charge.'

Mel was a proven and consummate liar, but Amy accepted her apology. No one could have faked her horror-stricken look, even if it was an overreaction.

'Why are you so bothered about it?'

'Well, it must be very stressful for you,' said Mel, not entirely convincingly.

'It is. Look—I don't suppose you'd make a voluntary statement on my behalf?'

She shook her head.

'I'll make sure they don't prosecute you.'

'I'd like to help, really, but all the other stuff is bound to come out—I'll be finished, in prison, which won't do Joey any good at all.'

Disappointing, but predictable.

'OK, I understand, but take my advice and don't stick around here.'

'I know—I'm leaving, but without Joey. He doesn't know yet.'

'I wouldn't bet on it—for someone with learning disabilities he's razor-sharp. How will you be for money—the fifteen thousand won't last you long?'

'I'll be OK. I've got a plan. Best I don't share it with you though…'

'And Joey?'

'It's a problem. He's happy here and it's not fair to move him. But I won't be able to see him so often.'

'I could pop in now and again,' Amy suggested.

'Yes, he'd like that.'

Now they had both acknowledged each other as fellow survivors of shit childhoods, there was an unspoken bond between them. Although Mel had broken the law, Amy couldn't condemn her outright—who knows, maybe she'd have done the same in Mel's shoes. And equally Mel now seemed more tolerant of Amy's City fat cat foibles. For once, Amy was empathising rather than judging—Jane's influence no doubt.

'I hope I haven't caused you too much trouble,' said Mel.

'Well, you've terminally screwed up my relationship with Dave Carmody and that's undoubtedly for the best.'

'Who's Dave Carmody?'

'A narcissistic, control freak of a policeman.'

'Ooh tell me more,' said Mel.

'Not now.'

Not ever—it was too shaming to admit how she'd been suckered.

As they returned from the Ladies', Joey was waiting patiently for them, having ordered himself another pint of beer.

'Cheers,' he said, holding the tankard up high.

'Oh dear,' said Mel. 'He isn't allowed more than one. Come on, Joey—let's go now.'

'The baby's called Joey,' he replied. 'I'm a big boy. Remember, call the baby Joey.'

They exchanged mystified glances.

'What *is* he on about?' asked Amy.

'Haven't the faintest—he'd always saying daft things nobody understands, but there's usually something in them when you figure it out.'

They hugged as they said their farewells. For all her promises to visit Joey, chances were none of them would meet again, though Mel provided Amy with her secret mobile number—just in case.

***

After Amy left, Mel made a call.

'You asked me to get in touch if I heard from Jane, or rather Amy. She came calling today.'

'She did well to track you down.'

'Yes, well, she's pretty smart, in a dumb kind of way.'

'What did you tell her?'

'Like we agreed—I did it for revenge,' said Mel.

'That's good—really good. And what will she do now?'

'Who knows? She didn't say.'

'If I find you're double-crossing me…'

'If I was double-crossing you, I wouldn't have called.'

'I'm so glad you did.'

58

Amy had been trying to forget Carmody. After their break up, she'd switched her phone off and deactivated her voicemail, but since reverting to the normal settings there'd been no contact. For all her animosity, she was somewhat offended by this. A declaration of undying passion followed by a violent jealous rage did not progress logically to radio silence.

During the long drive back to London, Carmody called four times and left a saccharine message, begging her forgiveness and promising eternal love. While this behaviour fitted with Amy's expectations, the message uncomfortably echoed her mother's empty promises to "make a start on the house" in years gone by. And now, no doubt, Amy's forgiveness would entail her denying, minimising and excusing Carmody's behaviour—the usual game abusers play with their victims. Well, she was done with being a victim, and done with playing the game. Her mother's invalidation of her feelings and opinions had shaped her life for years, and she refused to allow history to repeat itself in a different context.

As the motorway gave way to urban sprawl, Amy thought of a rationale for Carmody's silence—he'd probably been instructed not to communicate with her. Consequently, his renewed contact might indicate she'd been cleared as a suspect. She wondered when exactly Bligh would get around to telling her.

Someone else confirmed my suspicions.

Mel's words popped, unbidden, into Amy's mind.

Who was aware of Mel's secret and might have suggested that Amy had joined IPT to investigate her? Pedley?

It was certainly possible. Venner may well have confided his misgivings to his chum, giving Pedley some leverage over Mel. Enough leverage to manipulate her into stealing by playing on her fears? Perhaps so, although the timing didn't stack up. Pedley had fired Amy *after* Toby's death, and she doubted he'd be capable of hiding his anger if he'd learned the truth about her identity any earlier.

Even if the police were pursuing Pedley as a suspect, she doubted anyone would dig too deep into his motives—she'd already surmised that Bligh and his sidekick had little interest in Pedley's complex machinations. This seemed unfair— if Toby had died because he'd uncovered dangerous facts, shouldn't the whole truth be exposed? Otherwise, his sacrifice would be in vain.

If the police refused to pursue the truth, Amy would take up the challenge. She was under no illusions, though—with no inkling of Toby's "sensational" find, it would be hard to progress. She so wished she hadn't missed the crucial call from Toby, because unless he'd confided in someone else before he died, there seemed little prospect of unravelling the mystery.

Unless Toby had confided in someone—Celia perhaps?

It was a long shot, but worth following up.

59

The Marchpole residence closely resembled Amy's own house, one stop down the District Line. Amy didn't expect Celia to welcome her visit in all the circumstances. But hey—if she slammed the door in her face, Amy would take that as a sign from on high to dig no deeper.

A mosaic path led to a front door with fancy brass fixtures, including a large knocker. Celia answered the door promptly, as though she'd been awaiting a different visitor. Her shock at seeing Amy equalled Amy's own dismay at Celia's puffy-eyed misery. A cigarette-free, teetotal, blameless existence was powerless against the ravages of grief, it seemed, and even Amy's inner bitch derived no pleasure from Celia's suffering.

'Amy,' she said, in a tone impossible to interpret. 'You'd better come in.'

Once inside, the similarity between the two houses ended. Celia ushered Amy into a classic if rather fussy living room, with elaborate drapes, Queen Anne legs, and a large Oriental rug. None of it to Toby's taste, Amy supposed, but then how well had she known him?

'It's a long time since we met,' said Amy inanely as she took in the surroundings.

'Well, we loathed each other at school, so it's not surprising we lost touch.'

Celia's brusque realism was strangely wounding. Amy hadn't liked Celia, but it had never occurred to her that the aversion had been mutual.

'I always felt you were jealous of me, and hoping I would fail at something,' Celia continued, by way of explanation.

Which was perfectly true. Amy had declined to vote for Celia as head girl, and had badmouthed her to other girls in a subtly snide way, but without mustering enough support to sabotage Celia's success.

'Yes I was a bitch,' Amy admitted.

'Well we're grown-ups now aren't we?'

Celia's voice sounded bitter, as if growing up meant little more than hiding your bitchiness beneath a veneer of civility.

'I'm so sorry for your loss.'

'I'm sorry for yours,' she replied, with a trace of sarcasm. 'Can I offer you a glass of wine?'

Celia already had a glass herself, in conflict with Toby's description of her health-freakery, but who was Amy to criticise?

'Thanks, yes.'

Amy followed Celia into the kitchen. She guessed Celia wouldn't share her own phobia of wandering guests, and besides, she was nosy.

The room was less immaculate than she'd predicted, with one of those silly displays of hanging pans, repositories for grease and dust, and a butler ceramic sink. Kids' art adorned the walls. In the middle stood the obligatory island—the ultimate symbol of kitchen one-upmanship. Very dated, all the folksy rustic stuff, thought Amy, her inner bitch now back at the helm.

Amy had anticipated catching up on the past twenty years. But once they'd settled with their wine, Celia bypassed the social pleasantries and made straight for the jugular.

'I know you slept with Toby, so it's no good trying to pretend otherwise.'

'I'm not.'

'I assume the police have interviewed you.'

'Yep—formal interview with DCI Bligh, voluntarily, of course.'

'I must say, I preferred Carmody—at least he has an intellect—but I understand you have a personal connection with him.'

Her tone was accusatorial, leaving Amy in no doubt as to Celia's disapproval of her loose morals.

'Not anymore.'

Celia refrained from probing, and said instead, 'Why have you come here, apart from offering your insincere condolences?'

Amy suppressed a scathing retort, since a grieving widow confronted by her husband's lover deserved at least some compassion.

'I'm trying to find out what Toby unearthed in China— what was considered so dangerous he couldn't be allowed to live.'

'Frankly, it's none of your business.'

'But it is my business, because this may be my only chance to exonerate myself.'

'Exonerate yourself? Christ, you always were a little drama queen—nothing's changed, I see. This is not about you, Amy.'

Amy prickled. If she had been a drama queen back in the day, it had been to deflect everyone's attention from her secrets. And she was certainly no drama queen nowadays; merely someone who'd developed an alarming knack for getting embroiled in other people's dramas.

'Didn't they tell you about the money stolen from my bank?'

'Oh yes,' she said, sipping at her wine. 'But unfortunately, you won't be able to bask in the limelight as the truth seeker unjustly accused of murder. Because they already have a suspect in mind—someone who set up the whole charade with the photograph and your bank. Even Bligh isn't dense enough to believe you're implicated.'

This confirmed Amy's theory about having been cleared—would have been nice if someone had informed her though.

'Is the suspect Richard Pedley by any chance?'

'I refuse to discuss the case with you—I've told you too much already. If you need drama, why don't you go back to St Pauls and follow through with your pathetic suicide attempt?'

Such heartless sentiments would have been beyond the pale under normal circumstances, but Amy made excuses for Celia and held back the scathing retort on the tip of her tongue.

'OK—you're right—this is not about me. So let me tell you the real reason I'm asking these questions. Toby was passionate about getting to the bottom of the skulduggery at IPT. They may charge Pedley or whoever for Toby's murder, if they have a case, but they're not remotely interested in the motive. It's far too complex for their simple little minds. Why, their eyes glazed over as soon as I began to explain the financial shenanigans. If the truth isn't exposed, Toby will have died in vain.'

'Oh very good. Highly convincing, except I don't buy this heroic Amy crap. There's nothing heroic about a deranged woman who can't keep her knickers on.'

Amy had one last card to play in her bid to secure Celia's cooperation.

'Perhaps you'd be more inclined to help me if I shared some information with you.'

'What?'

'About the key in the porch?'

Celia's face froze. On some level, she already knew the answer.

'Toby told me you couldn't remember.'

'I lied.'

'Why?'

'To spare your feelings.'

'So what's changed?'

'I've decided you have a right to the truth.'

'And what's the answer?'

Amy dreaded to imagine the effect of dropping the bombshell on Celia in her present state. It was one thing for Celia to suspect the explanation—quite another to have it presented as a fact. Equally, Amy questioned her own strength to deal with the aftermath of exhuming long-buried memories.

'Jack, your stepfather, mentioned it,' said Amy. 'Just very casually.'

Celia picked up her wine and this time swilled down a big gulp rather than her earlier delicate little sips.

'Shit,' she said, taking a second swig. 'You too?'

Amy nodded. It was out—like the proverbial genie from the bottle.

There was a lengthy silence, and Celia's wan face only emphasised her red eyes.

'He took my virginity.'

'And mine,' said Celia. 'On my sixteenth birthday—he made such a big thing of waiting.'

'I always saw your life as perfect—I didn't ever suspect he was abusing you too.'

Somehow, Celia's tarnished life seemed to render Amy's own quest for perfection even more pointless than she already suspected. Did anyone enjoy the ideal existence she'd been striving for?

'Well there you go—your life looked pretty cool to me—I always envied you your freedom.'

Though the freedom had only arisen from her mother's neglect. It didn't seem appropriate to mention the hoarding—it might seem like trying to usurp the limelight. And yet the blasted hoarding had caused her to fall prey to Jack.

For once, she allowed her mind to drift back to the day Jack gave her a lift home and tailgated her into the squalid, hoarded house. Even now, Amy couldn't account for how he'd evaded her strenuous efforts to keep him out, but he was a skilled manipulator. Once he'd seen inside, he'd used her fear of exposure as a technique in seduction. He'd instinctively grasped her capacity for keeping secrets, and was therefore confident in entrusting her with a new one.

'Jack liked young girls,' said Celia. 'He married my mum for me, not for her. Seems like I wasn't enough for him though.'

Amy was disturbed to hear Celia berating herself for not keeping her abuser satisfied. It was redolent of her self-blame for her mother's hoarding.

'One victim is never enough for predators like him.'

'I know,' Celia agreed. 'I've had years of psychotherapy. And no chance for restitution—he died in a road accident in my first year at Oxford. Can't say I shed many tears.'

'Did you ever tell anyone apart from your therapist?'

'Only Toby. My mum would never hear a word said against Jack. Did you?'

'No one.' The memory was buried so deep it didn't even surface during the soul searching in the Priory.

'Thank you for telling me,' said Celia. 'I suspected as much. He'd come home smelling of your over-the-top perfume, and then the key. I can lay it to rest now.'

'That,' said Amy, pulling the psychological lever, 'is the power of the truth. Doesn't the same apply to Toby's death—wouldn't it be better to know?'

There was a long pause as Celia evaluated the merits of Amy's question.

'Yes,' she said, at last. 'It would.'

Sickened to the core by the cunning she'd used to achieve her goal, Amy topped up both their wine glasses.

'Anyway,' Celia said. 'You were quite right about the police.'

She seemed keen now to get stuck into the practicalities—her way of handling the trauma within, and not dissimilar to Amy's own coping mechanisms.

'They've not been pursuing the "why", except to lead them to the culprit. And yes, they do have Pedley in their sights,' she confirmed. 'His prints are on the photograph and they figure he roped in the Cronin girl too. She's conveniently disappeared, and he denies everything.'

'Is that so?' said Amy, in mock surprise.

'So the prosecution case is weak, but was reinforced by another of the directors, Nelson Chang, who disclosed Pedley's dodgy share transactions to Bligh. They reckon Toby was killed to prevent him publishing the sordid details. But they're struggling to tie Pedley to the actual murder.'

'It's a red herring—that's why. Toby turned up something in China—which he referred to as sensational. There's the real motive.'

'He used the same word with me, but he didn't elaborate. To be honest, I didn't give him much chance.'

She looked as though she might cry, but seemed to buck herself up before the tears started flowing.

'Though he mentioned he'd been robbed and his phone stolen,' she added.

Ah—this must account for the calls from landlines and Toby not answering his mobile.

'Could the robbery be linked? I mean he was always taking pictures. Did they steal his phone because of the photographs on it?'

'Entirely possible. I mentioned it to Carmody and he assured me they'd look into it, but the new team are more focussed on events in London. They say if what he learned in China was relevant, they'd have killed him over there.'

This was a fair point.

'Have they checked his iCloud account?' Amy asked. 'He once told me he backs up his pictures onto there.'

'They have. His MacBook is always signed in so it wasn't difficult.'

'And?'

'They found a variety of pictures, but crucially none shot on the day of the robbery. So either he took none, or they were deleted.'

'He was visiting the distribution centre that day,' Amy recalled. 'Did they check the internet search history on his computer?'

'Again, nothing, but apparently he was using a network thing to avoid Chinese censorship, so his browsing history is hidden.'

'Can I see the remaining pictures?'

'If you want, although I'm not sure how they'll help.'

Poignantly, first up was a shot of Toby and the children in the garden—presumably snapped by Celia—the son a red-haired miniature of the father. Amy skipped ahead to the Chinese pictures. Mainly they were photos of the insubstantial offices of Plumb Enterprises, and the shabby exterior of the hotel in which its alleged operations were based.

'We'd worked out this part already, but I'll have a closer look just in case. OK if I take a copy?'

'Fine.'

Amy downloaded the pictures onto a memory stick.

'Is there anything else?' Amy asked. 'Papers?'

'Yes, there were papers on his desk, relating to the share transactions. But the police removed those as evidence. You're welcome to look at the rest though.'

Amy found it weird sitting in Toby's chair, working in amicable partnership with Celia as they sorted through his papers. The documents consisted largely of the shipping records Amy had already seen and though it was unlikely they'd be relevant, she took them to be on the safe side.

'I must say, I prefer your investigative methods to those of Bligh and company,' said Celia as Amy packed up to leave. 'And I do hope you find something.'

'I'll do my best,' said Amy, 'and I'm sorry to bring you bad news.'

'Oh I knew all along really. And my head's in such a mess right now, it won't make much difference.'

Amy doubted this. Sooner or later Celia would suffer a huge emotional backlash.

'Before you go,' said Celia. 'There's one thing I should tell you. You perhaps realise this already, but Toby was in love with you.'

Amy didn't realise—she'd not even considered the possibility. Toby had shown no sign of seeking anything beyond sex. Besides, if it was true, wouldn't she have known, even without him spelling it out explicitly?

'Are you sure? He never said anything.'

'I'm certain—I felt it—you prompted him to question the whole direction of his life. Our marriage was over.'

'I'm sure that's not right. You're upset. Toby loved you, even if he wasn't great at showing it.'

'It's nice of you to say so, but I'm under no illusions.'

Amy could find no words of comfort, and further protestations would only strengthen Celia's conviction.

'I'll get in touch if I find out anything,' said Amy.

'Thank you,' said Celia. 'Please do.'

60

Back in Chiswick, Amy poured herself a gigantic gin on autopilot, even though she didn't really fancy one.

She hadn't thought of Jack in years.

Each Thursday he'd taken her to a hotel, and plied her with champagne. In retrospect, the most shameful aspect of the sordid affair was how much she'd enjoyed it. She'd felt giddy with the power—this handsome, mature man found her irresistible and she could make him do naughty things. And afterwards, when he'd returned to his Tudor-bethan palace, she'd have a nice long soak in the bath, dry herself off with white fluffy towels, and enjoy another drink or two from the minibar. Jack kept her secret and she kept his—an equal balance of power, it seemed.

She didn't discover the true imbalance until the end—the day after he caught her with Toby in the pub.

Jack met her as usual at the hotel, but the dynamic had shifted. His mood was ugly as he cross-questioned her. And when she lied, he'd slapped her around and told her she was a dirty little whore, and they were finished. Then he'd given her "one last fuck" so she'd never forget him. This was ironic, because she'd blanked out the memory until now, forgotten how she could barely walk for days, how she'd projected a cool and collected image while quaking inside.

'Oh God, you slut, you're loving it,' he'd said. 'You dirty little bitch.'

And then he'd put his hands round her neck...

Amy pulled herself back from the edge of the abyss. There was nothing to be gained by dwelling on the experience. She must try to shut it all back in the little sealed compartment in her mind, where it couldn't harm her. And she'd start by taking a leaf out of Celia's book and concentrating on practicalities. She headed up a blank piece of paper.

THE CASE AGAINST RP

1. RP knew where TM would be as he was meeting him (opportunity)
2. RP committed securities fraud and other crimes which TM knew of (motive)
3. RP didn't initially tell the police about meeting TM (suspicious)
4. RP may have instructed MC to withdraw money from bank (damning?)
5. RP fingerprints on photograph sent to CH (suspicious)

But as leading criminal QC Celia pointed out, it was a weak case for the prosecution.

Amy headed up a second piece of paper.

PROBLEMS WITH RP AS A SUSPECT

1. RP was aware TM was visiting China. Why not have him killed there? (Illogical)
2. Fingerprints on photograph (beyond dumb)
3. Acted normally after TM's death, so either a psychopath or fantastic actor (unlikely)

Bizarrely, she now veered towards thinking Pedley might be innocent. There was something just too neat and tidy about his alleged involvement.

Yet if it wasn't him, who?

Amy flicked through the pictures she'd copied from Toby's iCloud, hoping a detailed study of the available photos might shed some light on what was missing. But no luck, and confirmation of Plumb Enterprises' meagre substance, which they'd known along, in no way qualified as sensational. Though on closer inspection one photograph looked odd—a picture of a ship. Strange—because Toby hadn't visited any sea port. The name of the ship was just discernible—Jin Yin Hua, together with its equivalent in Chinese characters.

Intrigued, Amy googled it.

61

THE DAILY GLOBE 15 August
By Bill Gordon
Colombia detains captain of arms-trafficking ship headed for Cuba

The captain of Jin Yin Hua, a China-flagged cargo ship, has been arrested in the Colombian port city of Cartagena, charged with arms trafficking.

The ship was stopped on Wednesday after authorities found more than 4,000 artillery shells and 150 tonnes of gunpowder together with other munitions during a routine inspection. Papers presented by the ship's crew listed the contents of the ten shipping containers as plumbing products.

Rodrigo Martinez, an official from the Attorney General's office, told reporters a Chinese national identified as Kai Zhang had been arrested and was being held in custody. "The documentation for the cargo in the Chinese vessel did not correspond to the contents of the containers," he said.

On Friday, China's foreign ministry claimed the vessel was engaged in "normal trade" carrying ordinary military supplies to Cuba. It was not, he said, in violation of any international laws.

After stopping in Cartagena the vessel had been bound for Havana, Cuba.

Photos of the containers holding the shells, published by a local Cartagena newspaper, indicated they were destined for a company in Cuba, which according to several blogs is responsible for procurement for the Cuban armed forces. However, the company presents itself as an importer of industrial products. The supplier listed on the crates is TMT Materials, a Chinese distributor of piping and plumbing products.

Amid talks between the two countries aimed at normalising diplomatic relations, Cuba is currently pressing the US to remove it from a list of state sponsors of terrorism. Cuba was first included on the list in 1982, on the grounds that its communist government was sheltering members of the Basque separatist group ETA and left-wing Colombian rebels.

For the past two years, Cuba has been the site of peace talks between the Colombian government and leftist rebels. However, there was no indication that the weapons were at all related to the Colombian guerrilla forces.

As of Friday, a cargo-ship tracking website showed the vessel still docked at Cartagena, with its captain due to appear in court later that day.

62

Wow. If those were "ordinary military supplies", why disguise them as something else?

While the cover for the shipment was plastic pipes and plumbing products, the company involved was not Plumb Enterprises, but an outfit named TMT Materials. Convinced there must be a connection, Amy googled the second firm.

Bingo—TMT and Plumb Enterprises shared the same address, and the name looked vaguely familiar too. She darted back to Toby's pictures and sure enough, came upon a shot of a plaque with the name on it. Further searches revealed that Chang also owned TMT.

Toby had plainly googled TMT, read the article and downloaded the accompanying picture into iPhoto. But when? The commentary itself was three months old, but the picture's position in the album suggested a recent download, maybe after the missing pictures had been deleted.

There was no indication that the weapons were at all related to the Colombian guerrilla forces…

But why stop at Cartagena otherwise?

Amy consulted the world map. Coming from the Pacific via the Panama Canal the vessel would have exited into the Atlantic at Colon, and then taken a hard right to go to Cartagena. Cuba, on the other hand, was north-northwest on a straight course. In other words, you don't go to Cartagena from Colon unless you mean to.

The information was interesting, but material published in a mass-circulation newspaper could hardly be top secret, and seemed unlikely to have precipitated Toby's death. Still, Amy remained convinced she was on the right track.

***

Amy slept astonishingly soundly, and woke clear-headed with a definite plan of action.

At nine am sharp, she called the *Globe* and asked for Bill Gordon. If he had no further details himself, he might point her in the right direction.

There was only one problem. Bill Gordon was dead.

Amy suppressed all the wild theories zipping through her mind, and was put through to one of Bill's colleagues, a stroppy cow called Claudia with a strong Caribbean accent. She sounded fed up, as if she was a junior employee deputed to handle all the crank calls.

'When did Bill die?' Amy asked her.

'Oh nearly two weeks ago.'

'Exact date?'

'October thirtieth, I think.'

The same day as Toby. That couldn't be a coincidence.

'What happened?'

'Died in his sleep.'

'Of what?'

'Look, I'm not being funny,' said Claudia. 'But I've no idea who you are or why you're asking all these questions.'

'Sorry—I should have explained. I'm a friend of Toby Marchpole's, the journalist who was shot a couple of weeks ago. He was working on a story, and an article Bill wrote around three months ago seems relevant to his enquiries.'

'Why are you interested?'

'Because I think Toby died due to something he was investigating.'

Now she'd captured Claudia's interest, the girl was keener to assist.

'Which article was it?'

'About an illegal arms shipment from China—maybe linked to Colombian terrorists.'

'Oh I remember. I actually wrote it for him.'

'So can you add anything to the story?'

'Nothing. The news came through and I copied it—just filling the space, not cutting-edge journalism. How does it tie up with your friend's work?'

'Not sure. But now I've heard Bill's dead too, I'm beginning to wonder.'

'Now let me stop you right there,' said Claudia. 'Because I can guess where you're going with this. Bill had a heart attack. He drank and smoked like a lunatic and in fact it's amazing he lasted as long as he did.'

Like Venner.

'But it's odd,' she went on, 'because some dude called Bill about that piece the day before he died.'

The day before they both died, thought Amy.

'The dude may well have been Marchpole,' said Amy. 'Did you listen to the call?'

'Well, obviously I only heard one side of the conversation, but it sounded like the other guy was asking Bill to check something for him—shipping records I think.'

'And did he check?'

'Not sure—I left the office shortly after.'

'It's rather odd, isn't?'

'What?'

'That both Marchpole and your colleague died the next day?'

'Maybe, or maybe not. What story was your friend working on?'

'About IPT, the plumbing company. He believed the company was riddled with fraud.'

'Wouldn't surprise me,' said Claudia bluntly.

Amy sensed a potential ally.

'So are you interested in helping me?'

'No way—my editor would have me hung, drawn and quartered. I tried to run an exposé on IPT a while back and they warned me off big time.'

'Why?'

'Isn't it obvious? Those guys spend a fortune advertising with us, so we can't slag them off. Anyway, got to go—nice talking to you.'

She hung up hurriedly, thus lending weight to Toby's theories on mainstream media corruption.

***

So—Venner visited China and dropped dead. Marchpole retraced his steps and was shot. Marchpole's journalist contact died in a similar way to Venner. That was far too many coincidences.

She'd extracted as many details as she could about Marchpole's trip to Beijing, but there must still be mileage in finding out more about Venner's visit. Had he perhaps said something to Susan, which she hadn't recognised as significant?

There was only one way to find out.

63

Susan Venner appeared to have recovered completely from the loss of her husband—not that she'd seemed particularly distraught at the funeral.

They met for lunch at Harvey Nicholls. Susan wore a snugly fitting cornflower blue dress, black patent shoes and a matching handbag, with little diamond stud earrings and hair bouffed up to within an inch of its life. Although she looked a teensy bit "mother of the bride", she'd made too much of an effort for lunch, and Amy fancied she was going on somewhere afterwards.

'So how are you bearing up?' Amy asked, once they were seated.

'Oh fine, thanks. John left all his finances in an immaculate state, as you'd expect, so we've blitzed through it all in no time at all.'

'Well that's a mercy.'

Susan's silence on her emotional state was telling, as if John had meant nothing to her beyond a source of finance. They ordered a bottle of Sancerre, and two lobster salads.

'So,' said Susan. 'I assume you haven't asked me here for social reasons.'

'Not entirely, no, although it's lovely to see you,' Amy replied carefully. 'But I'm just wondering—did you ever find out what John wanted to tell me before he died?'

'Nothing like getting straight to the point,' she said, her voice laden with sarcasm. 'The answer's no, but I'm surprised it's still bugging you so much. Maybe I should rethink the list of girls he was screwing.'

This ill-concealed unfriendliness, not present at the funeral, mystified Amy, but she chose to ignore it.

'Thing is, Toby Marchpole is dead.'

'And I'm supposed to cry a river?'

'But I believe there's a link between his death and John's. Both of them died shortly after returning from China.'

'How can you say there's a link?' Susan said. 'John died from a heart attack.'

Amy now saw her line of questioning was misguided, and swiftly changed tack.

'Well not a direct link. But John uncovered something in China and I'm trying to establish whether there's a connection between that and Toby's death. You see, John might have said something to you about his trip that's more significant than you realised.'

'Well he died the next day,' said Susan in a matter-of-fact way which disturbed Amy. 'So we didn't have much time.'

'But he returned home, so perhaps you ate dinner together. You must have discussed it.'

'We did, but why should I share our conversation with you?'

'Look—at John's funeral, you were the one who wanted to know what he wished to say to me,' Amy reminded her. 'Aren't you interested anymore?'

'I've moved on,' she said. 'But evidently you haven't. So if you need answers, I'll try to help.'

'Thanks.'

'We did eat dinner together, but the conversation wasn't earth-shattering. He moaned about the internet in the hotel, and the taxi driver ripping him off. That was it, and then he disappeared off to his study with a bottle of wine and spent the rest of the evening poring over paperwork.'

'What paperwork?'

'Shipping logs, I think—is that likely?'

'Yes—very likely. And do you still have them?'

'No, because that creepy guy from the company came round to collect them.'

'Who?' Amy asked, already half-suspecting the answer.

'Why, Nelson Chang, of course.'

***

The documents she'd removed from Toby's house related to Plumb Enterprises, and it took Amy some time to locate the shipping records for TMT Materials online. But once she had, the regular trips to Colombia were plain.

So—a secret Chinese company, owned by Chang, was moving regular illegal arms shipments for terrorists, under the cover of supplying plumbing products. Quite why this knowledge should be dangerous enough to cause three murders eluded Amy for the moment, but she felt confident she'd work it out.

In the meantime, there was a subsidiary question. How much did Pedley know about all this?

Probably not much.

It puzzled Amy why Venner hadn't mentioned the arms shipments to Pedley *before* the AGM. Logically, wouldn't he have contacted his old chum at the first opportunity? They'd even travelled to the meeting together. But Pedley was clearly unaware of the truth, as otherwise he'd have lost trust in Chang, which hadn't happened.

Pedley likely understood that Chang owned Plumb Enterprises and relied on him to run the relationship with the company—so there was no reason for him to be aware of TMT's existence. Thus if TMT's secret activities lay behind Marchpole's killing, Chang looked a more likely suspect than Pedley.

In hindsight, this made perfect sense. Intuitively, Pedley had never been a credible murder suspect—he lacked the necessary brutality. But Chang, quiet, hard-working, loyal and devious—a different kettle of fish entirely.

Moreover, Roxanne's connection with Pedley provided alternative explanations for the evidence against him. Amy had always thought their relationship odd. Of course, Pedley was a lecherous old rogue, but a successful PR executive like Roxanne had no need of a sugar daddy. Mel had suggested that Roxanne wanted something specific from Pedley—could this be information to feed to her brother?

Amy picked up the notes she'd made earlier and jotted down some additional ideas.

THE CASE AGAINST RP

1. RP knew where TM would be as he was meeting him (opportunity)
   Yes, but so might NC via Roxanne
2. RP committed securities fraud and other crimes which TM knew of (motive)
   TM had found out about NC's involvement in arms smuggling—RP unaware but TM was planning to tell him. Query—how would NC discover that?
3. RP didn't initially tell the police about meeting TM (suspicious)
   But understandable given the history—maybe Roxanne put it into his head to keep silent?

4. RP may have instructed MC to withdraw money from bank (damning?)
Perhaps it was NC?

5. RP fingerprints on photograph sent to CH (suspicious)
Roxanne could have shown him the picture. Query—was it taken by her private eye?

PROBLEMS WITH RP AS A SUSPECT

1. RP was aware TM was visiting China. Why not have him killed there? (Illogical)
NC might have known this, again via Roxanne. Same issue with NC as a suspect.

2. Fingerprints on photograph (beyond dumb)
Not if Roxanne tricked him into leaving them.

3. Acted normally after TM's death, so either a psychopath or fantastic actor (unlikely)
Or because he was innocent?

As she reviewed all this, an alternative version of events unfolded in Amy's mind.

What if Chang had arranged for all three victims to be killed because he feared Pedley getting wind of his arms smuggling?

Why?

Because Chang would lose Pedley's trust, which he desperately needed.

Why?

Don't know—maybe Chang was scamming Pedley in another way, or possibly planning to take over the company.

The police alleged Pedley had set out to frame Amy. This theory had its merits, not least that a Luddite like

Pedley would likely pay a hitman in fistfuls of cash. But Amy had already worked out that the timing didn't fit, because he hadn't found out her true identity until after Toby's death. In addition, Mel had been allowed to keep the money. Suppose instead Chang had not only arranged for Marchpole's murder but also contrived an elaborate plot to implicate Pedley? In this way, he would eliminate them both.

Celia said Chang volunteered details of Pedley's illegal share dealings to Bligh. Why do this, unless to give Pedley a motive? Perhaps the killing took place in the UK rather than China to reinforce this false narrative? And had Chang collected the papers from Susan Venner in a further bid to obscure the truth?

But wait—Chang couldn't have known in advance what Marchpole would uncover in China. True, but he may have chosen to kill Toby as a precaution once he became aware of his impending trip—begging the question of how he'd gleaned that knowledge.

Easy—Marchpole had most definitely been followed that Saturday morning, and it could have been Chang keeping tabs on him. Moreover, Chang's surveillance of Toby might also have exposed Amy's identity. The notion of Roxanne setting a private eye on her because of her earrings had always seemed bonkers. Perhaps it was only a line she'd spun to Pedley to explain how she came by the photograph. After Marchpole was dead, Roxanne must have told Pedley about Jane being an imposter, whereupon Pedley had fired her.

Amy's tower of surmise might be shaky, but there was one obvious way to shore it up from the foundations. She dialled the secret mobile number Mel had given her in Whitstable.

'Amy. How are you?'

'Not bad. I seem to be off the hook for Toby Marchpole's murder at any rate.'

'Good news.'

'And you?'

'Out of reach from everyone now, thank God. I'll miss Joey, though.'

'I'll bet. I will pop over there now and again, like I said.'

'Oh that'd be fantastic—he really likes you.'

'Look, Mel. I think I've worked out who killed Toby Marchpole, but I need your help.'

'No. Sorry, but I can't—we discussed this before.'

'Not to make a statement, and I promise not to tell your secret when I go to the police tomorrow. I just want to know one thing.'

'What?'

'You didn't steal from my account off your own bat, did you? Somebody asked you to, didn't they?'

'OK—yes, they did.'

'Was it Nelson Chang?'

There was an extended pause, as Mel evaluated her options. 'Yes,' she said. 'It was.'

64

Enough evidence pointed to Chang for Amy's theory to be credible and she dialled DCI Bligh's number. It rankled that the imbecile should reap the fruits of her labour, but Toby wouldn't have wanted her to stand by and let Bligh nail the wrong man, even if it was slimy Pedley.

'Ah, Ms Robinson, I'm glad you called,' he said in a voice rivalling only Smithies' for pomposity. 'Couple of points. First of all, I'm pleased to say we've eliminated you from the enquiry into Toby Marchpole's murder.'

'Good of you to tell me straight away,' she said, with a hint of sarcasm.

'Secondly, can you give us a steer on the Melanie Cronin's whereabouts?'

'Well she *was* in Whitstable,' Amy replied.

'Indeed so, until you took it upon yourself to track her down and alert her to our enquiries.'

'She robbed me,' Amy pointed out. 'So she already knew you'd be anxious to speak with her.'

'Then why did you go?'

'To find out why she did it, because I couldn't see you plods getting on to it anytime soon.'

'You do appreciate,' said Bligh, ignoring the insult, 'that interfering with a police investigation is a very serious matter.'

'But I didn't.'

'So how would you describe your involvement then?' he asked with a sigh.

'Helping the police with their enquiries?'

Another sigh.

'And what did you learn from Ms Cronin?'

All Amy's ethical standards prevented her covering for a criminal. But Jane's were more flexible.

'Very little, but I can confirm that someone instructed her to withdraw the money from my account.'

'That's the explanation we're working on too,' said Bligh, brightening at the prospect of Amy agreeing with him. 'Pedley was trying to set you up while getting hold of untraceable cash.'

Bligh's optimism was to be short-lived.

'If that's what you think, you've been duped.'

'So you know better?'

'Almost certainly,' Amy said. 'The thing is…'

'I would rather not discuss this on the phone,' cut in Bligh. 'Can you come in at two tomorrow afternoon and make a formal statement?'

Amy agreed, although his lack of urgency spoke volumes.

'I shall look forward to seeing you then. Though I must say, I wish you'd leave the sleuthing to us.'

Sure, thought Amy, *because you're so much more competent.* She ended the call before she could say anything she might regret.

***

Despite Susan Venner's inexplicable hostility at their lunch, she'd still been willing to help. And as a matter of common courtesy, Amy felt obliged to let her know she'd solved the mystery.

'So what *did* he want to tell you in the end?'

Amy paused, remembering how everyone else who possessed this knowledge was now dead.

'For your own safety, it's better I don't spell it out. But I can tell you this. Nelson Chang has been shafting Richard Pedley, and he arranged for Toby Marchpole's murder while framing Pedley.'

She left out her views on Venner's death, in view of the lukewarm reception the last time.

Susan didn't probe further, but said, 'That figures. I told you he was creepy.'

65

The arms shipments were a lucrative side-line, but they'd caused Chang no end of trouble. The Chinese had told him he was helping to transport regular military supplies. How was he to know those dumb Cubans were supplying the weapons to Colombian terrorists, or still less that Venner would join the dots?

The first intimation of trouble had been the US government agents after his ass, threatening to kill him if he didn't stop the shipments. In fact, the Americans had done him a favour by taking Venner out, by some miracle before he spoke to Pedley. But when Chang told the Chinese he wanted to end the arrangement, they'd threatened him too. On balance, they scared him more than the Americans, so he'd taken a gamble and carried on.

Hot on the heels of the Venner fiasco had come Marchpole. At first he mostly focused on Pedley's misdoings, though Chang kept an eye on him to be on the safe side. But the Amy Robinson connection and Marchpole's trip to China disturbed Chang, and he decided Marchpole had to die. He also dreaded the Americans hearing of the continued shipments, which was why he'd arranged for Marchpole's phone to be snatched in China.

The execution was beautifully carried out, and Chang congratulated himself on his cleverness. And it was a masterstroke to set up Pedley as the fall guy. Not only was Chang's secret safe, but Pedley's downfall would allow him to seize control of IPT, as he and Roxanne always planned.

The only fly in the ointment was Amy Robinson, who was too smart for her own good.

Under different conditions, Chang would have warmed to Amy. Ed had tenacity in spades, but his intellectual limitations often frustrated Chang. Chang perceived that Amy would fight his corner against HMRC not just with guts, but with intelligence. However, he would never get to road test Amy's skills as a tax professional, because she'd chosen to apply her brain to more dangerous pursuits. And it had become essential to remove her before she shared her suspicions with the police.

Another shooting, or a disappearance, would be far too fishy. She had to die an authentic death, apparently unconnected with her appointment at the police station.

Amy's averted suicide had given Chang an idea. Perhaps if she wound up in the Thames, drugged up to the eyeballs? This wasn't a perfect solution, as questions would still be asked when her body washed up. But it was the best he could come up with and he was running out of time.

66

Amy came round in pitch darkness, aware only of a low rumbling noise and the sensation of motion.

One minute she'd been walking to the Tube, on her way to meet Bligh—and now this.

She retched as bile came up her throat.

Something stuffed in her mouth—blocking it.

Got to get it out.

But she couldn't. Her arms were numb and stuck in a peculiar position behind her back.

Bound and gagged.

Choking to death.

Moving—strange rubber smell and fumes.

Car boot.

Fuck—this looked awfully final.

The car stopped and she heard the drone of voices, too indistinct to make out the words. Shoes crunched on a gravelly surface.

The boot opened. An unshaven face leered over her, with spiky blond hair, white teeth and minty breath. His eyes were bright blue—intelligent but not cruel, Amy reckoned. The man hoisted her effortlessly over his shoulder, as the driver remained by the car, lighting a cigarette.

From the sun's position in the sky, Amy estimated she'd been gone for about two hours. Which meant she must be still in London, or very close by. They were in a derelict industrial site, she noticed, next to a gigantic heap of rubbish, like an oversized hoard. Her captor carried her into a building, upstairs to what must have once been an office area.

The room was empty of furniture, save for a broken chair and a tired sofa with springs sticking out. In what she chose to interpret as an act of kindness, the man gently laid her down on the sofa.

'Water?' His accent, she noted with bewilderment, was American.

He removed the gag and handed her a plastic bottle. Amy gulped at it greedily, not caring how much she spilled down her once-immaculate blouse. Though there was no shame left—she'd already wet herself.

'I don't understand why you brought me here,' she said, seizing the initiative, 'but I'm afraid there's been some terrible misunderstanding.'

'I love your British understatement, hon, but there's been no misunderstanding.'

'Why didn't you just kill me like the others?'

'What others?'

'Venner, Marchpole, and the other journalist.'

'I never heard of Venner or Marchpole. All I've been told is you stay here till you're needed.'

You're needed—an odd choice of phrase. He made to replace the gag, but changed his mind.

'Hey—I'll cut you some slack. You can scream as loudly as you like—there's no one out there. Not that you look like much of a screamer.'

True, Amy wasn't much of a screamer, although now seemed an opportune time to become one.

'So long, hon, and we'll be back for you real soon.'

Amy heard a key turn in the door, then receding footsteps, the crunch of gravel and the car driving off.

Relief washed over her. She was alive and alone—she still had hope. Amy remembered saying to Toby once that she could stand despair, but hope drove her insane. How absurd this statement seemed now.

A grimy roller blind covered the window, adding to the twilight gloom. The opposite wall was mostly taken up by a notice board, still with an assortment of yellowing papers pinned to it. A "No Smoking" sign hung crookedly above the door, while on the floor a saucer overflowed with cigarette butts. Amy would have loved a smoke, if only to calm her mind. But trussed up like a turkey, neither lighting nor smoking a cigarette would be possible, even if they'd left her with her handbag.

Escape seemed equally unattainable.

'You got teeth—use them.'

Oh God no—Little Amy—wearing a tracksuit and trainers.

'Go away.'

Adult Amy lacked the strength of will to deal with her teenage alter ego now. She closed her eyes and reopened them, hoping Little Amy would be gone. But no—she stubbornly remained, arms folded and looking smug.

'Our inner child is always with us, and we neglect her at our peril,' she said, mimicking the pious twaddle of the Priory therapist.

'You know what—if my arms were free and you weren't a figment of my imagination, I'd give you a damned good smack across the face.'

'That's nice,' she retorted. *Am I slagging you off for ending up in this mess? No. Am I criticising you for looking and smell-*

ing so disgusting? No. I'm honestly trying to help. You can escape from here, if you put your mind to it.'

'Any suggestions? I can't just disappear into thin air like you.'

As I said, use your teeth. Chew through the tethers on your ankles.'

'You must be kidding.'

Amy tried, but she was no contortionist. Equally, Little Amy was no defeatist.

'OK well, give me another twenty-five years and I guess I'll be as unfit as you. Onto Plan B—why don't you rub against that broken spring sticking out of the sofa.'

In fact several sharp springs protruded from the sofa. They had already scratched her legs and torn her trousers. She strained, but prolonged and determined rubbing made little impact.

'It's no good. This won't work.'

'OK, Plan C—you curl into a ball and pick at your ankle ties with your hands. And if that doesn't work, we'll keep on going until we've run out of letters.'

Plan C was more promising—Amy could at least touch the knots. But there's a limit to the strength and dexterity of hands bound together.

Plan D?

Shit—little Amy had vanished again, presumably because her ideas well had dried up. There was no Plan D, and so much for her promises to work through the alphabet. The final ray of hope flickered and died as Amy fell back sobbing onto the sofa.

67

DCI Bligh was less than impressed by Amy's failure to show up.

'Is she usually this flaky?' he asked Carmody.

'No.' Carmody instinctively sprang to Amy's defence. 'I'll call her.'

He dialled from the landline so she wouldn't realise it was him, though he didn't care for Bligh to see how far their relationship had deteriorated.

Voicemail.

'Perhaps she's stuck on the Tube,' he suggested.

But the Transport for London website boasted of a normal service on all routes.

'More likely she changed her mind,' said Bligh. 'Decided not to talk to us for whatever reason. It's surprising though, because she seemed so keen.'

Carmody felt a creeping unease. To his mind, there were two reasons for Amy's failure to show. One—she'd flipped out again and was lying in hospital somewhere, or worse. Two— she'd been forcibly prevented from attending the appointment. Realistically, the first option seemed more likely—their bitter argument had amply demonstrated her volatility. How he wished now he'd kept his cool and taken better care of her.

Carmody phoned all the local hospitals, but with no joy. Then, fed up with waiting around, he headed for the Underground. If Amy was traceable, he'd find her. And if she needed saving, he was the man.

68

Chang sat on the roof terrace of Ed Smithies' penthouse Chelsea apartment, puffing at his cigar as he sipped a fine cognac.

It had been a satisfactory evening on the whole. Over dinner at Rules, he'd beaten Ed down on the fee for the tax-efficient supply chain implementation, just as he'd planned. Familiarity with Ed's predictable negotiating tactics made it easy to outmanoeuvre him.

Yet his niggling anxiety about Amy marred the pleasure of a done deal. For now, she was in a safe place, but he still hadn't finalised his next steps, mainly for fear he was missing a more elegant solution.

He wondered if Ed had known Amy at Pearson Malone— unlikely, otherwise he would surely have recognised her when she'd poured the coffee at the meeting a few weeks ago. Still she had been in disguise, and Ed was notorious for his cavalier attitude towards "little" people. Anyway, there was no harm in asking.

'Been meaning to ask,' he began. 'Did you ever come across someone called Amy Robinson—was a partner in your firm?'

'Yes—I used to be her boss, for my sins. Why?'

Great—now he might gain some further insight into Amy's character.

'Her name cropped up in conversation the other day.'

'Is she working for another firm already?' Smithies asked, perhaps nervous of a competing bid for the supply-chain project.

'I don't believe so.'

'I'd keep well away if I were you,' counselled Smithies. 'She's mentally unstable.'

'Yes, so I gathered. Would you say she was suicidal?'

'God,' said Smithies, nearly choking on his brandy. 'I sincerely hope not.'

Strange—unlike Ed to care so much.

'Why—you guys having a fling or something?'

Smithies gave a self-conscious little laugh.

'Good God no—but it would be rather awkward if anything happened to her.'

'I hear she nearly jumped off the roof at St Paul's a while back.'

'Well, thank the Lord she didn't.'

'But she might try again?'

'Unlikely—from what I've heard she's stabilised now.'

A pity—still, once unstable always wobbly in Chang's experience.

'And why would it be awkward if she died?'

Smithies paused, apparently vacillating over confiding in his old friend.

'Let's just say she has something of mine which I wouldn't get back.'

'Tell me more.'

Chang leaned forward in anticipation. At first, Smithies was reticent. Confessing to Chang put him in a one-down position, and yet the urge to unburden himself of a troubling secret must have been overpowering. Chang listened intently as his friend described in graphic detail Amy's irrational hatred of him, her emotional outbursts, how she'd tricked him with recordings, and was now cruelly taunting him.

Chang lapped it up—this was way more useful than he expected. A hysterical reaction to her hated former boss constituted a proper motive for Amy's suicide, and ten floors up must be plenty high enough.

'I may be able to help you with those disks,' said Chang, looking out across the Thames. 'What if I could persuade her to come here and hand them back to you?'

Smithies visibly brightened at the prospect.

'That would be wonderful, but how?'

'Let's just say I may have some leverage.'

69

It was still dark when Amy woke. Her head thumped from dehydration, her bones ached and the bindings dug into her wrists and ankles.

With a sinking dread she understood that Mel must have betrayed her to Chang. For who else, other than Mel, had been aware of her plans to talk to the police? It had been a huge miscalculation to trust her.

In a moment of stomach-turning lucidity, Amy finally acknowledged her Achilles' heel. She didn't know who to trust.

Her enemies had instinctively preyed on her weakness. Greg, the ex-husband from hell, told her she trusted the wrong people. So did Ed Smithies. Why, casting her mind back, even Jack had highlighted it as an issue. And Carmody had said that Amy couldn't trust herself. By contrast, she'd suspected Toby, the least unreliable of the lot, at every turn.

All those people who'd abused her had been honest enough to explain *why* they'd picked her as a victim. Yet still, like an idiot, she'd repeated the same mistake over and over. And now she'd ended up here, in this hellhole, peering down the wrong end of a telescope on her life.

Why were they keeping here, instead of killing her on the walk to the Tube station? They'd implied that she would be "needed" for something later, but what?

For no rational reason, she felt a glimmer of optimism. Did Chang intend to cut a deal with her? If so, she'd grab it, whatever it was. She was no Toby Marchpole—exposure of the truth wasn't *that* important to her, not more important than life itself. A deal with Chang was her best option though, because there was little chance of a rescue. Bligh wouldn't sound the alarm just because she'd stood him up—he would merely assume she'd changed her mind—Crazy Amy strikes again. And sadly, no one else would miss her for some considerable time.

Amy lapsed back into a fitful sleep, punctuated by the image of a man lifting her onto the mantelpiece as a toddler. Was it a memory or some kind of metaphor for her life? The man morphed into Carmody, who laughed at her, before fading away into the darkness.

When she woke next a faint light showed through the window, and the first birds of the morning were chirruping. And little Amy had returned to taunt her.

'Are you still here?' she said, incredulous.

'Well yes—you bailed out on me last night, after giving me all that crap about plans A to Z.'

'That's because Plan C was working, but kind of slowly, so I popped off to do other stuff rather than waste time hanging around here.'

How absurd for a figment to claim an existence outside the mind that had created it. Yet Amy didn't challenge Little Amy, in case she disappeared again. For Little Amy, combined with the dawn of a new day, had brought fresh hope.

She began where she'd left off with Plan C, curling up and picking at her foot ties, only this time with more resolve than before. Her efforts with Plan B must have been more fruitful than she'd known, because now progress was evident. Her contortions were excruciating—the main reason she'd thrown in the towel before. But encouraged by the beginnings of success, she persevered.

Finally, one narrow strip of material bound her feet together. After several efforts resulting in deep scratches on her ankles, she wriggled on the broken spring until the weakened fibre split as she strained against it.

'Oh well done,' said Little Amy, in admiration.

Amy stood up and swiftly collapsed. She rose again, holding the wall for support, but her numb legs might as well have still been tethered together.

'Now for the wrist ties—same again.'

With her ankles freed, Amy edged herself into a suitable position, while Little Amy stood by, tut-tutting at the slow progress. Eventually though, Amy was free. Or relatively free. The door was locked—eminently predictable, given the sound of the key turning the previous evening.

'So what now, clever clogs—leap out of the window and break a leg?'

'Shall I give you a clue?'

'Pick the lock?'

Little Amy shook her head.

'The dumdums left the key on the outside. You can push it through onto a piece of paper and pull it under the door.'

As Amy cast around for tools to help her, her eyes lighted on a crumpled old newspaper in the corner.

Hands trembling, she straightened the paper out, and laughed at the headline.

WOMAN SAVED FROM ST PAUL'S SUICIDE BID

How ironic was that? Better not let Little Amy see.

Amy slid the paper under the door, and then searched for an implement to push the key through. She looked at Little Amy for inspiration.

'How about the broken spring in the couch?'

Amy tore at the sofa's covering. The foam beneath crumbled away in her hands, revealing the spring. She couldn't see where it was attached at the other end, and had no equipment to remove it, but no matter. She bent it back and forth until metal fatigue set in and it broke off in her hand.

'Does this work,' she asked Little Amy, 'apart from in the movies?'

'Dunno—but we'll soon find out.'

Triumphant now, Amy poked the broken off spring through the keyhole, and the key dropped obligingly onto the sheet of newspaper, which she slid under the door towards her.

Success. Amy staggered out, down the metal stairs, and could scarcely believe her luck as she saw the main warehouse building was open—no more locks.

***

She heard the car before she saw it. Damn—having got so far, had her luck run out? She couldn't allow them to recapture her, but outrunning them on jelly legs was a non-starter.

'Into that pile,' urged Little Amy.

The huge heap of rubbish she'd noticed the day before towered above her—a giant version of her mother's hoard. For a moment, Amy stood mesmerised by the memories the sight and smell evoked.

'Quick—quick or they'll see you.'

It was a no-brainer—the stinking, decaying pile was the only hiding place. Amy took a deep breath and dived in.

Through the gaps in the putrid garbage, she saw her two captors enter the building, along with Nelson Chang. With luck, she'd never learn what deal he'd come to broker. Amy waited, breathing as little as possible and after what felt like forever, the men left, cursing each other roundly for allowing her to escape.

'I told you she was smart,' Chang lamented. 'You brainless thugs underestimated her. And you'd better find her—or else.'

After they'd left, Amy waited as long as she could bear, fearful of a trap to flush her out. But before long, the foetid atmosphere overwhelmed her and she stumbled out of the pile, gulping at the fresh air.

Once on the road, she flinched each time a car passed, terrified her captors would return at any moment, and knowing she'd be powerless to escape if they did.

The police—she had to call them. Why the dearth of public phone boxes these days? Surely people got kidnapped and robbed of their mobiles all the time?

Amy paused at a bus stop to orientate herself. Bermondsey—south of the river. Of course—IPT's worthless derelict factory. A bus approached, labelled Waterloo, though the destination was irrelevant—all she wanted was the driver to make a phone call. He eyed her suspiciously as she boarded.

'Good night out?' he said, with a knowing wink.

The man must be stupid, thought Amy—*no one gets into this state voluntarily.*

'Please,' she begged. 'Call the police. Some men abducted me but I escaped.'

He looked at her as though she was a crazed loon, and showed an obvious reluctance to be drawn in. Amy didn't blame him—if she'd met Crazy Amy, stinking and emotional, she wouldn't have rushed to assist.

'Oh please, please help me. I get how it looks but I'm in big trouble.'

As she broke down in tears, the driver softened.

'Tell you what,' he said, relenting. 'I stop round the corner from Rotherhithe police station. We'll be there in ten minutes. Will that do?'

'Fine.'

The bus filled up, but the seat next to Amy remained empty. A few months ago she'd been a successful partner in a global professional firm. Now she'd become the smelly old bag lady everyone avoids, worse by far than her mother, who always looked presentable even though living in squalor.

'OK, love, we're here,' shouted the driver. 'It's just round there, can't miss it. And good luck—whatever's going on with you.'

70

Amy never reached the police station. A dark blue BMW drew up alongside her and the driver wound down the window.

'Hey, Amy,' the guy said in an American accent.

What was it with all these Americans?

Petrified, Amy tried to break into a run, before collapsing on the pavement. She screamed as the man approached her.

'Hey Amy, calm down—you've gotten yourself into an unholy mess, but we're here to help.'

He appeared sincere, friendly even, but that meant nothing. Amy peered at the car and observed that the female passenger wore her hair in an elegant chignon, and sported manicured pink fingernails. Illogically, she found those details comforting.

'Who are you?'

'I'm Ethan and my colleague is Michelle. We represent the US government.'

'You have ID?'

'Sure we do.'

He thrust a card in her face. It looked official enough, but anyone could mock up ID these days.

'What do you want?'

'We're aware of your situation and we'd like to help you.'

Michelle sprang from the car. In tight jeans and a leather jacket, she was slim and athletic.

'I can see what you're thinking,' she said, with a brittle professional smile, 'and I don't blame you one little bit. Why should you trust us after everything that's happened?'

'I don't trust you,' Amy retorted. 'And I'm headed for the police station now.'

'We wouldn't advise that.'

'Why not?'

'Because there's shit going on that's way over your head,' Ethan replied. 'And police involvement would be disastrous. Plus I know for a fact Chang is waiting for you outside the cop shop.'

'He is?'

Shit—Amy hadn't anticipated that, although it was predictable enough.

'Look—we haven't much time, but if you come with us we'll explain everything.'

Amy wavered. Chang might well be lying in wait, and there might be a cogent reason to avoid informing the police, even if she couldn't fathom what.

'Look, you've had a rough time, Amy,' said Michelle. 'You're badly shaken and confused.'

To say the least.

'We can take you somewhere safe, get you a shower, some clean clothes, something to eat. You can have a sleep, and then we can discuss everything.'

'Can't I go home?' asked Amy. 'And discuss it tomorrow?'

Tomorrow she might have more capacity for rational thought.

'Not a smart move,' said Ethan, shaking his head. 'Home will be the very next place Chang comes looking for you.'

Through all her suspicion, anxiety and woolly-mindedness, Amy saw the logic in what Ethan was saying. She so wanted to trust him, but her track record wasn't strong, even at the best of times.

'Look—what do you have to lose?'

'My life?'

Michelle laughed. She was a hatchet-faced bitch when you looked close up.

'Let me be honest with you, Amy, because I can see you're like me—someone who appreciates straight talking. Now, do you seriously imagine the US government habitually kills people?'

'How would I know? Hell, I'm not even convinced you're genuine government agents.'

'Well whoever we are, if we'd wanted you dead, wouldn't you be dead by now?'

This was a reasonable point.

'OK—I'll come with you, but I can leave at any time right?'

'Sure,' said Ethan. 'We're civilised people.'

He helped Amy to her feet and supported her as she walked over to the car, hoping to God she was not making the biggest blunder of her life.

***

During the journey, Ethan and Michelle kept up a stream of light-hearted banter, no doubt to keep Amy's spirits up. She didn't join in and, though she battled sleep, her eyelids closed within minutes.

She was jolted awake as the car stopped outside an anonymous semi-detached house. Although neat and inconspicuous, it had an uninhabited air.

'Hey, Amy—we're here.'

'Where, exactly?'

'One of our safe houses. We're in Hounslow.'

Not too far from home.

Inside, the neutral décor was at odds with the most bizarre collection of furniture Amy had ever seen.

'Not the most stylish furnishings, are they?" said Michelle, reading her mind. 'We buy them in job lots from house clearances. So—what now?'

'Shower, sleep and food, in that order.'

'OK—you got it,' she said.

Upstairs in the main bedroom, the bed was made and had various items of clothing spread out on it—two pairs of jeans, tops, socks, pyjamas, and underwear even. Amy checked the labels—M&S, but the size was spot on. In addition, she spotted fifty pounds in cash and a set of house keys laid out on the dressing table. Amy felt reassured—just as they'd promised, she wasn't a prisoner.

'The clothes aren't great,' said Michelle apologetically. 'I had to buy them in a rush.'

Amy mulled over how they'd learned her bra size, but was far too exhausted to ask.

'They'll do.'

'Looks like you lost an earring,' Michelle pointed out.

Amy hadn't noticed until now.

'Damn. They were my favourite. From Tiffany.'

'Too bad it's always the upscale stuff goes missing,' said Michelle.

The shower refreshed Amy and, after gulping down several glasses of water, she collapsed into bed and slept till early afternoon, dressing in her new clothes before venturing downstairs.

Michelle sat on the sofa, tapping away at a laptop. There was no sign of Ethan.

'Hi, Amy. Better now?'

'Definitely.'

This was a lie. Amy's head still ached from the residue of whatever drugs Chang's heavies had dosed her with, and she felt liable to burst into tears at the slightest provocation.

Michelle appraised Amy's outfit.

'The clothes don't look too bad considering everything.'

'They're OK—jeans are on the loose side though.'

'I'll call Ethan. Meanwhile, do you want food?'

She hadn't eaten in more than a day, yet didn't particularly feel hungry. But she ought to keep her strength up.

'Can you rustle up a sandwich?'

'Sure can, and I think I'll join you.'

As they were eating, Ethan arrived.

'How you doing, Amy?' he asked.

'Better than before, thanks.'

'You ready to hear us out?'

She nodded.

'OK—this is the mess we're in. You're in great danger.'

No kidding, thought Amy, but said nothing.

'Chang and his chums plan to kill you.'

'So why didn't they do it already? They had plenty of chance.'

'Might look suspicious if you wind up with a bullet in your head, or disappear. Chang likes things just as they are—with Richard Pedley in the frame for Marchpole's murder.'

'But Chang did kill him—right?'

'Yep—well not personally, but he hired the killer.'

'And he killed Venner too?'

'Whoa,' said Ethan. 'That's a big assumption. How much do you know of Chang's activities?'

'What you mean the Chinese arms shipments to the Colombian terrorists?'

Right after she'd said it, Amy realised it might have been smarter to play dumb.

'Yep. Now, fact is *nobody* wants that stuff broadcast around.'

'How do you mean *nobody*?'

'You think about it. Something like that doesn't happen accidentally—it requires *all* those governments to cooperate. As you've worked out, the shipment they stopped was not a one-off. But here's the lowdown. The Chinese are not denouncing it, because then they'd have to arrest Chang. And they're not keen, because he can tie all the consignments back to them. So better for them to claim these were regular supplies. No one will challenge them, least of all the Cubans. Same with the Colombian authorities—they staged a token arrest of the ship's captain because they had to but hey—they let him go.'

'So where does the US fit in?'

'You're aware of the US talks with Cuba?'

'Yes,' said Amy, remembering the newspaper article and suspecting just how far out of her depth she was.

'We can't let those be derailed by some silly arms transactions the Chinese have cooked up with Cuba—there's more at stake here, like the credibility of the US government.'

'Hence your involvement.'

'Correct.'

'So why should I avoid the UK police?'

'Well, technically,' Ethan said, 'Because Chang is a UK resident, some of the arms offences he's committed fall foul of UK law.'

'But wouldn't the UK government be equally keen not to embarrass our American cousins? Aren't we all on the same side?'

Impressive questions for someone who was struggling to think rationally.

'Sometimes,' Ethan replied evasively. 'And maybe you're right, but if they decide to sweep the whole arms-smuggling thing under the carpet, that's the worst possible outcome for you.'

'It is?'

'Sure—why be the loose end that unravels the carpet? Got to say, hon, I wouldn't bet much money on your continued survival in that scenario, with Colombians, Cubans and Chinese all keen to keep their secrets.'

Although she'd only taken two bites from her ham sandwich, Amy suddenly flipped from not hungry to queasy. She pushed her plate away.

'But if they don't sweep it under the carpet?'

'Not a great outcome for us—huge international embarrassment all round.'

'Not my problem, though.'

'True, but you can't predict which way they'll jump. Do you want to take the risk?'

'Well, no,' Amy admitted. She didn't want to take *any* risk, even though she'd jettisoned the risk-free option long ago. 'But how can you help me?'

'We can protect you, give you a new identity even, if you cooperate with us.'

The prospect of a new identity tempted Amy far more than she would ever admit. Her life had been such a sham it would be painless to start over, especially with a million pounds from her property sale.

'Can I keep my money?'

'Sure—no problem,' said Michelle. 'Wouldn't want to deprive you of those Tiffany earrings.'

Amy detected a bitter sarcasm in Michelle's voice—nobody likes a rich bitch, not even a spy.

'So—how do I cooperate?'

'By helping us eliminate Chang,' said Ethan.

Amy hesitated.

'What—you mean kill him?'

'He would have killed you, remember.'

Yes, though did that justify a pre-emptive strike?

'OK, but why do you guys want him dead?'

'Thing is,' said Ethan in grave tones, 'Chang has become a liability. We asked him politely to stop the shipments but he didn't. He's being squeezed by the Chinese because they're under pressure from the Cubans to keep up the supplies. It's only a matter of time before something goes embarrassingly wrong. So—we're forced to neutralise the threat.'

'Why not use the same stuff as whoever killed Venner?'

'Healthy young man dies suddenly—I don't think so. There has to be a convincing narrative, just as he'd worked out a credible way to stage your death.'

'What way?'

'You know a guy called Ed Smithies, right?'

'*Ed Smithies*,' said Amy, astounded by the mention of her former nemesis. 'Where the hell does he fit in?'

'Old buddy of Chang's apparently.'

Made sense. Birds of a feather.

'Chang planned to accompany you to Ed Smithies' penthouse apartment, drug you up, and have his hit man throw you off the roof terrace. So—here's the story. Woman has irrational hatred for former boss—goes to have it out with him, gets crazy angry, and jumps. A life tragically cut short.'

'What the…' Amy began, before Michelle abruptly cut her off.

'It's not like you don't have form, hon.'

Amy fixed Michelle with a beady stare, though she was right. What would be more plausible than Crazy Amy finally topping herself? There would be no shortage of people willing to testify to her insane and unjustified loathing of Smithies, her substance abuse and mental instability. Why the story would practically write itself. And even if Smithies witnessed her being thrown to oblivion, he wouldn't have the balls to tell the truth—he'd stick to whatever version of events suited his purposes.

'How come you know all this?'

'Because we've had Chang covered for a while,' said Ethan. 'You remember Rex—the blond guy who's working with him?'

'Yes,' said Amy, assuming he was the one who'd given her water and removed her gag.

'We turned him. He shot Marchpole and he's wanted in the US for a string of contract killings. We promised him immunity if he plays the game.'

Amy recalled her brief contact with Rex, and how she'd determined that his blue eyes weren't cruel. Wrong again.

'And what is the game?'

'Well, part of it was to protect you. So even without your great escape—on which congrats, by the way—you would have been OK.'

'It would have been helpful to know that beforehand.'

A night spent believing it to be her last on this earth left a scar that would not easily be erased.

'Yes but we needed you to be authentic,' said Michelle. The talk of killing hadn't blunted her appetite, Amy noticed, as she'd polished off her sandwich in short order. By contrast, Amy's food remained almost untouched.

'And why would I be visiting Smithies? I don't suppose I'm top of his guest list.'

'You have a disk he wants, right? You'd be handing it over to him.'

'Never,' said Amy. 'That CD is my insurance policy. I have it lodged with my lawyers and if anything happens to me it gets sent...'

'We know all that,' said Michelle.

Amy could only marvel at how deep they'd delved.

'But like I said, I'd never agree to do it. So no way would Chang get me into Smithies' apartment.'

'No? You've been held hostage overnight—that softens you up. The deal is you keep your mouth shut and you give Smithies all copies of the disk. Then they'll let you go.'

'But if I didn't agree.'

'Oh mostly people agree to anything if someone's holding a gun to their head,' said Michelle.

'I'm not most people.'

'Is that a fact?'

There was something sinister in the way she said it, as if she had experience of holding guns to people's heads, and might even be inclined to call Amy's bluff.

'They wouldn't shoot me anyway, if they cared about the contents of the disk.'

'That's just it—Chang doesn't give a shit about Smithies' dirty secrets. It's just a means to lure you onto that roof terrace.'

'That's interesting,' said Amy. 'But what have you planned for Chang, and where do I fit in?'

'Well,' said Ethan. 'We let Chang believe his plan is proceeding, but we turn the tables, so he ends up being shot by Rex.'

'Why?'

'Chang and Rex argue about killing you. Rex doesn't want to—he's taken pity on you—so he shoots Chang and then runs off.'

'And Smithies?'

To her surprise, Amy pitied him. The aftermath of a shooting in his immaculate new penthouse apartment would be hideous.

'Unless he chops the body into little pieces and flushes them down the toilet, he'll call the cops.'

'Fine. But what about me? I'm still in there—I can't just leg it. What do I say? I mean, the police will think it's weird, won't they?'

'It's weird—so what? You can be a gibbering wreck if you want—too traumatised to communicate. Or you could be honest—Chang abducted you and promised to release you if you gave Smithies the disk. In reality Chang had planned to kill you, as became apparent, but Rex didn't want to, and they argued.'

'But…'

Amy broke off, realising she'd been about to object to embarrassing Smithies. But hell, he thoroughly deserved whatever bad consequences might flow from colluding in a fraud.

'I'm still not convinced,' she said. 'Surely you guys can quietly do away with Chang without going through all this hassle. Why involve me?'

'That's a great question, Amy,' said Ethan gravely. 'We knew you were smart. Unfortunately there are aspects of this case we can't discuss due to the security implications.'

'Involving Ed Smithies,' Michelle added, in cryptic tones.

'*Seriously?*'

'Oh yes,' said Ethan. 'You wouldn't believe it even if we told you.'

This sounded intriguing—although no depths to which Smithies might stoop would surprise Amy.

'Is he in trouble?'

'He is, and indirectly you'd be helping bring him to justice. Basically, we're asking you to help us tie down a few loose ends in exchange for a brand new identity. Now will you do it?'

Amy wavered. The prospect of becoming someone else and disappearing was so appealing, particularly if Smithies finally got his just deserts.

'OK,' she said. 'Let's go.'

'Great—I'll call Rex,' said Ethan, 'He'll convince Chang that he picked you up at your house and persuaded you to cooperate. You're scared, but he's spun you a line about how you'll be released if you hand over the disks and keep quiet about Chang's activities.'

The conversation was short and functional. Half an hour later, Ethan's cell phone rang.

'Good news,' he reported. 'Rex spoke to Chang who spoke to Smithies, and we're a runner for tonight.'

'OK.'

'Rex will shoot Chang and then he'll leave. You stay and deal with the cops. We'll give you an untraceable cell phone, and if you call us when you're done we'll tell you where to go. Then we can get to work on your new identity, and winding down Amy's affairs. Does that make sense?'

Frankly, it didn't. Nothing made sense anymore and Amy's head swam as she tried to absorb all the implications.

Michelle suggested she and Ethan should collect some of Amy's things from her house, as "you won't be back there for a while". That might mean never, Amy realised, with an unexpected twinge of sadness.

'Sure, that'd be great. I haven't got my keys—they were in my handbag, but my estate agent has a set. I'd better call them in advance and give them the password, though.'

'The password?' said Michelle, wrinkling her nose. 'That's cloak and dagger, even by our standards.'

'Apparently access to their properties is a sensitive issue at the moment,' Amy replied, without elaborating.

Left alone in the house, Amy ruminated over her decision. She considered escape, but not for long. The doors were unlocked, and anyway she had keys. They trusted her not to run away, so logic dictated that she should repay their trust.

71

Mel had been twitchy ever since her conversation with Amy. Although she'd now made herself scarce, Joey was still in Whitstable, and potentially within Chang's reach. As she'd always suspected, Chang's well-mannered exterior concealed a devious and ruthless man prepared to do anything for his own advancement. She would only rest easy once he was under lock and key.

Two days had now elapsed, and there'd been nothing on the news. Surely Amy must have squealed on Chang by now. Why hadn't he been arrested?

She called Amy.

Voicemail.

There were many reasons Amy might not be answering her phone, but still an uneasy intuition nagged at Mel. An hour later she left a message asking Amy to call back urgently.

What if Chang had somehow weaselled his way out of arrest? She didn't give much for Amy's chances in that scenario.

Another hour passed, but Mel was loath to make official police contact, for obvious reasons. She remembered Amy's policeman friend—what was his name again—Carmody? OK, he'd broken up with Amy and sounded a bit of a knob, but he might still help on an informal basis. After being passed around half the Metropolitan Police force, and insisting it was a vital personal call, Mel eventually tracked the detective down.

'I'm calling regarding Amy Robinson,' she began.

The reaction confirmed all her worst suspicions.

'My God—is she OK?'

'I hope so,' Mel replied.

'Who's this speaking?'

'Just a friend.'

'Which friend?'

'Lisa,' said Melanie at once, usurping off the top of her head the false name Amy had used at The Larches.

'I thought you guys fell out months ago.'

There was suspicion in his voice now. Shit—this Lisa must be an actual person.

'Well, we're back on the same page now. And I know you fell out with her too, and she seemed kind of cut up…'

'She did?' Carmody cut in, a little too eagerly.

'Thing is I'm due to meet her and can't seem to make contact. I was wondering if you guys made up, and she's been with you.'

'Unfortunately not. She was meant to come to the station yesterday afternoon but she never showed.'

This was the worst news.

'Are you worried about her?' Mel asked.

'Not really—I'm sure there's a perfectly reasonable explanation.'

There was a mismatch between his nonchalant, almost dismissive words and his reaction when she'd first announced the reason for her call. He was hiding his anxiety, perhaps through embarrassment.

It also suited Mel to play down her own anxiety, which might raise questions she was unwilling to answer. She was particularly keen to avoid any formal interviews.

'Yeah—that's what I think too. She can act crazy sometimes, but hey—that's Amy isn't it?'

'Yes, that's Amy,' Carmody agreed. 'Hey, if she reappears, will you do me a favour and get in touch?'

'Sure thing and it'd be great if you did the same for me.'

She rang off before Carmody asked for her contact details.

***

Mel reckoned that if Amy was still alive, she stood a far better chance than Carmody of locating her. And if she wasn't, then she was beyond the help of either of them.

Amy's house was the only place to start. Mel had got an extra set of keys cut while masquerading as the cleaning woman. At the time, she'd questioned whether this was a worthwhile investment—anyone with a grain of nous would have changed the locks. But Mel suspected Amy wasn't as streetwise as she pretended, and would now test this theory.

After a tedious drive to Chiswick, Mel rang Amy's doorbell. As predicted, there was no reply. She tried the key—yep, same old lock. And the burglar alarm was still broken, further confirming Mel's views on Amy's naivety.

Today's newspaper lay untouched on the doormat, but Amy's passport and other documents were still in the desk drawer, proving she hadn't fled. In fact, with the laptop still switched on and the previous day's paper left open at a half-completed crossword, it appeared that Amy had expected to return very soon. And it was disquieting that she hadn't.

Fearful of detection, Mel hadn't lingered on her previous visit. But now she relished the ostentatious luxury. Mel had never aspired to such a lifestyle—her own horizons were limited to emerging from the care system as a functioning adult with a job. Many of her peers hadn't even managed that.

But seeing all the trappings of Amy's high-flying life made her question whether she should have aimed higher. Sure, in terms of pure intellectual horsepower, Amy had the upper hand. But brains weren't everything—the other skills Amy conspicuously lacked, like empathy and reading people, were of equal importance.

Upstairs, Mel explored Amy's wardrobes, astounded by the array of fine designer outfits. Amy's modus operandi was the opposite of Mel's. Whereas Mel's frailties were shrouded in a fog of invisibility, Amy's were hidden in a dazzle.

Why on earth had Amy abandoned this life?

The front door banged, breaking Mel's train of thought. For one deluded moment she nearly called out Amy's name, but stopped herself. In the distance, she heard voices of a man and a woman, both with American accents. Prospective purchasers perhaps? As they climbed the stairs, Mel dived behind the door of the en suite bathroom. And when they entered the bedroom, she hardly dared to breathe.

'Gonna take a heck of a long time picking all this stuff out,' said the woman. 'And it's not like she's gonna need it.'

'Don't,' the man replied.

'Squeamish?'

'Sometimes what we do seems kind of unnecessary. The other two I could live with—both old guys who would have croaked soon anyway. But Amy's different, and hey—all she did was blunder into something she shouldn't have.'

'Yeah, well, there's no room for sentiment in this job. She won't feel much by the time Chang's drugged her up. Why, hold a gun to her head and she'll fly off that roof terrace of her own accord—I mean she's flaky enough—that we do know.'

Mel suppressed a gasp. Whoever these people were, they were not prospective purchasers, but their intent was plain. And unless she wanted Amy's murder on her conscience, she had to stop them.

'I only hope we're done soon,' the woman went on. 'Venner, the other one, and now this. Enough already.'

'Red Luisa Spagnoli suit,' said the man, doubtfully. 'Why would she want that?'

'Power dressing. I bet she'll wear it tonight. So at least she'll be going out in style.'

Mel prayed that Amy hadn't asked for the towelling robe hanging on the back of the bathroom door. She could hear her heart thumping. If these people discovered her, she'd be finished.

'What's she written there?' asked the man, obviously trying to decipher Amy's handwriting.

'Back bedroom wardrobe.'

'Jeez, this girl sure loves her clothes.'

As the couple moved to the other room, Mel seized her chance to escape. Shaking with fear, she tiptoed downstairs and let herself out, pulling the front door quietly shut behind her. She took refuge in her car, a short distance down the road.

A BMW was parked in Amy's driveway—their car. If she memorised the registration plate and telephoned the police, they could likely track the Americans down. But even with London's proliferation of cameras, they'd struggle to locate Amy. Foolhardy as it was, only one option remained.

A few minutes later, the couple emerged carrying two large suitcases. And as the car set off, Mel pulled out in pursuit.

72

The presence of her own possessions comforted Amy. As the child of a hoarder, she'd always scorned any emotional attachment to stuff, but in her enfeebled state she felt differently.

All she lacked was a cigarette to calm her nerves.

'OK if I pop out and buy some ciggies?' she asked. 'I assume I'm allowed.'

'Yeah—no problem,' said Michelle. 'Turn right, then right again and there's a parade of shops.'

As Amy rounded the corner she felt a tap on her shoulder. Filled with terror, she spun around.

'Holy shit—Mel.'

Mel's presence meant only one thing—Chang had tracked her down.

***

Between Chiswick and Hounslow, Mel committed more traffic violations than in the rest of her driving history combined. She ran red lights, whizzed down bus lanes, blocked box junctions, and still came close to losing the BMW several times. Once she found herself in pursuit of the wrong car, and was forced to turn right from the left lane in a hazardous manoeuvre to get back on track. She hoped they weren't checking behind them, for her lunatic antics made her horribly conspicuous if they cared to look.

With relief, Mel pulled up some distance behind the BMW in the quiet Hounslow road. She parallel parked with aplomb and watched as the couple let themselves into the house. She saw no sign of a roof terrace, and so presumed Amy would be safe while here. But what should she do?

She was seconds away from calling Carmody when the front door opened, and out walked Amy. Mel watched as she ambled down the street, then set off on foot, closing on Amy as she turned the corner, before tapping her on the shoulder.

Amy twisted round, her expression first fearful then surprised. She had a haggard, haunted look, like a wild animal being hunted down.

'Holy shit—Mel.'

'Don't look so scared,' Mel said. 'I've come to rescue you.'

Strangely, Amy did not seem reassured by this.

'You're kidding me—do you honestly think I'd fall for a line like that?'

'I'm trying to help you, as a friend,' Mel reiterated.

'Shut it, Mel—I know you're working for Chang.'

Mel had anticipated Amy would be grateful, but it appeared that she'd misjudged matters. Why the heck did Amy believe she'd teamed up with Chang? She must be deranged.

'You've got it all wrong. Look—I assume you're trying to escape.'

'No—I'm popping out to buy cigarettes.'

'*What?*'

'I'm fine—I don't need rescuing, especially not by you. You betrayed me—you told Chang I was onto him.'

'I didn't.'

'Oh come on—you were the only person I mentioned it to.'

'There must be another explanation. What happened to you, Amy?'

'As if you didn't know already.'

'No—tell me.'

But Amy stubbornly refused to answer any of her questions.

'How did you find me?'

As Mel described her visit to Chiswick, Amy cut in.

'Ha—that proves you're in cahoots with Chang—Chang has my handbag with the keys. I bet he asked you to check whether I'd been back there.'

'I had a copy of the keys made last time.'

'You're lying.'

Mel switched tack—if she couldn't persuade Amy of her own integrity, she'd try to cast doubt on the others.

'Who are those people Amy—the Americans? Are they linked to Chang?'

'Wouldn't you know if they were?'

'What's happening this evening?'

'You know already.'

Mel rolled her eyes in exasperation at the illogicality and the wilful refusal to see reality.

'I *do*, because I heard them talking in your house. And whoever they are, they killed Venner and the journalist and they plan to drug you up and throw you off a roof somewhere.'

'There—you just proved you're aware of Chang's plans.'

There was no logic to Amy today—she appeared to be in the grip of an uncontrollable madness. But without the physical strength to grab Amy and force her into the car, Mel had no option but to continue her war of words.

'They were talking like you're going to die. You can't go along with it—you're in terrible danger.'

She spoke slowly and calmly, although frustrated by her inability to make Amy understand.

'That's rubbish. In fact…'

'In fact what?'

'Nothing—I can't discuss it with you.'

Mel tried again. Perhaps she'd failed to understand some essential aspect of Amy's predicament.

'How did you meet these people—did they abduct you?'

If they had, why wasn't Amy trying to escape? It was like she'd been brainwashed by a cult.

'Piss off, Mel—you're way out of your depth here.'

'*I'm* out of my depth! That's the pot calling the kettle black. Why do you trust these strangers more than me?'

Amy laughed in Mel's face.

'Isn't it obvious? You've already let me down. I'm pretty sure these guys are on the level. I mean—I'm free to come and go.'

'Duh—they're not worried you'll leg it because they know they've conned you into believing their shit.'

'You can't trick me, Mel. Fool me once, shame on you— fool me twice, shame on me.'

'I can't wrap my head round this. In a few hours, you'll be dead and I'm trying to warn you.'

'If I go with you—you'll lead me back to Chang and I'll be dead in any case.'

'OK—don't go with me. Call your policeman friend— Carmody—use my phone. What the hell have you got to lose?'

'If I tell the police, I'll never be safe. These guys will finish it. There's stuff you can't even begin to comprehend, Mel.'

'Because I'm the stupid fat girl, right! They'll finish you more like,' said Mel with a snort. 'Remember, I *heard* them talking about it.'

'Leave me alone.'

'Amy, use your brain for Christ's sake. Why would I be urging you to contact Carmody if I was with Chang?'

'There's nothing more to be said.'

'I can see I won't talk any sense into you.'

'Piss off, Mel—go find some other sucker to con.'

Amy walked off, towards the newsagents, as Mel wrestled with her conscience. Could she justifiably leave Amy to her fate? She'd done everything to convince her of the danger, but the crazy, headstrong girl wasn't having any of it. Ultimately you can't save people from themselves if they're hell-bent on self-destruction. On the other hand, if she didn't intervene, Amy would die. Could she live with that?

73

'Can I speak to DCI Carmody please? It's a personal call.'

Mel's voice held calm and steady, but an eddy of anxiety swirled underneath.

'This is Lisa again,' she said, when Carmody answered the phone. 'I've found Amy.'

'You *have*. Where is she?'

Mel related how she'd let herself in Amy's house and what she'd overheard, and how she'd tracked the Americans to Hounslow. She added that while Amy appeared to be there of her own volition, the balance of her mind was clearly disturbed.

'I tried to reason with her,' she told him, 'and persuade her to contact you of her own accord, but she's completely delusional. She may be traumatised, or brainwashed even.'

'Entirely possible,' said Carmody, not sounding surprised. 'So where is she?'

Mel told him.

'OK—we'll be right there. But one thing—this isn't Lisa, is it?'

Mel almost ended the call, but changed her mind.

'What makes you say that?'

'Because I tracked down the real Lisa to ask more questions, and it was evident she hadn't called.'

Damn.

'So I'm thinking—who else is there in Amy's life, who might have her own reasons for not coming forward? Perhaps someone my colleagues want to talk to about money withdrawn from Amy's account? Someone who knows more than she's prepared to let on regarding Toby Marchpole's murder?'

Mel nearly hung up again, before accepting the futility of avoidance. She could give a sanitised account of the events surrounding the cash withdrawal, but Chang would retaliate by exposing Mel's activities. It would be much better to pre-empt this with her own confession.

'Yes—OK. I admit it. I'm Melanie Cronin.'

'Anything else you'd like to tell us?'

It all tumbled out, and Carmody listened, like a priest.

'Are you prepared to give us contact details?' Carmody asked when she was done.

'OK,' said Mel, resigned to her fate. It seemed as if emerging from the shadows and facing the music was the price she must pay for saving Amy. 'But you will rescue Amy, won't you?'

'We'll do our best, Ms Cronin.'

74

Amy smoked two of the cigarettes in quick succession. She dithered over whether to mention her encounter with Mel to Ethan and Michelle, before concluding that honesty was preferable.

'You're right to be cautious,' said Ethan. 'We're well aware of Melanie, and you're right—she's definitely working for Chang.'

'So why would she warn me against you guys?' asked Amy, playing back Mel's argument.

'I doubt if Chang has told her what he has in mind. I'll bet he sent her to your house to try and lure you back, which was when she overheard our conversation.'

'But she inferred that *you* were planning to kill me.'

Michelle laughed, apparently unconcerned and unsurprised.

'Oh yes, I see how she may have gotten the idea. We were discussing how *Chang* planned to kill you—she must have misunderstood.'

Mel had given her away to Chang and wasn't trustworthy. But equally, who knew what bullshit he'd fed her? Michelle was likely correct in suggesting Mel didn't have the whole story, and she might well have misinterpreted the conversation. And yet…?

Michelle sensed her indecision.

'Look, if you're concerned, call the cops, but remember what we said about the risks.'

She held out her iPhone.

They wouldn't be offering her a phone call if they weren't on the level. And Little Amy hadn't shown up screaming at her not to be so stupid—also a promising sign.

'No,' Amy said. 'It's OK. I trust you.'

Amy dressed and made up carefully. She'd almost discarded the Luisa Spagnoli outfit several months earlier, but later decided there were times in a woman's life when only a red suit would do. A showdown with Ed Smithies was just such an occasion. She spritzed herself with Coco perfume and applied her most vampish crimson lipstick as a final dramatic touch. She looked in the mirror, satisfied by what she saw. With her war paint on, nobody would realise what she'd endured in the past twenty-four hours.

'Hey, check you out,' said Michelle, before turning to Ethan. 'See, I told you she'd wear the red suit.'

'Very chic,' he observed.

The doorbell rang. Rex.

'Hey, Amy—how's it going?'

How unnerving to look into those vivid blue eyes again, knowing they'd been the last eyes Marchpole had seen. With his neat, preppy style, Rex looked the very antithesis of a cold-blooded killer, doubtless an advantage in the profession.

'OK, thanks. I wish you'd told me I wasn't in danger, back there in the factory place. Would have saved me a lot of angst.'

'I considered it,' he said, without emotion. 'But you looked like a tough babe—I reckoned you'd handle the experience.'

Amy managed a smile. How ironic that a veteran assassin regarded Crazy Amy as tough.

'OK,' said Ethan. 'This is where we part company for a while.'

'What—you're not coming too?' Amy asked. Being alone with Rex and putting her trust in him made her uneasy now she knew his back story.

'No—we can't have a whole troupe of people showing up at Smithies' apartment, can we?'

'I guess not.'

'Now before we go—you ever fired a gun?' asked Rex.

'Nope.'

'You shouldn't need to shoot tonight, but I'm giving you a firearm, just in case.'

'In case of what?'

Amy tried not to sound panicked.

'If anyone else pulls a gun and I'm not around to help you.'

'That doesn't sound encouraging.'

'Hey relax, hon—I like to be prepared for every eventuality. We'll be fine.'

The gun felt heavy and alien to Amy. A niggling fear assailed her, but she pushed it back.

'You'll need a lesson in how to use it,' said Rex. 'So we'll stop somewhere on the way and have a little target practice.'

'OK?' said Ethan to Amy.

'I hope so.'

'Well good luck—we're relying on you.'

Which in itself was unsettling, thought Amy.

***

Fear shot through Amy as Rex drove into the car park of a disused school. A terrifying flash of insight told her she'd called this totally wrong. This was where it all ended. She'd been conned good and proper.

'Why are we stopping here?' she asked Rex as calmly as she could.

'Why—target practice, like I said. Edgy aren't we?'

She shivered as he stroked her arm with a gentle touch. 'Don't be. We'll be OK, you and me.'

Amy found the shooting easy, once she'd become accustomed to the gun.

'Not bad for a beginner,' said Rex. 'You've an accurate eye and a steady hand. We'll make a trained assassin of you yet.'

Amy found this creepy—especially as the profession must require some mental resilience on top of the ability to shoot straight. Did Rex, who'd called her a tough babe, really believe Crazy Amy possessed that too?

'Doesn't it get to you?' she asked. 'Killing people?'

'I'm a professional—I'm in control. Why would it get to me?'

Amy fired another round at the targets. Could someone switch off their feelings while they killed someone, or did they not have any to begin with? Did Rex enjoy a sense of professional accomplishment in a clean kill, where the victim didn't suffer? She, Amy, often lacked empathy, but she still didn't picture herself as a killer.

'You might find this gun easier to use,' Rex suggested, handing her his own weapon. 'It's lighter—more responsive.'

'Yes—definitely better,' Amy agreed, after another round.

***

DCI Bligh was far from convinced by Melanie, in spite of Carmody's best efforts to persuade him. After investing so much intellectual capital in the current line of enquiry, he showed a stubborn resistance to any other theories.

'She says Chang's the murderer,' he said over and over, as if constant repetition would make it more credible. 'But how does it fit with the other evidence, like Pedley's prints on the photograph, and his share dealings?'

'Search me—I'm merely relaying what Ms Cronin said. You can speak to her yourself if you want to confirm.'

'But all this seems so complicated,' said Bligh wearily.

Everything seemed complicated to him, thought Carmody uncharitably.

'Maybe so, but it's vital for us to act on the tip off. Amy's life is at risk.'

'I suppose so,' Bligh replied, with no enthusiasm.

They'd established that the Hounslow address had been rented in a false name, so no clues there. Carmody favoured mounting an operation to storm in and rescue Amy, but Bligh vetoed the suggestion.

'Look, the Cronin woman thinks Amy's safe for the moment. If we go charging in, we'll never solve the mystery. So let's send an unmarked car and watch and wait.'

'I have to disagree with your approach…' Carmody began.

'Who's running this enquiry—you or me? Your brain is addled where that woman is concerned, and you seem to forget there's a bigger picture here. Now butt out and go home.'

Carmody smarted at Bligh's insult, even though he had a valid point. But equally this might be their only chance to save Amy, and by watching and waiting, they might blow it.

Reluctantly, he left, but not to return home. Even the concept of his flat, where a fortnight ago Amy had lain in his arms all night, was unbearable.

He hoped beyond hope Bligh wouldn't mess up, so he'd have the chance to put things right with Amy. Hell, she wasn't perfect, but he had every confidence in his ability to tame her wild excesses if she'd let him. And he loved her, really he did.

He wandered around for the best part of an hour, before ordering a beer in a random pub. Halfway through his pint, his phone rang.

'I'm afraid we lost them,' said Bligh.

'Lost them?'

'Ms Robinson left with another man in a car.'

'Chinese guy?'

'Nope—blond hair, medium height. Unfortunately our guys got stuck at a red light.'

'Why not switch on the siren?'

'They didn't like to, in case it drew attention to them.'

'For fuck's sake!'

The risk of losing Amy in transit was just one of many reasons Carmody had advocated storming the premises. Now it looked as though his fears were well-founded.

'They were headed towards Central London, so we may pick them up on the ANPR cameras.'

But not in time, Carmody thought.

He took a swig of his beer. Why even bother telling him this? To torment him?

'Rest assured,' Bligh concluded. 'We'll keep you in the loop.'

Carmody sighed. If he'd had his way, Amy would be safe now and there'd be no loop. He finished his drink and went for a refill.

'One of those nights eh?' said the barman, tuning in to the gloomy vibes.

'You could say that.'

After two more pints, Carmody's phone rang again.

'OK,' said Bligh. 'We got them.'

'What—you mean Amy's safe? Thank God.'

But Carmody's relief was short-lived.

'No—we located the car, parked near Chelsea Embankment, but there's lots of new apartment complexes round here, so it's not easy. But don't worry—we'll keep searching.'

How ridiculous—how could he not worry? And he had a sneaking suspicion they wouldn't act until Amy hit the ground.

Chelsea Embankment and those swanky waterside apartment blocks rang a bell.

Ed Smithies.

'I've just completed on a super penthouse flat in that new waterfront development in Chelsea—my little city pied-à-terre. It's Churchill Tower—perhaps you've heard of it.'

Smithies had told Carmody this when he'd been fishing for information on Venner's death. There must be a connection, though Carmody couldn't imagine what.

'It has a super roof terrace, with some of the finest views in London.'

Carmody knew he ought to call Bligh and report his hunch. But the temptation to hotfoot it over to Smithies' apartment and check it out himself was overwhelming. He drained his beer and hailed a black cab—he'd be there in five minutes.

75

Amy was thankful to have arrived and—unbelievably—eager to see Smithies. An hour spent alone with a cold-blooded assassin put even Smithies' idiosyncrasies into perspective, and his presence would lend a semblance of normality to the evening.

She hadn't even known until Carmody mentioned it that Smithies owned a London property. She'd always assumed he resided full time in his tasteless mock-Georgian executive mansion in Virginia Water.

They waited in the car until Chang appeared fifteen minutes later, immaculately dressed in a navy suit, white shirt and a blue and red tie in an unusual chequerboard design. It was strange to think he'd be dead within hours, and even stranger to find herself as unruffled as Rex by the prospect.

'Hi, Amy,' he said. 'Well done on your escape—you're one feisty lady.'

On this occasion, Amy did not interpret feisty as a compliment.

'Pity you didn't just offer me the deal without all the aggro.'

'You'd never have cooperated. We had to show we meant business.'

'Well, you did that alright.'

'And you have all copies of the disk?'

In fact Rex had given her two blank disks, but Chang would never realise.

'I do—there are only two.'

'Incidentally, I have your handbag. Everything's in it, including the earring you dropped. I'll give it to you afterwards.'

'Thanks,' said Amy.

The earring was lost forever, as there'd be no afterwards for Chang.

Chang pressed the buzzer and the three of them took the lift to the top floor. Nobody spoke. Smithies was already waiting at the door, and ushered them in.

'Hope you didn't mind us bringing Rex along,' said Chang. 'He's a close friend of Amy's and she needed the support.'

Smithies looked at Rex suspiciously, as if surprised to find Amy associated with someone so normal looking.

In spite of her nervousness, Amy took in all the details. The apartment was ostentatiously furnished, in an avant-garde style at odds with Smithies' myopic outlook on life. If she hadn't known better, she'd have suspected the hand of a mistress. But since Smithies' all-consuming love affair was with himself, it seemed more likely he'd hired an interior designer.

'Ah, Amy,' said Smithies effusively, shaking her hand. 'How are you? You're looking well—early retirement must agree with you. And I'm *loving* the hair.'

The phrase "early retirement" grated on Amy, as he no doubt intended. Even when trying to be cordial, Smithies couldn't avoid causing offence.

'Yes, I'm doing well, thanks—pursuing various opportunities. How are you?'

'Prospering, thanks. As you can see.'

'Yes, super place you've got here.'

'Oh just a humble little bolt hole.' he said with mock humility. 'I've been working *such long hours* and it makes life so much easier to have a pied–à–terre in London.'

Even if he'd maxed out on his borrowing, Amy estimated it would be tough for Smithies to afford the apartment on top of the other components of his flashy lifestyle. She wondered if his excessive prosperity might be linked to those security implications Michelle had mentioned. Alternatively, and more likely, he was conceited enough to be banking on further career advancement to solve any cash flow difficulties. But wherever the truth lay, the apartment's main purpose was to trumpet Smithies' success rather than its convenience.

'I'm sure it does,' Amy agreed.

'Can I offer you a drink—something soft?'

A bottle of white wine, standing in an ice bucket on the sideboard, looked much more appealing.

'Actually, I'd prefer a glass of wine.'

'Of course—if you think that's wise,' he said, conveying a hint of pleasure at what he doubtless saw as her fall from sobriety.

'I'll have one too,' said Chang, making a beeline for the sideboard, and waving Smithies away. 'Don't worry—I can pour them. You too, Rex?'

'Sure—why not?'

'So what opportunities are you pursuing egg-zackly?' asked Smithies, signalling his scepticism.

'Oh this and that.' She was trying to keep an eye on Chang, but Smithies blocked her line of vision. 'A few non-exec directorships.'

'You could always step into Venner's shoes at IPT,' suggested Smithies, jokingly. 'I hear there's a vacancy.'

'Oh, Amy wouldn't be interested in an executive role,' said Chang.

'Absolutely not,' Amy said, with a grimace. 'Too much like hard work.'

'Don't stand on ceremony,' Smithies urged, as Chang brought over the drinks. 'Please sit down.'

Typical of Smithies to pretend this was a proper social occasion. To satisfy his deep-seated desire to be liked, it was not enough for her to hand back the disk with its damning contents. She had to appear to enjoy spending time with him in the process.

Amy positioned herself tactically at one end of the sofa next to a triffid-like pot plant on the floor. She joined in politely with Smithies' inane conversation about all his wonderful holidays.

'Yes, yes—Madeira is marvellous. Did you stay at Reid's Palace or the Savoy?'

Smithies launched into a monologue on the relative merits of each, and his disgust that British Airways passengers couldn't use the VIP lounge, such as it was, at the airport.

Rex also chipped in, although Amy suspected he'd visited most of the places mentioned for his grisly professional purposes rather than vacation. Odd how he was acting so normally, knowing he would shortly blow Chang's head away.

Amy took a tentative sip of the wine—it tasted dreadful—presumably because Chang had spiked it. While no one was watching, she discreetly emptied the glass into the plant pot.

'My goodness.' Smithies' eyes lighted on the empty glass on the table.' You've made short work of that. Another?'

'Lovely—please don't get up—I'll help myself.'

The second glass tasted as shit-awful as the first. Surely Chang hadn't poisoned the whole bottle?

'Oh, by the way,' said Smithies to Chang. 'Heard some juicy gossip on the grapevine. No idea if it's true but thought you'd know better than anyone. Apparently, and they're not going public yet because they haven't told the kids, but Richard Pedley is getting married to John Venner's widow.'

'First I've heard of it, but it may be true,' said Chang. 'My sister broke up with him last week—she'd had enough of all the innuendo surrounding the journalist's murder. In PR, you can't be too careful who you associate with.'

More likely the relationship had served its purpose, thought Amy, with Pedley now set up as Marchpole's murderer.

'How do you know so much anyway?'

'My lips are sealed. But my source told me they'd been having an affair for years.'

The source, Amy guessed, was Smithies' wife, via a loose-tongued friend of Susan's. Some of the Pearson Malone partners' wives were as poisonous as their husbands.

'What—you're saying he was cheating on Roxanne?'

There was something fake about Chang's outrage, perhaps as fake as Roxanne's relationship with Pedley.

'Now, Amy,' said Smithies, hastily changing the subject. 'Before I forget, I think you had two CDs for me.'

He said it as if she'd borrowed a couple of music albums and he'd suddenly remembered to ask for them back.

'Yes of course.'

'Excellent. I'm so glad common sense has finally prevailed.'

Was he really so stupid as to believe he was being offered back the one weapon Amy had against him? Apparently so.

'Yes well, I'm moving on with my life, so it's silly to hold a grudge. And it was unethical to record them in the first place.'

'Just tell me this. How you the hell did you get the bug planted in that trophy?'

Amy well recalled the "Top Professional Advisor" award from a trade publication—Smithies' pride and joy, and the one non-essential item in his otherwise minimalist office. It was a brilliant hiding place, and she had no clue how Venner managed it.

'It doesn't really matter now, does it?'

'No, of course not, let's call it quits.'

'Yes, let's,' said Amy.

As she produced the blank disks, she enjoyed the prospect of him finding out later he'd been hoodwinked. Not her problem though—she would never have to set eyes on his oily fat face again. And he might have more pressing issues to fret about shortly, based on Ethan's veiled comments. What on earth had he been up to?

'Thanks so much.' Smithies grinned inanely from ear to ear. 'And should you ever need a personal reference, it goes without saying…'

Well, I won't, thought Amy. *And if I did, I wouldn't ask you.*

'Shall we go out onto the terrace and have a celebratory cigar?' said Chang. 'I have some rather fine Havanas.'

He showed Smithies the packet.

'Oh marvellous,' he enthused, rubbing his hands, like a small boy excited at the prospect of Christmas.

'How about you, Rex?'

'Non-smoker, me, but I'll join you to be sociable.'

'Come on, Amy, how about a cigarette?'

'Yeah, why not?'

Amy shuddered involuntarily. It would be chilly on the terrace and worse, in a few minutes, she would have to witness Chang's murder. How on earth had she become mixed up in this? Didn't everyone, no matter how evil, have a right to life?

As she stood up, a horrifying realisation shot through Amy like an electric shock.

Mel was not the only one she'd told about her plans to inform the police. There was also Susan Venner—in a relationship with Pedley.

Susan likely spoke to Pedley. He'd have laughed it off, because he trusted Chang implicitly and assumed there was nothing in it. In fact, he might have found the notion so amusing that he'd said something flippant to Chang about Crazy Amy's crackpot theories.

Shit. Mel hadn't betrayed her after all, and she wasn't working with Chang.

Oh dear God no.

...fact is nobody wants that stuff broadcast around.

Not least the US government, at a critical juncture in their talks with Cuba.

In an appalling moment of mental clarity, Amy saw the truth. Neither she nor Chang would survive. She'd been played by a couple of pros dangling the irresistible carrot of a new identity, and insinuating she'd be helping bring Smithies down. They'd known precisely how to manipulate frightened, disorientated Crazy Amy. And all the tiny details she'd found comforting were part of the con too.

You might find this gun easier to use.

Her prints would be on the gun Rex had taken, and she'd have gunshot residue on her hands. She'd be in the frame for Chang's shooting, and unable to defend herself because she'd be dead. Admittedly, she hadn't taken the drugs, but they weren't essential—she was loopy enough without chemical stimulants.

And the narrative? Crazy woman shoots—shoots who? Chang, yes—but Smithies surely wouldn't survive either. Correction—Crazy Amy shoots hated ex-boss and client before committing suicide. Rex disappears to kill another day.

With hindsight, *none* of what the Americans told her had stacked up logically—how had she been so addled as to accept their crap so uncritically? And Mel had tried to warn her, but she'd refused to accept the truth. Same old problem, rearing its ugly head for one last hurrah—she'd trusted the wrong people.

'Come on, Amy, what are you waiting for?' said Rex.

She could refuse to go outside—say she needed to visit the little girls' room, then emerge with the gun and shoot Rex and Chang dead. But Rex was a trained assassin, and he knew she had a firearm. Hell, it probably wasn't even loaded—just provided to give false reassurance. She didn't stand a chance.

Never were the dangers of smoking more grave and imminent. She stepped out onto the terrace, swaying subtly to emulate the effects of the drugs. Her sobriety might yet prove to be her one strategic advantage.

If living as Crazy Amy was frustrating, dying as her was unthinkable. All her sensible achievements would be erased, and she'd be forever remembered as a madwoman. Amy lit a cigarette, possibly her last, and inhaled deeply as she looked across the Thames to the London skyline. She couldn't believe it would end like this.

A buzzer sounded.

'Ah—I'd better get that,' said Smithies, leaving his cigar

burning in the ashtray. 'It might be a courier bringing papers requiring an urgent signature.'

'Don't be too long,' said Chang. He and Rex exchanged a glance.

At once Amy was seized with an unjustified optimism—this was not the final chapter—somehow, she would extricate herself from this mess.

76

En route to Smithies' apartment, Carmody reconsidered the wisdom of going it alone. For a start, he would lay himself open to disciplinary charges. But more importantly, lives were at risk, including his own. Melanie Cronin had allegedly overheard something about putting a gun to Amy's head, meaning he'd be walking unarmed into a shoot-out. So he telephoned Bligh and told him he would need armed reinforcements. Bligh sounded doubtful, but since they had nothing else to go on, he acquiesced.

On arriving at Churchill Tower, with his heart in his mouth, Carmody rang the buzzer with Smithies' name on it.

'Ed—Dave Carmody. You suggested I might like to come round sometime, and I was passing, so I decided to drop by.'

'Ah, Dave,' droned Smithies over the intercom. 'It's not terribly convenient, I'm afraid—I have visitors.'

He sounded a touch uncomfortable, as though anxious to conceal something. And on the assumption that Smithies was not smoking crystal meth while entertaining teenage rent boys, Carmody suspected it was Amy's presence.

'Is Amy with you?' he asked.

The short silence told Carmody all he needed to know. She was there, and Smithies was deciding whether to lie.

'Yes, but…'

Carmody weighed his options. Smithies might be part of this web of criminal activity, in which case tipping him off would endanger Amy. But on reflection, he pegged Smithies as a stooge, not a mastermind.

'Now I don't want to panic you, but Amy's in grave danger. We've received a tip off that she's about to be thrown off your roof terrace.'

'What? How insane…'

'And you may be in danger too.'

'Oh my God!'

The panic in Smithies' voice clinched it. He wasn't involved—he wasn't capable of putting on such a convincing performance.

'Leave the door ajar—I'm coming in with armed reinforcements.'

'But…'

'Don't argue—go back in and act as normal.'

***

Smithies returned, and puffed nervously on his cigar. Without anyone saying anything, the dynamic had shifted, and all those present sensed the change, even if they couldn't pinpoint the cause.

'Was it the courier?' Amy asked, feeling sure it hadn't been.

'Yes—bloody nuisance. These days you're on duty twenty-four-seven—no escape.'

'Hey, Nelson,' Rex said. 'Would you take a look at this?' He pointed towards the river.

Chang turned, and immediately a shot rang out. He crumpled to the floor and ended sitting propped up by the wall, with a neat hole in his forehead, and an expression of slight bemusement.

The colour drained from Smithies' face and as his eyes flicked from Chang to Rex, they registered unadulterated fear. Another bang and he too hit the floor.

333

'Collateral damage,' said Rex, before turning to Amy.

'You next, hon. Sorry, but we all have to go sometime.'

The shocking comprehension of impending death hit the reptilian epicentre of Amy's brain, not the part that intellectualised death, but the little central kernel powered by pure emotion.

FEAR

An overwhelming primeval and visceral dread ripped at her guts, and she felt the warmth of urine running down her legs as she punched and scratched at Rex. Amy wouldn't go without a fight. She made eye contact with him for an instant before he lifted her up. Nothing—no shred of humanity in those bright blue eyes—all the friendliness had been an act, a coldly calculated charade to gain her trust. A scream rose in her throat, but died, replaced by a desperate retching.

Little Amy appeared, naked except for a fluffy white towel wrapped around her, as if she'd been interrupted while showering.

'Please, God—no! Let her go—she can't leave me all on my own!'

Grown Up Amy kicked and flailed, damned if she would make this easy.

Rex inexplicably tottered then fell, dragging Amy on top of him.

As she pulled herself up, the bloody crater where Rex's face had once been met her eye. A red jelly-like substance slopped to the floor.

What the…?

Dave Carmody stepped onto the terrace, like an apparition, with armed officers a few steps behind.

Only then did Amy realise Rex had been shot.

77

THE DAILY GLOBE 17 NOVEMBER
By Claudia Knight
TOP ACCOUNTANT AND CLIENT BRUTALLY SLAIN IN CHELSEA

Last night, armed police stormed the exclusive Church-ill Tower off Chelsea Embankment after reports of gunfire emanating from a penthouse apartment.

The owner of the apartment, Edward Smithies, 40, a senior partner in the global accountancy firm of Pearson Malone was found dead from gunshot wounds, along with his client Nelson Chang, aged 33. The killer was gunned down by police before he could escape. He has been tentatively iden-tified as Rex Spindler, a US citizen wanted by the FBI in connection with a number of contract killings. A female former colleague of Smithies, who has not been named, was reported to be shaken but otherwise unharmed. So far, she has been unable to shed any light on the killings.

Mr Chang was a director of IPT, the plumbing components and piping company which has been the subject of much controversy in recent months. His death comes barely two months after finance director John Venner dramatically col-lapsed at the company's Annual General Meeting, and just two weeks following the killing of Toby Marchpole, a blogger critical of IPT. A police spokesman declined to comment on whether these events were in any way connected.

***

Amy laid down the newspaper in disgust.

Toby had been right—the mainstream press was full of shit.

78

Carmody was Amy's biggest short-term problem.

He'd been so solicitous in the following days, smothering her with thoughtful gestures, that Amy didn't have the heart to tell him straight away.

She was, of course, grateful to him for saving her life and taking care of her in the chaotic aftermath of the shooting, but this didn't glue them together. Even in her darkest hours, Amy detected the same dangerous undercurrents as before, plus some new ones now swirling treacherously beneath the surface of their relationship.

Amy had played dumb with Bligh, much as Ethan and Michelle had suggested. And while those two had fed her a load of bullshit, she feared the threat to her life was real. In the circumstances, silence was her best hope for survival even if, ironically, this entailed sobbing hysterically every time Bligh asked her a tricky question. It also seemed wise to steer clear of the CDs, to avoid questions about why she hadn't disclosed their existence earlier. Besides, Smithies had paid for her silence with his life.

So she had no clue who the Americans were, or why she was at Smithies' apartment. She couldn't imagine why there was a gun (unloaded as she'd suspected) in her handbag, or why Rex's murder weapon had her prints on it.

'I was confused,' she wailed. 'They kidnapped me and messed with my mind. They said they'd let me go.' And scarily, this wasn't far from the truth, because the more Amy dwelled on it, the more she realised just how unstable she'd been in the safe house.

After a while Bligh gave up. He'd pinned down Rex Spindler as Marchpole's killer, acting under Chang's instructions. Case closed—no trial. No trial for Smithies' murder either. So Amy's inability to provide a coherent explanation was of little importance.

Carmody knew Amy was hiding something though—her gibbering wreck routine didn't fool him for a moment. And he no doubt considered that if he pressed her on the matter, eventually she'd crack and confess all.

Another bone of contention was Mel, who'd conveniently disappeared again. Carmody was convinced she'd disclosed her whereabouts to Amy. And although he was wrong, his suspicions injected a further toxic ingredient into the mix.

After a week tiptoeing around, everything came to a head.

'We could charge you with illegal possession of a firearm,' he said menacingly after yet another attempt to elicit further details.

'Go ahead—persecuting a traumatised crime victim is clearly a smart move for you both personally and professionally.'

He then switched to emotional blackmail.

'Aren't you grateful I saved your life?'

Amy looked at him in disbelief. Did he seriously expect to use her gratitude to extract a full disclosure, or even to tether her to him for life? She rather suspected he did—his kindness merely reflected his ownership of her, his right to transform her into an idealised Amy worthy of the power of his love. Her feelings, as she'd always known, were irrelevant. And her mental health would never recover while shackled to him.

'Yes,' she replied. 'But I can't live it with you.'

He left later that day, but Amy guessed he'd return before long. He seemed to regard her as a long-term project, a personal challenge he would never abandon. And her resistance merely provoked him to try harder.

79

Had he not been cremated, Toby Marchpole would have been turning in his grave.

The US government agents had escaped prosecution and Chang was beyond justice. Meanwhile, Pedley's flagrant market manipulation continued unchecked. Roxanne had slithered off like the snake she was, and now played down her connection to both Chang and Pedley. And even if he'd known she was working in alliance with her brother, Pedley was most unlikely to call attention to the matter.

Sadly, the only person who seemed likely to face prosecution, if and when they traced her, was Mel. Because even Bligh could get his pudding head round fictitious employees.

Judged by her exposure of the truth, Amy's enquiries had been an unmitigated disaster, and her experiences had severely knocked her self-esteem. Through her own gullibility, she'd come within a whisker of death. She could never rewind the chilling moment when she'd eyeballed the Grim Reaper, and her life journey had stalled.

Each evening she slumped in front of the television, sick of life yet scared of death. Even the comfort of gin and cigarettes left her nauseated, and with little appetite—though that didn't stop her, for she knew no other way to numb the pain. The Americans were welcome to assassinate her any time, provided they killed her while she slept.

What ate her most was the disappointment at having let Toby down—the one person she *ought* to have trusted, and who, if Celia was correct, had truly loved her. For his sake, she ought to salvage something from the debris of the investigation.

Ironically, it was Celia who provided the answer. She called round unexpectedly one Sunday—just passing, she claimed.

Amy, still in her pyjamas at two pm, had been loath to answer the door—particularly when she saw Celia through the window. But she'd have to face her sooner or later—if only to apologise for missing Toby's funeral in her dazed and raw state. And she knew in her heart that she couldn't continue with her hermit-like wallowing forever.

To judge by appearances, Celia had pulled herself back from the brink.

'It's OK,' said Celia. 'You don't have to say I'm looking well or any of that shit. You and I both know what it's like to present an illusion to the outside world when inside your soul is dying.'

'I can't even manage the illusion at the moment,' Amy admitted, as if it wasn't readily apparent. 'You're obviously way better at it than me.'

'What happened to you was worse, plus the kids help, and work of course. There are times when I can pretend the whole ghastly business never happened. Whereas you're stuck here…'

Amy caught Celia eying the scene of devastation. Unwashed cups, plates and glasses lay interspersed with empty bottles. An overflowing ashtray made an unattractive centrepiece on the coffee table, and newspapers were spread over all surfaces, including the floor. Amy stung with shame. How had she allowed the place to descend into this squalor? Was she turning into her mother?

'Apologies for the mess. Like I said, I've not been myself recently.'

'You've been through a hugely traumatic experience,' said Celia, clearing a space on the sofa. 'Surely you didn't hope to bounce back unscathed?'

'Actually, I did. And then I beat myself up for not making the grade. You have no idea how much all this,' she said, gesturing to the chaos, 'disgusts me.'

'Have they offered you counselling?'

'Yes, but none of this therapy malarkey seems to do me any good.'

'What troubles you most—now—this minute?'

No navel gazing, self-insight or dialogue with inner child was required to answer this trenchant question. In a flowing narrative, Amy articulated her disgust at the loss of life, inadequate justice and the utter futility of her endeavour. She hesitated before mentioning the arms smuggling and her associated fears, but ultimately found it cathartic to let it out.

Celia listened, perceiving not judging.

'OK—I'm assuming the Americans appreciate your silence and heck, if they'd wanted you dead, they'd have killed you by now. So you'll be safe enough provided you hold your tongue on the weapons. But that doesn't affect anything else.'

'What do you mean?'

Celia's suggestion seemed so obvious that afterwards Amy failed to grasp why she hadn't considered it earlier. Perhaps her obsession with secrecy over the weapons shipments had overshadowed everything else. Fact was, she still had all Marchpole's papers on the bogus company acquisitions, the insider trading and the phony transactions with Plumb

Enterprises. There was more than enough evidence to convict Pedley of securities fraud, if the authorities chose to pursue the case.

'So,' said Celia. 'Why don't you simply pretend you never came across the Colombian business and dish the dirt on Pedley to the SFO as Toby planned all along?'

***

Amy worked tirelessly through the night to fill the gaps in the documentation. Toby had never expected anyone else to pick up the trail, and he'd carried many vital facts in his head. But even with these obstacles, by the morning Amy had pieced together what she considered to be a robust case against Pedley.

The SFO website said they could not "accommodate drop-in callers", so Amy filled out the online reporting form, anticipating they would contact her in a few days. Ten minutes later, the phone rang. Could Amy come in for a meeting, bringing any paper trail in her possession? Yes, she'd be there in an hour—vindicated, triumphant.

Amy struggled, without success, to fasten the skirt of her Armani pinstripe suit. Strange, because she hadn't been overeating—must be the lack of exercise. Vowing to hit the gym before long, she switched to a looser but a rather less business-like Nicole Farhi jersey wrap dress and a navy jacket. It felt strange to be wearing proper clothes again, and even stranger to leave the house.

As Amy opened the front door an icy blast of cold air hit her—winter had arrived with a vengeance while she'd been hiding from the world. She hastily replaced the jacket with her black Vivienne Westwood overcoat. The last time she'd worn the coat she'd been up there, at the pinnacle of her

343

career, with no intimation of her impending fall. The coat still smelt of prosperity and success, a reminder of the life she'd left behind.

As she passed Trafalgar Square on her way to the SFO in Cockspur Street, some of the old swagger returned. Who, looking at her, would guess she was no longer a mistress of the universe?

A glacial woman wearing a navy skirt suit came down to reception to greet her. Tall and blonde with a regal bearing, she looked vaguely familiar, although Amy couldn't readily place her.

'Amy Farquhar—I'm an investigator here.'

'Amy Robinson.'

They both smiled awkwardly.

She ushered Amy into a meeting room and listened to her story with keen attention, before flicking through the papers.

'Hey, you're good at this,' she said. 'We should offer you a job.'

'Thanks, but most of it was down to Toby Marchpole.'

'Impeccably organised though. And I'm betting that was you.'

'It was,' Amy conceded.

'We appreciate you dropping by, although we're already aware of some of this.'

'*You are?*'

'You say you were with Pearson Malone.'

'Yes.'

'Did you know John Venner?'

'He was my boss.'

Amy blushed. Her disloyalty to Venner, however justified, pricked at her conscience, even though there'd be no prosecution.

'Were you shocked by what you found?'

'Yes,' said Amy. 'I worked with him for years—I was certain he wouldn't do anything like this.'

'And you were right.'

Amy stared—not comprehending.

'But here's the proof.'

'Let me explain. Venner was working for us.'

A conflicting range of emotions gripped Amy as she digested this—joy, surprise, vindication and scepticism.

'But he took the backhander.'

'He had to avoid raising suspicion—it was all held in escrow and we guaranteed him immunity.'

'So—you told him to apply for the job at IPT?'

'Oh no. We would never do that. After he took up the position, he spotted various anomalies and reached out to us. His assistance was strictly off the record, and we would have denied any involvement.'

'So why are you telling me now?'

'Because I have a hunch you're good at keeping secrets.'

'You're not the first to say so.'

'And in return you can tell me what else you've been holding back.'

Farquhar peered at her with piercing, intelligent eyes, and Amy looked back with wide-eyed innocence.

'But I've disclosed everything.'

It was a lie, though in the grand scheme of things, a necessary one.

'Apart from what Venner wanted to tell Amy.'

'But I still don't know. Does it matter?'

'For obvious reasons, we let everyone go on thinking Venner was referring to you but…'

The revelation hit Amy like a sledgehammer in the chest. It had been Amy Farquhar he'd wanted to tell, not her.

'It was you.'

If only she'd known at the beginning, she'd never have got sucked in. Toby would still be alive and Mel happily siphoning off Joey's care home fees undetected. And Amy would have been spared all the pain. If only…

'I believe so, yes,' said Farquhar. 'There was something he wished to share with me as his contact. We were scheduled to meet right after the AGM.'

There'd never been any logical reason for him to discuss anything with Amy Robinson—only her egocentricity had persuaded her otherwise. Still—this revelation resolved one minor mystery. Venner hadn't told Pedley what he'd learned in China because it would have been tipping him off.

'Do you really have no idea?'

They were straying onto dangerous territory, but there was only one answer.

'I'm sorry—I'm afraid not.'

Farquhar subtly shifted her line of questioning.

'Was it Chang who killed Venner?'

'I'm not sure.'

'It's important—if Chang had discovered we were onto him…'

'Chang's dead.'

'But the shoot out—you were there. Why was Chang killed?'

'As far as I can tell,' said Amy carefully, 'there was a falling out between Chang and his hired assassin, over killing me.'

'Yes, but what were you *doing* there?'

The questions were far more probing than Bligh's, and Amy wondered how long she'd be able to continue stonewalling.

'Chang wanted me dead because I'd tied him to Marchpole's shooting—I was lured to the apartment on false pretences. That's all.'

Her explanation seemed to satisfy Farquhar, who nodded.

'If you truly suspect Venner was murdered,' Amy added, 'you should contact the police.'

'Oddly enough, they approached us shortly after Venner's death and asked whether he'd been in touch with us. Of course, I was told to deny it. But later on, I came clean in an off-the-record chat with a DCI Carmody.'

It was then that Amy remembered where she'd seen her before—with Carmody on the night out with Mel. Off-the-record chats were a Carmody speciality, thought Amy bitterly, especially with women. So the bastard had known Venner didn't mean Amy Robinson, but never said a word. Would anything have changed if he had? Maybe not, but his deceit provided further indication, if any was needed, of his self-seeking approach to life.

'And what happened?'

'He told me there wasn't enough evidence to justify any further action.'

'That figures,' said Amy. 'Although it's not important, is it? Irrespective of Venner's fate, you have plenty of material to nail Pedley.'

'Well, I'll certainly do my best,' said Farquhar.

Epilogue

As the weeks passed, Amy's optimism about her chances of continued survival grew, along with a renewed zest for life. She cleaned the house, hit the gym and considered applying for jobs. In retrospect, she even appreciated the pleasing symmetry to events. The story had begun and ended on a rooftop and with knowledge that should have been imparted to Amy.

But as her emotional state improved, her physical condition deteriorated. She vomited daily, for once not because of over-drinking—quite the reverse. Even the smell of alcohol on people's breath now repulsed her, as did the mere thought of drinking it. She wondered if she was suffering a delayed reaction to the Priory brainwashing, but then smoking appealed even less. And despite throwing her guts up, plus returning to a sensible exercise regime, she'd lost no weight.

After a particularly vile day of nonstop nausea, something Joey had said in Whitstable sprang to mind.

'Call the baby Joey.'

Then the words of The Larches' receptionist.

'He notices tiny details no one else does, a bit like Sherlock Holmes.'

What minute sign had Joey detected that day? She might never know, but now, in horrifying crystal clarity, she finally grasped what Mel's brother had been on about.

THE END

Thanks so much for reading EXPOSURE. I hope you enjoyed it and if so, I'd very much appreciate a few words of support on Amazon or Goodreads!

Crazy Amy will be back in 2018 in another gripping adventure. Meanwhile, if you haven't read it yet, why not check out CONCEALMENT (Crazy Amy Book 1) on Amazon to bring yourself up to speed with Amy's back story.

Also, do look me up on Facebook Rose Edmunds - Author Page, and join the Crazy Amy VIP Fan Club, where you'll have access to free bonus material not available elsewhere. You can also discover more on www.roseedmunds.co.uk or on Twitter @roseedmunds.

Finally, if you check out the Mainsail Books website at www.MainsailBooks.co.uk, you'll find many more tales of corporate skulduggery to keep you going until Amy's return, and an exciting free offer!

25047573R00206

Printed in Great Britain
by Amazon